REALM OF STONE AND STARLIGHT

C. L. MECCA

Boldwood

First published in Great Britain in 2026 by Boldwood Books Ltd.

Copyright © C. L. Mecca, 2026

Cover Design by JD Smith Design Ltd

Cover Images: Shutterstock

Every effort has been made to obtain the necessary permissions with reference to copyright material, both illustrative and quoted. We apologise for any omissions in this respect and will be pleased to make the appropriate acknowledgements in any future edition.

A CIP catalogue record for this book is available from the British Library.

Paperback ISBN 978-1-83656-317-4

Large Print ISBN 978-1-83656-316-7

Hardback ISBN 978-1-83656-315-0

Trade Paperback ISBN 978-1-80656-158-2

Ebook ISBN 978-1-83656-318-1

Kindle ISBN 978-1-83656-319-8

Audio CD ISBN 978-1-83656-310-5

MP3 CD ISBN 978-1-83656-311-2

Digital audio download ISBN 978-1-83656-313-6

This book is printed on certified sustainable paper. Boldwood Books is dedicated to putting sustainability at the heart of our business. For more information please visit https://www.boldwoodbooks.com/about-us/sustainability/

Boldwood Books Ltd, 23 Bowerdean Street, London, SW6 3TN

www.boldwoodbooks.com

To anyone trying to find their way without losing themselves...

1

TERRAN

Thaeron, Elydor

"Kill him, Terran."

I would do no such thing, despite that the order had been given by my father, the king.

The Aetherian captive was haranya, and there was no glory in killing one who'd not lived yet one hundred years. I met the ice-blue eyes of the warrior, one whose hands were tied behind him with vines from an ancient tree of my ancestors. Binds that would not break.

"He was delivered to me, and I will deal with him."

That his father would even grace this corner of the palace underscored the importance of this particular captive. Here, in the eastern-most caverns of the mountain, the only one above ground as much of the Gyorian palace was built underground, the men were more loyal to me. The Gyorian nobles and diplomats from other clans rarely ventured this far east either. It was my domain. That my father made an appearance meant there was more to the story than the guards had told me.

"He is an Aetherian spy." My gaze met the water-wielder. He didn't acknowledge my father's claim in any way.

"Perhaps," I said. "But until your men's claims are verified, he will remain as my prisoner."

One of the guards who'd brought him here cleared his throat, his discomfort obvious.

My father's jaw flexed, the ground under his feet rumbling. That he allowed his anger to show in front of an audience was not surprising. The Gyorian king was not known for his stoicism or patience.

Few Gyorians were known for such a virtue, including myself. But the king less than most.

Watching Father's fingers, I envisioned what might happen next. He could twist them so subtly, most would not see them move. And as the most powerful Gyorian, not only would the Aetherian be dead in moments; my father would likely cause a fair amount of destruction to the courtyard where we stood.

Challenging him would not end well.

"He's been questioned," I said with a glance at the guards who handed him over to my men. "But not by me."

I let the implication hang in the air. I would question him and *then* kill him.

"My lord?" The youngest of the guards who had caught the apparent spy, one not much older than the Aetherian himself, spoke.

My father looked sharply his way without responding.

"He was found speaking to Ilyas Rho just outside the gates, but Rho was nowhere to be seen when the traitor was apprehended."

I didn't know the guard well, but my opinion of him soared. He knew well how to appeal to my father. Naming him a "traitor" would appeal to a man whose hate against the Aetherians had grown to a fever pitch of late.

Traitor.

I couldn't think of the word without envisioning the face of one familiar to me. So familiar, I saw it each and every time I peered in a mirror. There was little time to dwell on my brother's treachery. We were a heartbeat away from war. According to some, it had already reached us.

"Terran." The reprimand was sharp. The one who delivered it, inflexible.

Perhaps more inflexible now than ever before, the father I'd known for so many years was nearly a stranger to me. Sometimes, I wondered if duty was simply what my father used to mask fear. Fear of change. Fear of what we might become if we didn't hate the Aetherians quite so much.

My jaw flexed. I'd not apologize. Weakness among a Gyorian was unacceptable, especially for a prince.

"I will question him first," I said to the guard.

With that, my father spun angrily away, accustomed to having his orders followed. His men walked away with him as quickly as they'd come, leaving me and my own to deal with the Aetherian.

I sighed.

Young. Defiant. He stood on a copper slab mined from the very mountain in which we gathered. A defense against erosive air magic, mined from the ground beneath us, would ensure that even if the vines that bound his hands broke, he would find it difficult to summon magic.

"You have been accused of infiltrating the Gyorian court as a spy."

I could detail the reasons why such an accusation was leveled against him. But sensing it would not matter—the look in his eye telling me that the Aetherian would either not speak, or confess all—I instead said nothing more.

He met my gaze.

The air stilled as we both held our ground.

"The Gyorian court," he said finally, "is no longer what it once was."

My nostrils flared in defiance. Not because his words were untrue.

But because they were.

"What do you know about our court? Are you yet a century old?"

The warrior's chin lifted.

"Fifty years. One hundred years. Three hundred. What does it matter when the facts stand as they do? Prince Kael sees what you do not. A king who would damn us all."

It was the wrong thing to say.

"Do you"—my fingers twitched—"deny the accusations against you?"

Cheeks as slim as his shoulders, he was so unlike my brethren who were as brawny as this Aetherian was slight.

Justice.

My father demanded it.

My honor, after the Aetherians killed my mother, demanded it.

"Nay. I do not," he said finally.

There was one penalty for traitors. All knew it. Including the young Aetherian spy.

"Release him."

"Price Terran," my right-hand man began.

"Release. Him."

My voice boomed. The tone I used was my father's.

Dren did as he was told.

The moment the spy's hands, and then his feet, were unbound, he lifted his hand and attempted to use a gust of wind so powerful it would have swept most off their feet.

But not me.

With one last exchanged glance, his eyes wide with surprise that I still stood, I swept my fingers in a small arc. The vines leaped to his feet and hands once more, binding him for the last time. With a twist of those same fingers, the stone beneath his feet trembled just before it opened and sucked him down to its depths.

Closing my eyes at the site of the chasm, I said a silent prayer to Terranor for his safe passage and then twisted my fingers once more, closing the crack and damning him to a death so few immortals faced.

Keeping my eyes closed, I cursed my father. My brother. The Gods.

Myself.

And then opened my eyes.

Some of my men appeared proud at the ease with which I'd killed him. Others, more inexperienced, likely knew not what to think.

Only Dren's shoulders dropped as he looked at me.

Disappointed? Proud? Awed? Even after all these years, I could not tell. Nor did it matter.

Kill him, Terran.

And I had.

2

LYRA

"Those stilts look as if they might give way at any moment."

Peering out of the window of our table at the window of The Siren's Rest tavern, I watched as wave after wave crashed against the worn wood, expecting to plunge into the sea below us at any moment.

"They did once."

My head whipped back toward the speaker. Ilyas Rho, our shrewd smuggler-turned-rebel and local contact, grinned at my appalled expression.

Unlike Marek or Issa, the water-wielder and his sharp-eyed human partner who also sat with me, I knew little of Ilyas Rho aside from the fact that he was our contact here. We'd only met just before this meal.

"Pardon?" I asked, Issa seemingly just as surprised as me.

"They are fortified with featherleaf which, as you might know, cannot break. But local legend tells of one Gyorian king who was so enraged that his queen took a lover that he demolished the original Siren's Rest by splitting each of the stilts on which it was built in half and plunging her and her lover, along with the other patrons, into the sea."

Marek, amused as always, shook his head in disagreement.

"Nay. 'Twas not a lover but a woman who planned to challenge him at the Rite of Stone and Soil."

The smuggler frowned. "What does a Thalassari know of Gyorian legend?"

Marek, unfazed by the question, took a swig of ale. "When the woman in question was half-Thalassari? Plenty." He leaned forward, clearly relishing his new role as storyteller. "Her mother was Gyorian, her father, Thalassari. Though none knew of it until she was able to escape from a watery death with ease. She was the reason Gyoria, unlike the other clans, instituted The Sovereign Clause."

The Sovereign Clause. Only a full-blooded Gyorian could challenge the current king or queen.

"What happened to her?" Issa asked.

I was curious as well, never having heard the story.

"She survived and never challenged the king. Some say though, because she was more powerful than he, The Unbalance sparked The Shattering."

I rolled my eyes. "The Shattering was caused by two heirs who fought for the throne, and magic chose neither."

"So say those who wish to erase her history."

"The problem with a Thalassari," I said, ignoring for this one brief moment the gravity of our mission, "is that one can never discern whether or not he, or she, spins tales or relays real history."

"That is not the only problem with a Thalassari," Issa said wryly, to which Marek did something under the table to her that made the human shriek.

I was about to comment on their interaction when a Gyorian

woman walked by, brushing Ilyas's arm. The movement was so slight I'd not have noticed except I saw the tension in his spine. Without a word, he stood and followed her.

Marek leaned his head to the side, watching Ilyas's retreat.

"That was... abrupt." Issa sat back in her seat, peering in the same direction as her partner.

The Siren's Rest was precisely as Marek and Issa had described it.

Though I'd never been here—Gyoria, a region I typically avoided—I could admit it was exactly as they had explained. Located over the sea in a port known for smugglers and the like, it was the only place in Gyoria where a Thalassari, an Aetherian, and a human could sit together unnoticed.

When one's activities were illegal, they were less likely to question the actions of others.

"The Gyorian woman," I said. "With her hair in a circlet braid—"

"I saw her," Marek responded before I could finish. "With the weathered leather doublet?"

"Aye."

"Did she summon him?" Issa asked.

It was no wonder this was the team Mev and Kael had assembled for a mission as important as ours. Marek noticed what most would not. Issa surmised what others would have waited for me to explain.

"I'm assuming she did," I said.

"Do you think she is our contact?" Issa asked.

"Uncertain," I admitted. "But since we arrived a day early, I do not believe so."

"Agreed." Marek looked around the small tavern. "But the sooner we can make contact, the better."

None would argue that point.

As we ate, and drank, in silence, waiting for Ilyas to return, my mind wandered back to the king's directive. One which my parents, two of the most influential nobles in the Aetherian court, had no knowledge of as they were now retired from the king's employ.

Go to Gyoria. Infiltrate the court. Get the Stone of Mor'Vallis.

No easy feat for someone such as me.

An Aetherian noblewoman and friend to Gyoria's most notable traitor, the king's son.

Kael was less welcome here than all three of us combined, but that didn't mean he had stayed away. After the third artifact had been recovered, he immediately left Aetheria to treat with his brother Terran and attempt to convince him to switch sides. To choose peace over war. Love over hate.

For his efforts, Kael had nearly been discovered by his father's men and almost been killed.

And so we were here to finish the mission Kael started. Retrieve the stone, bring it back to Aetheria and reunite all three clan artifacts. Only then could we reopen the Aetherian Gate, the portal to the human realm that King Balthor had closed nearly thirty years ago.

"There is a... complication."

Ilyas, who'd returned to the table a moment ago, sat.

"What is it?" Marek asked.

"Seryn was discovered. And executed."

I froze.

Seryn was one of two Aetherian spies Mev and Kael relied on for information. But Seryn was more than just a spy. I'd suggested him for this mission. After proving his worth by summoning and dispersing a storm on the Sky Pinnacle at Aetheria's most sacred festival, the Trial of the Tempest, King Galfrid had asked me to train him. He was a more adept air-wielder than most, and for a time, I thought perhaps his magic might even surpass that of the king's.

It did not... though I suspected there was one alive now whose magic might make that claim. Even so, he was clever. Kind. And supremely talented. And now he was dead.

"How?" I asked, my fists clenching.

"He was discovered—"

"How was he killed?"

Ilyas, Marek, and Issa exchanged a glance. The smuggler frowned.

"He was brought to the king. But it was Prince Terran himself who commanded the mountain to swallow him."

Prince Terran. Kael's stern younger brother, if only by minutes, and a powerful earth-wielder.

My heart sank. If it was any other, I'd have found the culprit myself and ensured his immortal life was ended. But I could not kill Kael's brother.

"Fortuitous," I said, all three now watching for my reaction, not even knowing my ties to the young life forsaken.

"I could almost feel pity for him," Issa said, watching me.

She likely knew what I was thinking. It mattered little that Issa was human and not Aetherian and could not hear my silent whispers. But she knew the path to the Stone of Mor'Vallis went through Terran.

"He will pay," I promised. "I am assured of it as I am we will retrieve the Stone."

"I do not doubt it, Lyra," Issa said. "For I've not seen you unsuccessful on a mission yet."

"This," I vowed, resolute, "will *not* be my first time."

3

TERRAN

She stood alone beside the river.

I watched her for no other reason than a young one was such a rare sight to behold. I understood the balance that kept Elydor from overpopulating. Having so few young ones was the price we paid for immortality. This particular cherub belonged to one of my father's warriors and his partner. When she was born, all of Gyoria rejoiced.

I should have been training, but spotted the young one on my return to the training yard.

Beyond her, Gyoria spread out like a living tapestry of stone and fire. Our beauty wasn't delicate like Aetheria's or fluid like Thalassaria. It was carved, earned, and enduring. Towering cliffs rose behind the strongholds which comprised Gyoria's capital Thaeron. Ironwood trees lined the ravines. The river, fed by ancient springs beneath the mounts, shimmered in the daylight.

"Too rare a sight."

I heard Dren coming, his step unmistakable. The former scholar turned warrior's footfalls—courtesy of his partner having been executed many decades ago—were heavier than most.

"Aye," I agreed. "Her magic is progressing nicely."

"Indeed?" Dren asked. "It seems to me she's been attempting to summon riverlilies all morn."

Also true. But at least she persevered despite her failed attempts.

"Your father's Council met earlier. I heard you did not attend?"

My father's Council was nothing more than a collection of Gyorian nobles who agreed with everything he said and did, regardless of the merit of his actions. Over the years, as he became more and more embittered after my mother was killed by a human plague that somehow managed to take hold here in Elydor, even though such diseases did not usually find their way through the Gate, the Council had become a mirror of their king.

"I did not."

Dren sighed as we stood side by side, watching the young one.

"He will be angry."

"My father is always angry."

Dren shifted his weight, his leather jerkin creaking, reinforced with obsidian-scaled plating and char-stained from the forges beneath Thaeron. Like all Gyorian armor, it was built to withstand blade, flame, and the weight of expectation. "Perhaps. But more so recently."

The young one tried again, and failed.

"First Kael," I said, trying not to think too hard on my brother. "And the recent unrest, as well as Adren's defection to Hawthorne... Father has had his share of traitors and spies of late."

She was becoming frustrated. Willing her not to give up, I watched, belatedly realizing Dren had gone silent.

"What is it?" I asked, my eyes still on the young one.

"Your anger will rival your father's if I speak my mind."

With a sharp look, I diverted my attention to the Gyorian who had been my right hand for many years. He rarely hesitated to speak openly to me, meaning there was just one topic he wished to broach.

"There will be no talk of Kael," I said, leaving no room in my tone for discussion of my brother. My twin. The only shield against an increasingly angry king who had once been a loving father but whose bitterness and hate for the humans who killed his wife—or so he believed—had turned him into the ruthless ruler he'd become.

Dren fell silent once again.

The young one's shoulders slumped in defeat.

Try once more.

Instead, she sank to her knees. It would be years until she understood that all that was needed to make flowers bloom where there were none was there already within. She had but to learn to harness it. To block out all other thoughts and, most especially, doubts.

Stand up.

Like most Elydorians, the thought of having my own babe to raise, to teach, to nourish, was but a dream. One that I'd given up on long ago. Were she mine, I'd spend my days attempting to show her that the light within her only faded if she allowed it.

She stood.

Needing a victory, even a small one, this time, when she raised her arm and swiped her small fingers into an arc, I did the same with my own. A single bloom from the stonebloom plant at her feet appeared. A bright-yellow riverlily, stark against the browns and greens of the landscape around it, peeked out as if to greet her.

The girl leaped into the air and then fell back down to her

knees to inspect it. Smelling the flower, her elation evident, she rose once again. This time, when she raised her hand and swiped, a second bloom appeared, one I did not produce.

I smiled. One which fled immediately when I spied Dren's amusement.

"She'd not have done it otherwise."

"Likely not."

"Why do you smile like a fool?"

"No reason, my lord."

Knowing I'd regret it, I relented. "Say what's on your mind."

"Is he a traitor? Truly?"

Every muscle in my body tensed, the urge to reach out for magic and destroy something, particularly Dren, one I fought to succumb to.

"How can you ask such a question?"

"He is not the only one who disagrees with your father's stance on the Gate."

We'd spoken little of my brother since he left, with good reason. Thinking of him, of how easily he'd forsaken me and his men...

"Agree or disagree, he is a traitor to Gyoria."

"Perhaps. But not to his own convictions."

He spoke barely above a whisper. Dren had suffered more than most, a suffering that bore visibility even after so many years.

"Convictions," I spat, impatient with the conversation. "His only conviction was loyalty to a woman he hardly knew."

"Love does such things."

I would not argue with that appalling fact, for I'd seen as much with my own eyes. "Which is why it should be avoided."

Surely, an argument Dren could agree with since love had cost lifetimes of peace.

"It has the ability to transform us, aye. As it did your brother. And father. Though in very different ways."

"Enough."

Dren sighed heavily. "The Council warned your father of Thalassari raiders off the southern coast."

"Odd. We've not dealt with them in many years."

"Precisely. But the waters around the Maelstrom Depths seem to have calmed, making them more daring. Your father is sending men to investigate."

Interesting. "First, the Gate reopens for the lost princess to return but then promptly closes once again. Then a new Thalassari queen is chosen and now anomalies around the Depths. Not to mention signs of a new imbalance. One my father seems overly concerned about."

"Concerned?" Dren snickered. "Not the word I would use for your father's recent behavior."

"Obsessed, then," I said, acknowledging Dren was right. "I will speak to him." I was convinced there was more to the situation and not trusting recent events were isolated. Coincidences, I'd learned in the hundreds of years I'd been alive, were rare.

With one final glance at the growing bed of flowers being summoned, I turned toward the palace, each step I took toward the formidable structure, and the man who reigned over it, heavier than the one before. The burden of calming the King of Gyoria—my father—and his increasingly erratic actions was heavy before Kael left. Now, it was nearly unbearable.

But it was my duty. And unlike my brother, I'd not forsake it.

4

LYRA

"I leave you here."

Mounted beside Ilyas, I thanked him for his aid. "You've been invaluable," I said, the smuggler an unlikely ally in our mission to reopen the Gate. "Thank you, Ilyas."

"Had Marek not saved my life, I'd still be glad to serve you. Unlike my family, I understand the value of diplomacy and believe, as you do, the key to survival in Elydor is to foster alliances, even with those who have been enemies for generations."

"I don't consider you an enemy," I said honestly. "Even if others disagree."

The warrior sat straighter, turning his mount back toward the coast. "Nor do I." With a fisted hand over his heart, the Gyorian greeting and parting signal of respect, he spurred his mount forward, leaving me alone on the road.

Precisely as planned.

As I began the trek to Thaeron, one that would see me reaching it before nightfall, I thought back to the day our final phase of the mission that could finally see the Aetherian Gate opened and its unlikely gathering of individuals at King Galfrid's Council table.

For days, the debate had raged. Kael wanted to return, to be the one to confront his brother and father. It took everyone present to convince him that was the least likely way to retrieve the Stone of Mor'Vallis, the remaining artifact needed to open the Gate. Especially after the disaster that was his last visit.

In the end, it was the king and his daughter, Mev who had devised a plan, one similar to my own in the days after Marek and Issa returned Aetheria's Wind Crystal back to its rightful owner. I would visit the palace as an emissary. It would raise few suspicions as I'd done so many times. I'd been trained, as my parents both had before me, as an Aetherian diplomat.

And also trained well beyond that role too in another few knew about.

The spies we had in place knew me well. It had taken some time for me to convince the others to allow me to travel alone, but since King Balthor was highly suspicious of all Aetherians and tolerated my presence, they had finally agreed. Marek and Issa would escort me to Grimharbor, and Marek's friend Ilyas Rho would take me as far as he could without being spotted by palace guards.

We'd quickly set the plan in motion. The easy part was complete.

Gaining entry to the palace would be easy. It was retrieving the stone that would prove a challenge. Kael thought his brother could be turned. The others disagreed. But all trusted me to assess the situation, make contact with the Aetherian spies, though only one now remained, and decide how to proceed.

"I know what you're thinking, Lyra. Do not do it."

Kael's warning rang clear in my mind as I approached the

formidable structure built into the side of a mountain. Impenetrable. A fortress like none other.

How Kael had known the secret plan I hatched, I could only guess. Apparently, I was not the only one who noticed the way Terran looked at me throughout the many years we'd been thrust together. Though I dealt more often with Kael, or even the king himself, Prince Terran and I had had many, many encounters.

"My brother cannot tolerate a liar," Kael had said. "Be honest with him from the start. Convince him to join us. But do not do it under the guise of mock-interest."

It was that last bit Kael had wrong. There would be no need for me to feign interest in the second son of King Galfrid. From the moment we first met, when he'd accompanied his father to a Council meeting, well before the Gate had been opened, something about him had intrigued me. He was Gyorian, no doubt. Even less easy than his brother to coax a smile from. But when it did happen, there was a genuineness about him that most lacked.

I shuddered as a Gyorian guard stopped me.

Thaeron was a fortress disguised as a city. Slate-gray stone buildings huddled beneath the palace, their rooftops shingled in dark metal that reflected the overcast sky. The palace gates were massive, hammered from dark iron and opened for me. Much of it lay beneath the mountain, hidden and impenetrable.

I rode beneath a familiar archway of obsidian stone. Inside, the entry hall was vast, with high ceilings supported by twisted trees, roots clawing the floor, and branches cradling flickering lanterns above.

Draped in the calm mask of diplomacy that I'd learned to exude, even in the face of fear, I stepped into a small antechamber reserved for guests such as myself. Carved from stone, the windowless space wasn't meant to be welcoming.

Candles buried in every crevice gave the chamber a glow that would never dim. Land magic made use of so many minerals that, even after all these years, I knew only a sampling of their powers. Their flames were sustained not by wax, but by slivers of pyrolume, an amber-veined mineral found deep within Gyoria's mountains.

I sat under the constant watch of a guard who knew me well but still stared at me as if I would attempt to murder his king at any moment. No offer of a meal. Or lodging. In previous years, before the Gate, I'd have been offered both. Even after, when relations strained between our clans, a cordiality remained among official envoys. But those days were past. I would be forced to talk my way into remaining at the palace long enough to secure the stone.

Though I'd asked for an audience with the king, they would never give it to me so easily. Aetherians were often accused of slyness and deception, but the Gyorian court also wielded both as weapons. I would be strung along for at least a day, or more, before gaining such an audience. Which suited me fine. My first goal was having Dell learn about my presence and make contact. Who could have imagined the Aetherian spy who'd been placed in the Gyorian palace more than a decade ago would become the greatest asset in our history?

"To what do we owe the pleasure of welcoming the daughter of the most prestigious noble family in Aetheria?"

Before he fully appeared, I knew that voice. Prince Terran filled the entrance, his frame even more imposing than his brother's. Some had difficulty telling them apart, but I did not. Both dark-haired and skinned, both relentlessly handsome, there were differences too. Even when Terran smiled, creases never reached his eyes. He looked at everyone, especially me, with mistrust.

Arms uncovered, his training garb as presumptuous as his demeanor, Terran dared opponents to injure him. No armor, just leather pants and a sleeveless black tunic that clung to the sharp lines of his torso. Bronze cuffs encircled his forearms, more ornamental than practical, and dust from the training yard still clung to his boots. He was every bit the warrior prince, unapologetically unguarded, as if daring the world to strike first.

"I am more than simply a daughter now." I stood. "Perhaps you've not noticed."

His gaze perused me from head to toe, as I knew it would. Terran taunted with every part of him... his words, his eyes.

You are wrong, Kael. Your brother can never be turned to support Aetheria.

"I have noticed."

And there it was. The jittering in my stomach, my core, whenever he was near. I'd asked for it, goading him as I had.

I'd dealt with the more difficult immortals in Elydor with more cool than I was able to muster when Terran was near. But this time, the stakes were too high. There was no room for error.

"I requested an audience with your father."

"He is unavailable."

As expected.

"I will wait."

His brows shot up. "For how long will you wait, Lyra?"

He drew out the second syllable of my name, making it sound more like a lover's caress than an insult. But it wasn't the way he said, "Lyra" that had me decide on a course of action. Tossing Kael's warnings aside, and praying to the gods it wasn't a miscalculation, I narrowed the distance between us, taking two steps toward him.

"I have an eternity, Terran."

The undertone of my voice was unmistakable. Not surprisingly, he reacted.

"What game do you play?"

I blinked, as if innocent, which I most certainly was not.

"No game, my lord."

"So deferential, suddenly?"

"I don't have a deferential bone in my body, Terran. As well you know."

As expected, he couldn't resist the challenge. The darkening of his eyes told me as much.

"You will, by the time we're finished here."

Ahh, Terran. It was almost too easy.

"Aye?"

He closed the gap between us.

"I will have you begging before this game is through, Lyra. Do not test me on this."

"Begging? For what? An audience with your father?"

He smelled like the land. Like strength and warrior. A heady combination for someone who could respect his power, even if it was a danger to me and my people.

When his hand shot out, I didn't stop him. It was not the first time Terran had touched me, his finger lifting my chin to meet his gaze. But it was the first time in many years, and never in a conversation such as this one.

A dangerous game, indeed.

"I am impervious to temptation, Lyra. Especially when I'm being manipulated."

I leaned in, just enough to feel the tension coil between us.

"Then 'tis a good thing I'm not trying to tempt you."

His hand dropped, but Terran didn't step away. We were close. Too close. If anyone walked past, they would think something was happening between us, but Terran didn't seem worried. Instead, he held his ground.

If I were sensible, I would have stepped back. Terran smelled of rain-cooled stone and the metal tang of his magic. I could map his tells now: the way his jaw tightened when he swallowed a truth; the way power gathered at his left hand first; the way his gaze dropped to my mouth when he was about to say something he should not.

I had been trained to exploit weakness. The trouble was learning where his ended and mine began.

"Why are you here, Lyra?"

I stepped back, my senses already heightened with the threat of Gyoria all around me. An unsettledness I'd expected, but even so...

"To speak to your father."

"Speak to me instead."

I gestured behind him, the entrance still flanked by guards. The corridor open for any to walk past. "We're too exposed."

I didn't drop my gaze until Terran turned from me. Without another word, he walked out, as quickly as he'd come, saying something to one of the guards and then stalking away, his strides taking him quickly out of my view.

Prince Terran leaving without a proper fare-thee-well was unsurprising, but it stung nonetheless.

"Come with me," one of the guards said.

I expelled a breath, my shoulders untensing for the first time since I'd heard Terran's voice. Where we were going, I had no notion. But wherever it was, only one thing mattered. And it wasn't my feelings, however misguided they might be, about Kael's brother and son of Aetherian's greatest enemy.

5

TERRAN

"Why is she here?"

My father wasted little time questioning me. The moment I walked into the throne room where he'd just finished doling out both rewards and punishments to villagers who revered, and were terrified of their king, he began his interrogation.

Unlike my brother, I disliked the cavernous and cold throne room. He saw the floor, carved from a single block of dark stone, embedded with bloodstone and onyx, as a symbol of the power and wonders of Gyoria.

To me, it represented the man who sat on its throne, one who I was forced to defend even as his actions became indefensible.

"I am uncertain."

Unfortunately, Lord Valdric stood as if he were my father's sentinel beside the throne. His closest advisor, the Gyorian nobleman was never far from his king. I liked him less than Kael, and Kael despised Valdric enough to challenge him openly once, incurring our father's wrath.

"Uncertain?" Valdric's beady eyes narrowed. He cared about

little except his own ambitions which were unmatched. He'd been given land, status, titles... I didn't know what more he wanted but was fairly sure there was something. Otherwise, he'd not be here. He agreed so readily with my father that he'd stopped questioning the king's motives.

"I've sent her to the Watcher's Keep and will question her further there."

"Why?"

My father's tone was underlined with the harshness that came from centuries of mistrust of any Aetherian.

"She's traveled far and is a guest."

"A guest?" Valdric spat. "You confuse guests and enemies, my prince."

Despite the nod to my title, his words were anything but deferential.

I don't have a deferential bone in my body, Terran. As well you know.

There was little time to dwell on those words, or any other, Lyra had spoken. First, I needed to ensure her safety.

Not bothering to conceal my displeasure with him, I turned my attention to Lord Valdric.

Known for his deep connection to the land and his strategic mind, the nobleman was valuable to my father's rule. He had also harbored a deep mistrust of outsiders for as many years as I'd been alive and strongly believed in Gyoria's isolationist policies that began even before the Aetherian Gate opened. Or so I was told.

"She is an emissary of a neighboring clan, one whose land will border ours for as long as Gyoria endures. Were we an island, perhaps we could afford the arrogance of turning away a respected noblewoman without food or shelter. But I was not raised to mistake pride for strategy."

"Two insults in one fine speech," he shot back. "Well done—"

"Enough," my father bellowed. "Learn why she's here and find out what you can about the Tidebreaker Fleet defending a human holding."

I'd already planned to do as much. Most importantly, I wished to know if my brother had an inkling his right hand was half-human. The entire incident with Dren did not sit well, especially coming on the heels of so many other strange happenings.

Princess Mevlida among them.

"Aye, my lord."

My father's eyes narrowed. "And then bring her to me."

I'd planned to do that as well, but something about the way he commanded it...

There.

Valdric's eyes shifted to my father, for the briefest of moments, in a way that did not sit well. There was something more to this exchange.

"In the morn, I will escort her to you myself."

"Bring her to me tonight."

Father often kept visitors waiting, a habit born from calculation. I had no notion what he planned to say, or do, to Lyra, but something was most certainly amiss.

"She's requested an audience," I said evenly, "but we gain nothing by dragging her in tonight, weary and unguarded. Let her rest, and tomorrow, we present her on our terms with the dignity this court demands."

It was a weak argument, but until I understood better what piece of the puzzle I was missing, I would not allow my father to put our entire kingdom at risk. Would he actually harm Lyra? Perhaps not. But his actions had grown increasingly unpredictable.

"Very well. Return with our guest," he said the word with

unmasked disgust, "after you break your fast. In the meantime, she remains under watch."

"By my guards."

Valdric's hand twitched. I'd not seen him this unsettled in some time. Since it was customary for the king's heirs to govern our own halls, there was little my father could say without breaching tradition.

His quick nod of approval, though expected, was clearly not welcome by Valdric.

Without another word, I bowed to my king and spun from them both, taking deep strides to move quickly out of the throne room. Taking a left at the arched corridor just beyond the throne room, I passed the towering banners of Gyoria, the echo of my boots sharp against the polished stone. The weight of the conversation clung to me, but I didn't slow. My chambers lay just beyond the eastern wing, and her modest, but guarded one had been placed close by under my orders.

Guards straightened as I approached. I offered only a curt nod, my focus fixed on the door just ahead. Rapping on the heavy iron-cladded door, I was surprised how quickly it opened.

Alive for centuries, the beauty of one Aetherian woman—my enemy—should not have the ability to stop me short, especially when I'd seen her not long ago.

But it did.

Always had.

Elegant and graceful, Lyra's long silver hair flowed behind her as if the wind she commanded had just blown through it. Piercing, pale-blue eyes waited for me to speak.

Dressed as she'd been earlier, Lyra wore a flowing tunic of deep midnight blue belted at the waist with silver cord, the fabric catching the firelight like moonlight on water.

"May I enter?"

It was a formality as I'd planned to do so no matter her response. I wanted answers, and would have them.

She stepped aside.

If she were not Aetherian, I'd have asked about her travels. Her comfort. If she'd enjoy the meal that had been brought to her. But her family had campaigned to have my father removed from his position. Her king's actions had destabilized Elydor, killed my mother, and taken my brother from me. So instead, I asked the only question that mattered.

"Why are you here? And why is my father so intent on speaking with you?"

Instead of responding, Lyra raised her chin stubbornly.

Feigning a calm I did not feel, I glanced around her chamber. Though modest by royal standards, it was warm and well-appointed. A carved stone hearth crackled softly, casting a golden glow across the woven tapestries lining the walls. A narrow writing desk stood near the window beside a small table set for two. The bed, draped in deep green and silver linens, was simple but inviting. It was the kind of room chosen with quiet intention... close to mine, yet private enough to avoid suspicion.

"Lyra," I warned.

"We have much to discuss."

"Aye, we do," I agreed.

She looked at me as I did her. With suspicion. A measure of trepidation. And perhaps a hint of longing.

"I expect you sent a copious amount of honeymead and an extra mug for this purpose?" she asked.

A quick glance at the table confirmed her words. Silently thanking my men, I neither confirmed nor denied her words.

To a Gyorian, there was no worse offense than a lie. Unfortunately, the same could not be said for Aetherians, who were as slippery with their words as they were with their allegiances.

"If you're offering, I accept," I said, striding toward the table. Pouring two ales, I waited for her to join me.

"A comfortable chamber," she said, sitting. "So close to your own quarters. I assume used for such purposes as this?"

Whether she intended to goad me or not, I couldn't be certain. But I took her bait gladly.

"This?" I deliberately misunderstood her insinuation. "It's rare I host an enemy so close to my quarters. More often, 'tis the opposite."

I sat across from her. The chair, unlike most things in Gyoria, was soft. Meant to cradle and relax. It had been created by my great-grandfather, a leatherworker, and his designs permeated our palace.

"Do you host many... guests?"

We did have much to discuss, but I would play her game first.

"Why do you ask? Jealous? Or do you wish to join their ranks?"

I expected her to laugh. Or offer some coy, Aetherian response. Instead, Lyra sipped her ale, long black lashes framing those mesmerizing eyes above the mug's rim.

"So elusive, as usual. Let me be clear, Lyra: I would lay you down on that bed and make you scream louder than you have in the long life you've lived and be happier for it. You know well the urge to do so, against my better judgment, has been there for as long as we've known each other. What I don't understand is the reason, for the first time in memory, you pretend otherwise."

The urge to unsettle her was so strong, I would likely say, or do, anything to make it happen. Alas, she remained unaffected.

Would anything rattle this woman? I doubted so.

It would be entertaining, however, to discover if such a thing were possible.

"I've never pretended otherwise, Prince Terran. Not this eve, nor earlier, nor any time we've been in each other's company these past many years. But I'm not here because I find you unsettlingly attractive, despite your foul demeanor. We've more important matters to discuss."

Unsettlingly attractive.

Foul demeanor. Her words did little to improve it.

"Then cease fluttering your lashes, Lyra. And answer my question."

There. A spark of... something. Finally.

Did she guard herself so carefully because it was an honored tradition in her clan, especially among the nobility? Or because Lyra hid something deeper that she allowed few to see? With no evidence for the latter, I'd always imagined it might be so.

What, I could not be certain. But the urge to prod her to reveal more had never quite gone away, even though I'd willed it to do so many times in the past.

"I do not," she insisted, "flutter my lashes. As well you know."

A fact that mattered little. Leaning into her irritation seemed prudent.

"Nay? You've done all but say, 'Fuck me Terran,' since you've arrived," I said, using the crude human word a'purpose.

"You are confusing your own desires with my own," she said coolly.

"I've not denied mine, unlike you." Leaning forward, I reminded her of an interaction she likely had forgotten, but I had not. "The Festival of Tides, at the ceremonial banquet. You watched the water dancers, barely clothed, as their erotic movements which stirred more than one cross-clan coupling—"

"You stood behind me," she said, as if we spoke of the most mundane of topics.

I gave her the same look now as I had that eve. If Lyra had turned toward me, away from the dancers, I'd have taken her into my arms, and my bed, that very eve.

I had known it. She had known it. The look that passed between us was one of night-time awakenings after dreams of a kiss that never happened.

"You remember."

I was no Aetherian, but even I could sense that the rate of her breath had increased.

Three times in as many moments, I'd struck gold. And would not relent. Unfortunately, Lyra had caught onto my game and was no longer playing. The cool facade was back, and it seemed we'd be back to discussing matters of more import.

"Well done, my lord," she said, sarcasm dripping from every word.

"Now tell me why you've really come here."

She refilled us both. Slowly. Smoothly. Every movement like a whisper in the wind. We could not be more opposite. Perhaps that was why she intrigued me so.

Sitting back, Lyra studied me.

Measured me.

"If you're thinking of a way to say what you've come to say without revealing your true intentions, reconsider," I said, understanding her better than I should.

"You are my enemy. Would it not be wise to carefully consider my words, Terran?"

I thought back to my father's behavior these past days. Lyra's arrival was no coincidence. Something was afoot and had been since Princess Mevlida arrived. Which meant it could be just one thing...

"It's tied to the Gate? To reopening it. Aye?"

She was clever, but the briefest blink of her eyes told me I was right. There was no victory in my guess. King Galfrid had been attempting to reopen it since the day my father closed the portal to the human realm. His daughter's arrival brought more questions than answers, for our spies in Aetheria confirmed it had not reopened for anyone but, apparently, the princess.

"Lyra—"

"I will tell you, on the morrow."

That was not what I'd expected.

"Why not now?" She was up to something. Aetherian's always were, but I could not guess this one's game.

"I am weary from travel and need to gather my thoughts first."

I downed my ale, watching her as intently as she did me.

"We will break our fast here, and you'll tell me then. Before I take you to my father."

She revealed nothing.

"Am I confined to these quarters?"

What are you up to, Lady Lyra?

"You are a guest, not a prisoner. Go where you may. But be aware... my father and his men are not as gracious a host as I."

Her elegant brows raised, but she said nothing.

Leaning forward, I made myself more clear. "You are free to go about as you please, but remain in the Watcher's Keep if you value your immortality. 'Tis not a threat, Lyra. Whatever reason brought you here agitates the court in ways I've not seen in many years."

I had her full attention.

And liked it.

Damn her, but something about this particular Aetherian stirred me like none other.

"Your father would start a war if he harmed an envoy."

Standing, I told Lyra what she already knew. "The war has already begun. I will be back at sunrise. Good eve, Lyra."

I waited until she rose, as was custom, to take my leave.

"Good eve, Terran."

Nodding, I left her chamber. There would be little sleep for me this evening. Preparations needed to be made.

War wasn't coming. It had arrived. In the form of a beautiful, but deadly, adversary.

6

LYRA

I moved through the courtyard, unable to rid myself of an uneasiness that had settled over me during our conversation. I'd long ago dismissed our interaction at the Festival of Tides as one I imagined. If it seemed, with one step toward him, Terran would have ravaged me... surely it had been more in my own mind, the dancers having influenced my thinking.

You've done all but say, "Fuck me Terran," since you've arrived.

Why should I be surprised a Gyorian, and one as bold as its prince, would say such a thing? He did it to unsettle me. And it had worked.

The courtyard was quiet, lit by a few low-burning torches that cast long shadows across the stone. The air was cool but not harsh, still carrying the faint scent of something darker, like storm-soaked earth.

Jagged cliffs loomed beyond the outer wall. Strange silver-leafed trees lined the path, their leaves clicking softly in the wind. This place didn't breathe like Aetheria, but there was magic here too. It was just buried deeper, quieter. Waiting.

I kept my steps light as I moved through the garden. No one had stopped me. Yet.

Terran would most certainly know I was out here. But unless he were to openly declare me a prisoner, there was no recourse for him or his guards who watched me even now.

Talk to me.

Dell had been here for too long. Eleven years apart from Aetheria, breathing Gyorian air and walking on the land of a magic so different from our own, his whispers had grown quieter. They didn't travel the way they used to. Not through buildings, not across long distances. His reach had dulled, like a blade gone soft at the edge.

Dell?

I sent the silent message along the air currents, praying he might be waiting. Dell would know of my presence, but he'd been silent when I arrived. And this was the first time I had been able to make my way outside the palace walls.

It's no longer in his crown.

I closed my eyes against the darkness, taking a deep breath, smiling.

Where is it?

Out here, in the open, his whispers were clear.

I do not know.

My smile faltered. That did not bode well.

Seryn?

Was discovered and taken before I was aware of what happened. The king ordered Prince Terran to execute him.

It was as I'd heard.

Tell me what you know.

To the guard, I was strolling through the courtyard, perhaps unable to sleep. In truth, I was gathering the most important intelligence in more than a century.

It had been kept in his crown until recently. The day before Seryn was killed, I obtained an audience with him and the stone was... missing. I've not yet been able to gain additional information on its whereabouts... and then Seryn.

Dell went silent.

Seryn was discovered. And killed. By Terran.

It is too dangerous for you here any longer. Go to the Veiled Market and find Ilyas Rho. Avoid the Warden's Hold at all costs. They were out in force on my way in.

The Wardens enforced Gyorian law and would be more vigilant than ever, taking their cues from an increasingly unstable, and suspicious, king.

I would not presume to leave you alone here, my lady.

I'd stopped and the guard noticed. Resuming my meandering, I put Dell at ease.

Were you not here alone while Seryn was trained?

Ah, but...

Careful, Dell. I was outsmarting kings before you learned to whisper.

His response was immediate.

Apologies, my lady. I meant no offense.

Dell would not perish as Seryn had. If he thought me offended, better than having him remain here out of a sense of duty. So instead of saying, *"None taken,"* as I might in other circumstances, I ensured his safety instead.

Prove it.

More silence. I understood his dilemma. Aetherian warriors were taught to protect, not abandon. But Dell knew what was at stake. He had known since the day he chose to stay behind enemy lines, and that he remained alive was a testament to his abilities.

You've done extraordinarily well. Let me prove my own worth, now. And join you on our voyage back home.

Home, he whispered finally. *It feels as if I have two homes now. But only one clan has my loyalty. I will do as you request, my lady.*

This is what we fought for. Returning to the days Dell would be openly welcome in Gyoria. A united Elydor with wide-open borders. Someday, perhaps he could enjoy two homes in this land.

May the winds guide you to safety.

And you as well, Lady Lyra. Trust no one here.

A warning I didn't need.

Ensuring he was finished, I waited a moment longer and made my way back inside. From the look of the first guard I passed, and the second, I was surprised not to find Terran standing at my door, waiting.

Instead, I opened it, thankful to find my chamber empty, and sank back into the chair, my mind racing with the events of the day. And more importantly, calculating my next move.

Terran wanted the truth. Instead, he would be given a partial one. And that only because it was becoming clear, without him, the Stone of Mor'Vallis would be impossible to obtain.

I would lay you down on that bed and make you scream louder than you have in the long life you've lived and be happier for it.

This wasn't the first time since we'd first met that the Gyorian prince had stirred a part of me that I had little inclination to explore. With little time for entanglements and complications which undoubtedly arose by having a partner, meeting my basic needs had always been sufficient. And perhaps, with Terran, that's all it would be. A coupling, perhaps better than most, but a coupling, nonetheless.

And yet... the unsettling flutter in my core at his words told me otherwise. Something about this particular Gyorian warrior gave way to a warning I'd always been able to ignore. But our situation was different this time. I needed him, and he wanted me.

That was my answer. And in truth, my excuse too.

To let down my guard without admitting that's what I was doing. Because wanting him had never been the problem.

Admitting it?

That was another story.

7

TERRAN

I knocked. And waited.

Respecting your enemy was more difficult than not doing so, a lesson my father taught me before his mind had become twisted with hate. He had been, in fact, a wise and fair ruler. I'd never have used the word "kind" or "caring," even though my mother once described him as both, sending my brother and I into uncontrollable laughter... but wise? Aye.

But the man he'd become since Mother died? He was as much a stranger to me as Kael who had fled to Aetheria without a second thought, leaving his men, leaving me, behind.

"You are looking particularly dour this morn."

Lyra, on the other hand, was not. She was breathtaking, as always.

Her fitted bodice dipped slightly at the neckline, edged with fine silver threading. Long sleeves tapered at the wrists, where sheer, cloud-like fabric draped delicately past her hands. Her gown moved like air with layers of soft blue and pearl white that billowed with each step.

"Preparing myself," I said as she stepped aside, "to navigate the web of half-truths you are no doubt preparing to offer me."

If I wasn't mistaken, the corners of Lyra's mouth raised just slightly.

"A meal arrived moments ago. How much do you believe I eat?"

The table was set with thick slices of dark rye bread, toasted and slathered with salted butter. Beside them, a platter of roasted vegetables and dried stoneberries along with a carafe of spiced black tea which steamed gently, flanked by a stronger drink: dark, bitter kova poured into small, hammered-metal cups.

"Gyorians eat well, despite what you may think."

We sat in the same chairs as the night before, pulling food onto our wooden trenchers. It was something oddly... fitting, despite our mutual distaste for one another.

"What do you believe I think?"

"Of my people?"

"Aye."

"What all Aetherians believe," I said. "That we are inferior in every way to your clan."

She finished chewing a stoneberry. "I don't believe that."

My laugh was immediate, and laced with bitterness. "Your first lie of the morn."

Lyra said nothing but watched me, as she often did. "Do you believe all Aetherians so pretentious?"

I pretended to think on it. "Nay. Though I do find them elitist and condescending."

The look she gave me proved my point.

"All the same."

"You would know," I shot back. "You have the books hied away in your libraries and the minds, the greatest thinkers, to understand such nuances of language. I've naught but brute strength to recommend me."

Not true, of course. But that's what her people believed.

"Terran," she said, her voice not the only thing that lowered. "You've much more than that to recommend you, and know it well."

Her perusal of me was as blatant, leaving little to the imagination. Her tone, too, had taken on a flirty edge.

"Do you aim to seduce me, Lyra, into forgetting to ask about your midnight stroll? Or the true reason you're here?"

"This again?" Her question was tinged with impatience.

For a moment, I could almost believe her compliment was true. But this was an Aetherian who sat across the table from me. And not just any Aetherian but one from a noble line known for their cunning.

Her lips squeezed another berry, inviting an unwanted vision of those very same lips wrapped around me. Would a woman such as she even engage in the act? More likely, she would toss her silvery hair back and demand to be serviced instead.

And service her I would.

"Terran," she warned.

As if I would heed a warning. Instead, I took a bite of fresh-baked bread and sat back in my chair. "If you'd prefer I pretend to be unaffected by you, then so be it."

I was certain Lyra was unaccustomed to such directness. Her startled look told me as much.

"Kael said I would have difficulty gaining your trust."

My hand froze. My body stiffened. If she was attempting to put me off balance, Lyra knew precisely how to do it.

"I would prefer not to speak of my brother."

"He also warned you would say as much."

I poured another cup of kova and drank deeply.

"He told me once," I shot back, "you were the most trouble-some of all Aetherians."

Kael served on the Council with her for many years. Deter-mining who could, or could not, pass through the Aetherian Gate was considered an honorable position, until my father closed it, of course.

"Because he found it difficult to manipulate me. Still does."

I hated wanting to ask but did so anyway.

"He is... well?"

"Happily partnered? Aye. In love? Very much. But well? I would not presume to use that word. Kael misses you, and his men, very much. He longs to belong, something Aetheria cannot yet give him."

Each word was like a dagger pushed deeper into my chest.

"Misses," I mumbled. "I am here. As are his men. Waiting, for what I do not know? He abandoned us both easily and will not be returning."

"Easily? I think not. Kael, it does not have to be this way."

Her words were spoken so softly, I could have missed them. Except I didn't because I happened to be staring at her lips. They were fuller than any others' and demanded attention. Even when my attention should be elsewhere.

"There is no other way," I said. "As long as the Gate remains closed, my people will be hated by yours, by the humans. Elydor has been broken for some time."

Lyra blinked, watching me.

Was I baiting her? Aye. If her coming here, along with the other strange happenings these past months, did *not* have ought to do with the Gate, I would be surprised. Since Princess Mevlida came through, and was apparently unable to return, I could only assume her father's attempt to reopen it had intensified.

Yet Lyra revealed nothing. I might as well have been asking her if the meal was to her satisfaction.

She was good.

Very good.

"Terran—"

"Why are you here, Lyra?"

She'd been about to weave a tale. How I knew, I couldn't be certain. But she had, and my patience for her was at an end.

"Your father is not well, Terran. Kael knows it. *You* know it. His hatred of humans has poisoned Elydor—"

"Your king opening the gate and allowing them here poisoned Elydor."

It was an age-old disagreement that would not be solved at this table.

"They'd not have been allowed in if the humans weren't worthy. They were *called* through the gate for a reason, Terran. Not by accident, not by whim. Magic chooses what logic cannot. You may not trust my king, but do you truly believe the magic of Elydor itself is wrong?"

It was an argument they'd used many times. One I rejected.

Lyra made me want to choose something I'd never been given permission to want... myself.

"My mother was not the only one they killed."

"Life hangs on a thread, Terran. For them. Even for immortals. We may live longer but can be killed just as easily by one another."

"If they'd not have come—"

"What threatens our world now is not the humans but what we've become while hating them."

She spoke firmly, and I'd be lying if I said part of me wasn't enthralled by this version of her. Less measured. Perhaps a bit of passion simmered underneath that cool exterior after all?

What I would give to find out...

"The Stone of Mor'Vallis. Whatever legend you were told, there's more to it than as a relic that intensifies the king's power. It's reacting to something old. Something dangerous. I didn't come here to start a war. I came to stop one."

The Stone of Mor'Vallis.

That's why Lyra had come.

The relics had existed long before the Gate was ever opened, before the humans set foot on Elydorian soil. Forged by ancients to temper the raw, wild magic of this realm... A stone that could strip power from the strongest mage, a crystal that stirred the skies and a pearl that spoke to the tides. Only able to be used by the most powerful in each clan.

And yet... something had shifted.

The Stone of Mor'Vallis had grown restless. I'd felt it. Subtle, but pulsing, like a warning in my blood. The land felt different too. Off balance. As if the elements themselves were waiting for something.

I didn't know what Lyra wanted. Not fully. But as much as I wished to completely discount Lyra's words, I couldn't.

"What do you want, precisely, Lyra?"

She looked at me, straight in the eyes, the words she was about to utter likely true if I were any judge of character.

"I want you to take the Stone of Mor'Vallis from your father."

8

LYRA

His laugh was immediate. Harsh.

Worse, Terran stood, looking down at our finished meal.

"Come. My father grows impatient for the audience you requested."

"Terran—"

"There'll be no more talk of the Stone of Mor'Vallis, if you value your life."

How could I have thought, despite Kael's warning, Terran could be turned into an ally?

I poured a cup of tea and took two sips, obeying his hastily given order on my own terms. Pushing it away, I plucked the woven cloth from my lap, folded it neatly and stood.

Speaking to him now would not do. But perhaps the very person he tried to protect could unknowingly convince him to speak to me.

Formulating a plan, I followed Terran through the corridors of a surprisingly pleasant wing of the palace I'd never seen. Unlike the cavernous and imposing one which I was accustomed to staying in, Terran's quarters used the stone surrounding us not to intimidate as a background against a warmth that felt personal, coupled with woven rugs, sun-filtered glass, and the soft scent of cedar.

But there was no time to admire my surroundings. Mind racing, I considered every angle. My goals. Terran's. The king's. And refused to be intimidated as we walked into my least favorite throne room of all clans.

King Balthor sat upright, imposing as ever. He was alone, thankfully. His right hand, Lord Valdric, was one of the least favorable to me in all of Elydor. Sharing his king's hatred of humans but with no other reason behind it than personal gain made Balthor's prejudices pale in comparison.

There were few in Elydor who could intimidate me.

King Balthor was an exception.

Appearing as if he'd been forged from the very stone that surrounded him, the king's dark hair and green eyes were the only things he had in common with his sons. His nose was wider, cheeks less defined. Terran and Kael took much of their appearance from their mother, a noble Gyorian woman renowned for her beauty.

Greeting him in the customary Gyorian way, fist over heart, but with a bow to my head to denote his status, I wasn't surprised that the king didn't return the gesture. Not one for pretense, he wouldn't hide his hatred of me, or my people.

Give grace not because it's returned but because it's who you are.

My mother, one of the greatest emissaries in Aetherian history, offered sage advice. Some, like that particular one, were harder to execute than others. Especially when dealing with one such as King Balthor, who had caused much misery and pain for Elydorians these past years.

"You requested an audience. Be quick about it, Lady Lyra. There are few here who welcome an Aetherian in these walls."

A not-so-thinly veiled threat.

"There have been concerns, my lord, over elemental disturbances that could affect all of Elydor. I serve as an emissary from King Galfrid to open discussions on such matters."

"Disturbances? I know of no such disturbances."

While keeping my eyes trained on the king, I felt for any shift in air currents around Terran. As I suspected, an intake of breath told me what Kael had already said. Their father kept from both princes that he had hidden the Wind Crystal in the Maelstrom Depths. Likely Terran also did not know the crystal Balthor "returned" after he stole it to close the portal was a fake.

Exposing him as a liar to his son was my only goal this day.

"You've not suspected... anything might be amiss? That Elydor's magic may perhaps be shifting in some way? Or that the Maelstrom Depths have been acting... strangely?"

Denying it would outright brand him a liar. The very same celestial event that created our realm imbued it with an energy that gave Elydorians immortality and the ability to wield elemental magic, but that also demanded a balance which had been shifting since the humans came into Elydor from their own realm, and even more so since they were locked out.

But never more had the subtle signs of disturbance been evident than with Mev's appearance from a "locked" Gate. And of course, the manufactured one Marek's retrieval of an artifact that belonged in another clan had initiated.

My question angered him, of course.

"Do not play me for a fool. The princess." He said the word as if it was a slur. "Came through a closed portal. Is that the disturbance you refer to?"

He knew it wasn't and wielded unspoken words as weapons, just as I did.

"One of many," I responded, evading him and taking a more

direct tactic. "I don't remember seeing you without your crown before, your liege."

His nostrils flared. King Balthor wanted me tossed from his throne room, or worse. Would have done so already if he courted full-fledged, open war. Most telling, his eyes darted to his son.

"You play dangerous games, Lady Lyra," the king said.

Would Balthor let me leave this hall with Terran? I would ensure it.

"Executing me will not serve the same purpose as doing so with Seryn."

I glanced at Terran, whose eyes widened.

"Your king would do the same, were a Gyorian spy found in your midst."

It was time to stir the sleeping storm.

"We would not be so reckless as to allow one in Aetheria."

The ground rumbled beneath my feet. Impressive, as I'd not seen his fingers move. Drawing a slow breath as this was advanced magic, I focused on the charged space between earth and sky. With a flick of my wrist and the tightening of will, I thinned the air at my feet, lifting the pressure just enough to still the quake beneath me.

The rumble dissipated, as if exhaling through stone.

Both the king and his son were duly impressed, as they should be. It was a tricky bit of magic my king perfected and shared with us.

"Do you mean to cause a war? Is that why Galfrid sent you here?"

"*King* Galfrid sent me here to remind you that you've already begun this war, though not with soldiers but secrets. The borders have become so unstable, few will pass. We are more separated than ever before. Your own son recognizes," I said quickly, and boldly, knowing he would stop me soon, "Princess Mevlida's appearance, coming through a closed Gate, means that she belongs here. Just as the humans who—"

"Enough," he bellowed. His cheeks red, eyes glaring, the king's fingers flexed. Terran had taken a step toward me, though Zephra and the other Gods alone knew his purpose. "If you wish to leave this hall unharmed—"

I would not be intimidated.

"Your hatred of humans—"

He stood, scowling. "Tell your king, if it's war he wants, it's war he shall have."

"Father—"

"Do not," he continued to escalate, "interfere in this."

I didn't dare look at Terran. Instead, I met the king's gaze with a calm that seemed to anger Balthor even further, though it was difficult to forget... the king before me was the most powerful in Gyoria. If he wished me dead, my resistance would prove futile.

"King Galfrid wants to avoid war, not court it."

"By sending his envoy here to convince me the diseased humans were innocent in coming through that interminably damned Gate?"

There will never be peace in Elydor with him as king.

Knowing it, as well as I knew my own name, meant little. As long as Galfrid was alive, he would remain the King of Gyoria.

"Get out of my hall. If you are not beyond our borders by tomorrow—"

How I would secure the stone and fulfill that particular decree remained unsure. But one thing was certain: one of my goals here had been met. I turned, still giving the king the parting gesture he did not deserve, and left the hall with Terran.

He escorted me back the way we came. I said nothing, allowing him to replay the meeting in his mind.

Finally, just as we stepped into the corridor which led to my chamber, he stopped me.

"Lyra."

Halting, I faced him, revealing nothing.

"Aye, Terran?"

"Gather your belongings. It isn't safe for you here."

It was his expression, not his words, that told me I'd been successful. There was more there as well. A softness in his eyes usually lacking from Gyorians. But something else too. Something very, very Gyorian... though typically only for their own.

Even the slightest bit of protectiveness for me was more than I could have hoped for.

"Very well," I said in acquiescence.

"And wait for me in your chamber. Do not answer the door for any but me."

At my quizzical look, he added, "We must talk."

Indeed, we must. But that wasn't all Terran and I needed to do this day.

9

TERRAN

My father was lying.

About what, precisely, I couldn't be certain. But there was more to that meeting with Lyra than either of them outwardly admitted. Having just recounted the entire conversation to Dren, I waited for his assessment.

He knew every book in the Gyorian library from cover to cover. Was more intelligent than most, and I was wise enough to know my limitations. When it came to putting puzzle pieces together, none could do it as well as my right hand.

"I cannot think with you dizzying my mind. Stop pacing."

I kept at it. "Do not look at me."

"As if such a thing were possible."

Because I wanted his input more than I wanted to argue at this moment, I sat across from him in the iron-riveted chair carved with Gyorian runes. I had an identical one in my own chamber, a symbol of our close bond.

Only two others like it could be found in the palace, neither of which were currently being used.

Prince Kael sees what you do not. A king who would damn us all.

"My brother is a traitor, not a visionary."

Dren looked at me strangely.

"The Aetherian said, 'Kael sees what you do not: that my father is a king who would damn us all.'"

As he did often, Dren inhaled as if praying to Terranor for patience.

"Pretending you do not know Lady Lyra's name will do little to convince me you're immune to her."

The problem with living forever was not being able to hide your true self to those around you. I didn't deny his claim.

"Also... she's right."

I knew he'd say as much. When I met Kael on the road as he fled north with the princess, my father's order to retrieve them both had left Dren and I at odds on how to handle the situation. In the end, I allowed Kael to flee but it was Dren who counseled caution as Kael and I battled ever since.

"He is my father," I said, not for the first time. "You know the laws. As the most powerful Gyorian, he will remain king until his death. One I would not precipitate, even if we disagree more now than ever."

"I know the laws well. I also know, as you do, the Aetherian" —he grinned—"as you call her, is also right about the disturbances. We've all felt them since Princess Mevlida came through the Gate. That your father denied as much is telling."

"Denied it to her, his enemy."

Dren frowned. "Balthor is as transparent as aevumite. Think on it, Terran. The Gate opens for her. The land rumbles impatiently beneath our very feet. The Maelstrom Depths are disturbed for the first time in decades. Your father is more elusive than ever. And then Lyra arrives for some unknown purpose—"

"She wants me to take the Stone from my father."

Dren's mouth hung open.

"Do not say it."

"The Stone that he's worn in that crown atop his head for as many years as either of us has been alive but which has suddenly vanished?"

"Aye. That one," I admitted grudgingly.

The flicker of lanternlight played over shelves lined with ancient texts. Dren leaned against his desk as I stood and began to pace once again.

"You're looking at me as if I have already chosen a side," I said.

"Perhaps you have."

"Aye," I agreed. "My father's. There is no other choice."

"You always have a choice, Terran."

"In this, I do not."

"If not in this, then in nothing. What could be more important than your willingness to carry out duties and remain loyal to a king who is not forthcoming?"

"Not just any king. My father."

"Gods, Terran." Dren became impatient. "I know the fact well."

"What is he keeping from me?"

It was the only question that mattered.

Dren shook his head. "I don't know. But there is someone who likely does. Perhaps you should ask her. If she's still alive."

None would dare to touch her in my quarters. But the thought of it did not sit well.

"Do not venture far," I told him. "I will be back with orders by daybreak. See what you can discover in the meantime."

"Certainly, my lord. I will uncover your father's plot and ascertain the secrets he keeps from even his own son and heir. Easily done, my lord."

With a parting look that told him how much I appreciated his humor at the present time, I headed to Lyra's chamber. Before I could even knock at the door, the air around me thickened suddenly. I attempted to open it, but the door pressed back with increasing resistance the harder I pushed.

"Who's there?" Lyra called from inside.

"Terran," I said, unable to get inside.

Suddenly, the pressure vanished and the door came off its hinges as I continued to press. It was a thick door with wood made from silver-barked draylen trees found only in the high reaches of the Gyorian mountains.

She stood well beyond the fallen door, arms crossed, staring at me.

"You warded the door."

"Of course. I tend to take such precautions when my life is threatened."

Reasonable.

"Could you not have simply announced your presence and allowed me to let you in?" she asked, looking at the damaged door.

I despised her, aye. But did not want her dead. Picking up the door, I leaned it against its opening and turned back to her, ignoring her question.

"As I said, we need to talk."

She raised her arm, circled her hand and finger eloquently, and then waited.

"A veiling drift?"

"Aye. Since there are now large gaps in the door frame," she said, almost smiling. "Where anyone might listen through, courtesy of your unconventional way of entering a room."

Lyra was many things.

Beautiful. Graceful. Intelligent. Skilled. Manipulative.

But funny? It was not a quality I associated with her before, yet I'd been tempted to smile more in her presence than since my brother abandoned us.

"I thought you might be in danger."

Her smile faltered.

"Why would that matter to you?"

"I don't wish you dead, Lyra."

That damned chin rose. "Killing me would not bode well for Gyoria."

I added "defiant" to the list of Lyra's qualities with no doubt she believed her statement to be true.

"The last fight between a skilled Aetherian and Gyorian did not end well."

Her eyes flashed. "Seryn—"

"Was not skilled. I don't refer to that."

"Yet you murdered him anyway."

Had she known him? The spy was young, a haranya, just over a century old, but had been handsome and clearly clever enough to have gone undetected.

Thinking of them together did nothing to calm my mood. Not that it should matter.

But it did.

I took a step toward her.

"Would you care to test your theory? How easy Gyorians can be subdued?"

She didn't step back.

Of course she didn't.

Instead, Lyra tilted her chin even higher, fingers twitching at her side as a breeze stirred in the closed chamber. "You'd lose," she said, voice low.

"I don't lose," I replied, closing the space between us.

The air pressure shifted, subtle but undeniable. A flirt of wind brushed past my cheek like a whispered dare. Then came the sudden snap of force. I caught the invisible strike before it landed, my own magic flaring in response. Stone hummed beneath our feet.

Her eyes widened, just slightly. I could understand why. Few could detect and prevent such a strike.

She flicked her wrist, and the wind coiled around my arm like a rope. Meanwhile, Lyra's expression barely changed. I reached through the air rope and gripped her wrist before she could cast again, twisting her gently toward the wall. She didn't resist. Not at first.

But then a burst of air slammed into my chest and sent me a step back. She spun away, Lyra's hair whipping around her in an arc.

I caught her by the waist before she got too far.

We were both breathless. Flushed.

Close.

"Still think you'd win?" I asked, my voice rougher than I'd intended.

Her smile was slow. Dangerous. "You're the one panting."

Once. Just once, I wanted to see her lose control.

"Not from an effort exerted by using magic, I can assure you."

"Release my wrist."

I did, reluctantly. Wishing instead to use it as leverage to see what might happen if this dangerous dance continued.

"Explain the conversation between you and my father," I said, stepping back. "Why do you want me to take the Stone, rightfully his, from my father?"

Her lips were made to be kissed.

It was a damned inconvenient time to have such a thought, but there was no way to unsee a vision of me pressing her against the wall, wrists pinned above her head, and capturing those lips in mine.

I regained focus.

"You've sensed the imbalance. Mev... Princess Mevlida... came through and yet the Gate remains closed to all others. You know well, nothing in Elydor happens by chance or without repercussions. If you still do not believe humans belong here and wish to eradicate them, as does your father, explain how a thaelon was able to come through?"

"Half-human, aye. But she is also half-Aetherian. 'Tis likely the reason."

"She was not the only Elydorian trapped in the human realm when your father slammed the Gate shut without warning. Why have the others not come through? Surely they've tried?"

I'd told her this many times, but Lyra had never believed me. Even so, I would say it again. "We did not know he intended to sever the ties between our realms. My father's quest to close the Aetherian Gate was his alone."

"I know."

Nothing she could have said would have surprised me more.

"Kael said as much, and I believe him now."

"Ahh, how lovely for you that you've grown close enough to my brother that you trust his word over mine."

Lyra's expression was deadly. A combination of secrecy and seduction.

"Jealous?"

My response was honest and instantaneous.

"Yes."

She laughed then, a tinkling, distinctly Aetherian sound.

"I have no need for pretense, Lyra. As I've said, I *do* have a need for the truth which you've skirted around since you arrived. You wish for me to obtain the Stone of Mor'Vallis, Gyorian's most sacred relic, from its rightful owner—my father and king, who is the only one capable of actually wielding it. Subsequently incurring his wrath and likely joining my brother in being banished from my own lands. So the truth? If you would, please?"

Her brows arched as I spoke.

"You've heard that the Maelstrom Depths have calmed, have you not?"

"I've heard tales, but not believable ones. Lyra, what do the Depths—"

"Your father stole the Wind Crystal to close the Aetherian Gate. He returned it, or more precisely, your brother did, but unbeknownst to Kael, the returned one was a fake. Your father hid the real Crystal at the bottom of the Depths, turning legend into reality as they rebelled against the presence of such a powerful artifact, and one which belonged in Aetheria. It has recently been retrieved and returned to its rightful owner, something your father likely suspects but could not know to be fact. That is why the Depths have calmed and allowed sailors to approach closer than before. It's also the reason your father became so angry at me for not confirming his suspicions."

Every word she spoke surprised me more than the one before it. As my enemy, it was my duty not to believe her, and yet... she spoke the truth. I thought back to the events that later led to King Galfrid's queen being taken, to the Gate's closure.

I didn't say it aloud. Not yet. But the realization sat heavy in my gut. If what she said was true, and the Wind Crystal had played a role in sealing the Gate... then she was after the Stone for the opposite reason. To undo it. To rip open the veil between realms once again.

That should be reason enough to stop her.

And yet...

My father had stolen the Wind Crystal, wielded it like a weapon, and then lied to everyone. Including Kael and me? How much more had he hidden from us?

I would not aid her in reopening the Gate. But I had no choice but to help her restore balance, or at the very least, uncover the truth my father buried along with that damn Stone.

And if she planned to use it to destroy us?

Then I'll be there to stop her.

"If you are lying..."

"I am not. And you know it already. You're smart, Terran. For a Gyorian," she added.

"You flatter me," I said, sarcasm dripping from every word.

"Help me," she said, her tone softer. "Not for me. Not even for Aetheria. But for the realm your father broke, the truth he buried, and the power he stole from both our peoples. If we don't reclaim the Stone of Mor'Vallis, he won't just keep ruling by deception but will be tipping the balance until there's nothing left to save."

Pretty words, but in reality, I would help her for one simple reason. The Stone was more than a relic my father could use at will to intensify his power. It was, had always been, much more than that, and my father should have told me. Told Kael.

Gyorians with honor did not lie, and he'd done so in grand fashion. Did Kael know this when I confronted him on that road? If so, why did he not tell me?

"We will retrieve the Stone, but it remains with me until I understand more."

Or until you tell me the full truth, I added silently.

"We?"

"If I sent you from Gyoria, would you return?" I asked, knowing the answer already.

"Aye."

"And be killed for your efforts."

"Likely not."

Those two words were chilling. Even Lyra allowed for the

possibility that she could be overwhelmed by my father's men, and for certain by the king himself, if he chose to make good on his threat.

If I kept her close, controlled the terms, perhaps I could learn the entire truth too.

"*We* will retrieve it. But I'll have your word, you will not attempt to take it from me."

A vow I didn't expect her to keep, though breaking it could reveal her true character.

She hesitated for the briefest of moments.

"You have my word."

"Gather your belongings."

"Uh, Terran. Just one particular problem: We don't know where it is."

"*You* don't know where it is," I clarified. "My father may have kept important things from me, but I am the Prince of Gyoria, and his son, and have a strong suspicion where it might be."

Better than a suspicion. I was certain I knew where he relocated it to. But knowing would be easier than retrieving. Or than learning the full truth from Lyra about what her king had learned from Princess Mevlida's appearance and the cause of the present imbalance.

Those revelations would come later. First, I had to keep Lyra alive and retrieve the Stone without raising my father's suspicions.

No easy task indeed.

10

LYRA

"Absolutely not."

When Terran told me to gather my belongings, I hadn't expected him to lead me to a door in the very same corridor which I had previously occupied. Perhaps that was the reason he'd told me to hang back while he looked out first. And then shuffled me into... his bedchamber.

Somehow, from the moment we entered, I could sense it was his. And after our encounter, it was the last place I wished to stay. Knowing my own limits was a strength, my parents said. And in this particular case, Terran was a limit. Innuendos and harmless flirting were one thing. Being alone and sufficiently tempted into actual relations with someone who had occupied my thoughts throughout the years more than I wished to admit was another.

He stirred my ancient Aetherian blood like no one else. A Gyorian. The son of Balthor. My enemy. And yet...

"You have little choice." He closed the door behind him.

I glanced around the expansive chamber, expecting it would have been cold, severe, perhaps sharpened by stone and steel. But this... this was something else entirely. The fire was already lit when I stepped inside, casting a warm glow over dark walls softened by deep-green tapestries and shelves filled with worn books and small, strange relics. A low-slung leather chair sat near the hearth, creased as if someone spent time here. A large, arched window overlooked the cliffs and forest beyond, the kind of view that made you feel untouchable, removed from the chaos. It wasn't just a chamber. It was a sanctuary.

"What is the smell?" I asked.

It was entirely pleasant. Warm, earthy... like sandalwood and something darker beneath it, unfamiliar but not unwelcome.

Terran didn't answer right away. He was busy lighting a second taper, as if he hadn't heard me. But I saw the twitch of his mouth.

"You noticed," he finally said.

"Of course I noticed. It's... distracting."

Another almost-smile. "My mother's blend. Oils from the southern forests. I burn it when I want to think."

I inhaled slowly, letting the scent consume me. "And now?"

He looked up. "Now I burn it because you're here."

Even as I put down my leather satchel, I said, "That comment is precisely the reason I will not be staying in your bedchamber, Terran."

He approached me. "Because I don't pretend, as you do, that there is something between us?"

I ignored the flutter in my chest. "I am not jesting."

"Nor am I, when I say I've a notion where my father hid the Stone. And if I'm right, we'll have to remain in the palace to find it. Since you were ordered to leave Gyoria, there is little choice."

Could it really still be in the palace? If so, I was closer to it than I imagined. When I whispered back to Aethralis to speak to Mev, Kael guessed that his father may have brought it to The

Forbidden Tunnels, but it seemed the Gyorian relic may be more within my reach than I expected.

"I'll make inquiries and must train with my men lest they grow suspicious. Make yourself comfortable, and I'll return as soon as I'm able."

He wasn't jesting.

"You mean for me to stay locked inside your bedchamber while you go about your day being"—I waved my hand with a flourish—"Prince of Gyoria?"

Terran blinked.

"What would you have me do instead? Not attempt to locate the Stone? Escort you beyond the border, as my father ordered? Or perhaps you can accompany me to the training yard so that word of me disobeying that order gets back to him?"

That he was disobeying his father's order alone was so surprising that I considered his words, and my options. Though I'd utilized my audience with the king to begin to unravel some of the secrets Kael learned his father had kept from him and his brother, I still hadn't expected Terran to acquiesce so soon in any way.

He'd felt the shift. And likely knew his father to have grown unstable.

"Also, you are not locked in my chamber. None would dare to enter here, and you are free to leave whenever you will. Although I've no doubt you could do so anyway, if I did choose to lock the door."

Unable to help myself, with a flick of my fingers, I used the air current to lock his chamber door.

This time, Terran's smile wasn't a hint but a bold statement.

"Not sure I have time to play, but..." He shrugged. "If you insist."

With one swift, assured motion, the Gyorian lifted his tunic from his body and tossed it to the floor.

"Terran," I warned. He glanced at me with such a raw, unfiltered look of desire that I forgot what I'd been about to say. "You are outrageous," I managed. "Put your tunic back on and leave as you intended."

I reopened the lock.

Laughing, the brief intensity replaced by a rare moment of joy —it was the first, to my knowledge, that I'd been in the presence of Kael's brother actually laughing aloud—he did as I suggested and covered his linen shirt with his tunic.

"Come," he said, and I followed him through a carved stone archway draped in deep-green velvet. A vision of him in this bath chamber, shirtless with water glistening along the edges of his collarbone, assaulted me.

Refocusing, I marveled at the large space warmed by candlelight, a flicker dancing over dark stone walls veined with pale quartz.

"Lumenbind keeps them lit," he said. "The enchantment is said to have been developed by the first Gyorian king as a symbol of the 'light that would never dim,' as a reference to our clan."

I had much to say about that... If any king in history had done more to dim the Gyorian light, it was Terran's father, but I remained silent and stared at the soaking tub. It was sunk into the floor and easily large enough for two, perhaps three.

"Its rim is polished obsidian." Terran moved closer to me. The scent of bergamot and something darker, like crushed cedar and spice, reminded me he was near. As if I could forget.

A Gyorian crest was carved into the wall above the basin, half-wreathed in ivy, and I realized this wasn't simply a place to clean oneself. It was a retreat. A private escape for someone who didn't let many people in.

I looked up at him. "I've bathed in the palace before and have never seen anything like it."

"My quarters, and Kael's too, are unlike my father's in many ways."

"Fitting, for you both." I left the rest unsaid.

Terran's expression hardened. "Do not mistake me for someone I'm not, Lyra."

Deciding it was time to push, I did just that. "You will not convince me that tearing apart Elydor by punishing innocents was your doing."

"Innocents? Your king knew the risk of opening that portal. Legends foretold it."

"Humans brought their own sort of magic—"

"Conjecture and supposed prophecies?"

"Your hatred of them blinds you."

"Your love of them softens you."

I moved my hand quickly to show Terran precisely how soft I was and never expected him to grab my wrist in time. He was surprisingly nimble.

"Do not use Aetherian magic here."

His hand wrapped easily around my wrist. Shuddering at the feel of it, shockingly immune to wishing he'd let go, I asked one simple question.

"Why?"

His gaze moved to the intricate carvings on the chamber walls: spirals and branches that seemed almost alive in the glow of the candles. Releasing my wrist for the second time that day, he exhaled.

"Why?" I asked, quietly this time. "What are they?"

"My mother," he said finally, "was quite skilled. They're her carvings."

Terran's mother. The former Queen of Gyoria.

I knew less of her than I did the king or her sons. When she was alive, my parents were ambassadors to Gyoria, though I'd learned more about her from Kael when we served on the Gate Council together.

"Kael never mentioned that particular skill to me. My father remembers her as kind and welcoming. Back then, he enjoyed coming to Gyoria. Said it offered a kind of peace not found in the north."

He hardly reacted to my words.

"She was kind to all. Kael is fond of saying what's become of Elydor, in her name, would devastate her."

"Do you agree?"

The demons Terran wrestled with were not ones I envied. He stared at the walls, not answering, for a long while.

"You are welcome to freshen yourself in here while I'm away. I will bring food, and hopefully information, that will allow us to seek the Stone this eve. I would prefer to do so quickly, before you're discovered."

"Will it matter if I'm discovered when your father realizes what you've done?"

"For you, aye. It could be the difference between life or death. I do not doubt my father will wage a war between our clans and will have little qualm about taking your life, Lyra."

I knew as much, but to hear him say it...

"For me? Nay. He will see it as a betrayal, for it is one. But perhaps it will be the catalyst needed to learn the truth of what he knows about the current imbalance."

So he had felt it.

"Keeping me here," I said, not wanting to dissuade Terran from his plan, but to ensure he carried it through, "allowing me to aid you in retrieving the Stone might be seen to some as a betrayal equal to your brother's."

He didn't get angry. Or clench his fists. Or even look at me with the disgust that I'd come to expect from most Gyorians, and especially him and his father.

"Ignoring the truth is also a betrayal," he said softly. "To my mother."

With that, Terran left the bath chamber. Moments later, I heard the large, wooden door of his bedchamber click open and then shut.

He was gone. And I was alone in the private retreat of one of the most feared Gyorian warriors, its prince and sworn enemy. Then why did I suddenly feel so at peace? One that warred with a measure of fear I'd learned to ignore and the near-constant flutters of excitement at being alone in Terran's bedchamber... flutters matched only by the ones ever-present when he was near.

A question better left unanswered.

11

TERRAN

"I'm about to commit treason."

For his part, Dren hardly reacted. For a Gyorian, he was unusually calm unless a battle brewed. I was certain I could tell him most anything, and he would simply tilt his head to the side and consider my words before responding.

We'd finished training, a shorter session than normal given my... other activities. Having spoken to Lord Valdric's scribe, I was certain my guess was right.

The Stone was in Gyoria's Royal Vault.

"Go on," Dren said, as if I'd informed him obsidian was black.

"Lyra revealed little to my father, but her presence alone seemed to rattle him. When she mentioned The Unbalance, he all but threatened to kill her... after denying such a thing occurred."

"Quakes without causes, sudden cracks in centuries-old rocks... surely he does not believe we cannot see the truth of it ourselves."

"I've long ago stopped attempting to understand his thinking.

Also, my father all but admitted there was something amiss in the Depths, and thanks to Lyra, I know what that something is."

We walked from the training yard, an expansive field cleared for such a purpose, back to the palace. Righting the crevices and dirt disturbed during training along the way, I contemplated how much to tell him. I trusted Dren with my life, and had literally done so on more than one occasion.

The thought prompted me to continue.

"Apparently, he stole the Wind Crystal in order to close the Aetherian Gate, returned a fake to Galfrid, likely around the time of the Battle of the Eastern Border, and hid the real crystal in the Depths."

At "stole the Wind Crystal," Dren had stopped walking, his expression going from curious to disbelief.

"He... did what, precisely?"

"My guess, thinking more on it," I said, fixing the final patch of dirt with a twist of my fingers, "is that all three relics were needed to open it in the first place. My father would never have willingly given permission for Galfrid to use the Stone, and I have no knowledge of it being stolen, but it's the only explanation why my father would need the Crystal."

I could see Dren thinking.

"Elydor's way of ensuring all of its clans agreed to opening such a portal?"

"Perhaps."

Dren's head shook in disbelief. "How did Galfrid get your father to agree to use the Stone? Or Queen Lirael to use the Tidal Pearl for such a purpose? And your father? How could he have possibly stolen the Wind Crystal from Aetheria? And what of the Tidal Pearl? Lirael would have been even less likely to allow him to use it for such a purpose than she would to aid Galfrid in opening it." His rapid-fire questions were the same as mine had been. "And the Depths? Impossible. How could your father hide the Crystal there? And who retrieved it?"

With each question, I watched Dren's expression. As I had been, it was initially a surprise, but as the full impact of my father's deception sunk in, anger began to manifest.

"I know none of those answers, but intend to," I said. "More importantly, Lyra claims the Crystal's retrieval is the reason the Depths have calmed. She believes the Stone is not safe with my father and begs me to retrieve it from him."

"For what purpose?"

"She claims only to safeguard against an Unbalance that began when Princess Mevlida came through the Gate. Or maybe even when my father closed it."

Dren looked me in the eyes, unwavering.

"What do you believe?"

There was just one logical conclusion.

"That she's been sent by Galfrid, and my brother, to obtain the Stone of Mor'Vallis to reopen the Aetherian Gate."

"Did you ask her about this intention?"

"Nay. I doubt she believes me, or a Gyorian, could work out such a conclusion."

"Aetherians," he muttered, as if it were a slur. Which, of course, it was. They believed, with their vast libraries and scholars, they were the sole keepers of knowledge, superior in intellect over all other Elydorians.

"The act of treason you mention," he said, Dren's voice lowered despite that none of our men were within range of being able to hear our conversation. "You intend to obtain it for her?"

"Retrieve our clan's most precious relic for an Aetherian? Nay." I gave him a look that told my right hand how little I cared for his suggestion. "But I do agree that my father's actions have borderlined on zealousness, his lies concerning me more than even his behavior. And that having the Stone in my possession may be necessary."

"You cannot use it," he said, an obvious fact I'd not refute. Only my father, the most powerful Gyorian, could wield it.

"I don't intend to try. But I will allow Lyra to come with me to retrieve it."

That, apparently, was one step too far for Dren, who finally showed his impatience.

"I agree, as you know, your father has become dangerous, even to Gyoria. And do not disagree, taking the Stone may be wise; though if he finds out, I would not wish to be a part of that conversation. But why take her? I thought Balthor had banished her already? I assumed you escorted her from the palace?"

We resumed walking once again, the palace walls looming before us.

"She is inside my chamber."

Dren's jaw dropped.

"If Lyra really wants me to retrieve the Stone only to 'rebalance the realm,' she'll act accordingly. If she tries to take it or use it in a way that reveals a greater plot, I'll know. Bringing her will test Lyra's trustworthiness and expose Balthor's true plot."

"Test her trustworthiness? She is Aetherian."

I reminded my friend of words he'd spoken more than once.

"And yet, my brother has partnered with one." I used Dren's tone of voice. "Perhaps Prince Kael sees what you do not. A king who would damn us all. Are those words not yours?"

"Aye, but... Terran," he argued, "if you are caught. If she deceives you and takes the Stone—"

"I will not be caught. I know where Father hid the Stone and mean to test my theory. As for Lyra, I would not worry about her taking it from me. Do you truly believe an Aetherian noblewoman can overpower me?"

I was not fond of Dren's hesitation to answer the question.

"If she were any other? No. I do not. However..."

His voice trailed off as I glowered at him. Dren thought better of finishing the thought.

"Your brother partnered with an Aetherian woman. They are seductive. The one inside your chamber, particularly so to you."

That he'd noticed also did not sit well.

"It matters not."

"You don't deny it?"

I nearly laughed aloud. Deny Lady Lyra was seductive? It would be akin to denying my father had descended into madness beginning the day my mother died.

"I do not ask permission," I told him as we entered the palace gates. "Merely to advise you of my plan as I will need your aid."

Dren didn't hesitate. "Tell me what you need, and I'll see it done."

"Tonight," I said, "I retrieve the Stone of Mor'Vallis. Here's what I need you to do..."

12

LYRA

With little else to do but wait, I utilized Terran's bathing chamber, marveling at the display of lights and coziness of a space even the grandest of Aetherian bathing chambers could hardly rival. After dressing, I wandered his bedchamber, enjoying the soft, thick woven rug beneath my feet which softened the blackstone floor. I stared a bit too long at his large canopy bed which stood at the chamber's center, framed in dark wood with clean, strong lines.

How many had he taken in that bed over the many years he'd been alive? Were they all Gyorian? Likely so. Pulling my thoughts away from what it would be like to ride one such as Terran, or find myself beneath his thick frame as he attempted to dominate me, Gyorians known for liking control both in the bedchamber and outside of it, I perused the rest of his chamber.

Along one wall, shelves held maps, old tomes, and a carved box bearing the royal crest. It was a warrior's room, aye. But not an unfeeling one. Terran's bedchamber was, in fact, so different from the wings of the Gyorian palace where I had stayed previously, it was difficult to believe they were one and the same.

The door slammed open.

I turned, unsurprised to see Terran filling its frame.

"Do you plan to dislocate every door in the palace? Or are you capable of opening one as most do, without pulling it from its hinges?"

Closing it, he inspected the very much "in place" hinges, making his point. Covered in dirt, he strode past me toward the bathing chamber.

"You would do well to hide yourself to the solar for a time. Supper will be arriving shortly."

Hardly glancing at me, he stopped at the bathing chamber's entrance. "Unless, of course, you wish to hide yourself in here. With me."

"I would," I lied, pretending I'd not imagined him in that tub with me, "but I've already bathed."

"As I can see. But 'tis much more enjoyable with a partner than alone. Perhaps you need another?"

This seduction had become a game between us. One I did not intend to lose.

What will you do when I call your bluff, Prince Terran?

Pretending to think it over, I headed to the solar, giving him a moment to disarm. But just as he disappeared under the archway's curtain, I spun and followed him inside instead.

Heart pounding, I entered the chamber as water began to fill the cavernous tub.

"I've changed my mind," I said, startling him. "Perhaps a second bath will do after all. It was quite a luxurious experience, one I would not have expected here. In Gyoria."

Eyes narrowed, he watched me, clearly not believing my actions would match my words.

How far will you go to prove a point, Lyra?

With him? Too far, likely.

Without looking away, Terran took off his tunic once again.

This time, as he began to remove the linen shirt beneath it, I didn't stop him. Instead, I unfastened my belt. Every bit of skin he revealed was tanned. And muscled. Like most Gyorians, he was large... Terran's strength one of his|greatest assets. Rows of ridges on his stomach. His biceps, and shoulders, flexed as he tossed his shirt to the floor.

He was, in a word, glorious.

"Like what you see?" he taunted.

I would not feed an ego that had already been inflated by countless others. Instead, I used the skills of the graceful Aetherian dancers who enticed and seduced with their slow movements. Teasing, never giving. Starting with the jeweled pin that held my hair in place, I reached behind my head, and with one long pull, my hair tumbled down around me. Cleaned, still damp in places, curling in others, it was wild and untamed... perfect for this particular occasion.

He pretended to be unaffected, but Terran was anything but.

He was a competitor, though, and knew the game well. Somehow flexing every muscle in his chest and arms as he reached for his boot, Terran untied one and then the other. I watched, heart racing with every movement, as he stood before me in naught but the tight breeches that Gyorian warriors were known for. And, of course, the thick, muscled legs beneath them.

Summoning every bit of feigned indifference, I ever-so-slowly untied the sash at my waist that held my pale-blue tunic in place. Terran's gaze slipped down to my waist as the silken belt was undone. When he took two steps toward me then, closing the space between us, I held my breath, expecting the one thing I'd wanted from him for some time.

Despite that I should hate him.

Despite his treatment of my people.

Despite my mission here, one that was so much more important than this silly game.

But he didn't lean into me. Attempt to kiss me. Instead, his hand shot out, Terran grabbing the silk sash before I could stop him. He didn't say a word. Instead, he reached for my wrist and, stepping forward, pulled it behind my back.

My fingers immediately itched to wield air to stop him. But remembering what he'd said earlier about not using it in this chamber, I resisted. Even as his finger wrapped around my other wrist and brought it back to join the other, I didn't stop him.

Terran continued to hold my gaze, imploring... daring.

Stop him, Lyra.

I had every reason to resist as the silk began to thread around my wrists, but instead, I looked up at him, fascinated.

The prince of Gyoria was tying my hands behind my back, and I was letting him.

Standing so close that our bodies were nearly touching, a thrill of anticipation coursed through me as if I hadn't just summarily lost this game. As if I weren't on a mission to secure the artifact that could reopen a portal to the human realm.

As if nothing else in Elydor mattered but this moment.

He tightened the sash, and though I could release it—my finger was easily able to summon air currents—I didn't.

"Aye," I said suddenly, remembering.

His eyes narrowed quizzically.

"You asked if I liked what I saw."

Terran reached up to trace the outline of my cheek, his finger surprisingly gentle as it trailed down to my jaw, where he stopped. His thumb touched my lower lip, tugging on it. Parting my lips.

"As do I." For a change, his tone wasn't taunting, as if Terran meant the words. "Do you know what I believe, Lyra?" he asked, his voice low and reverberating.

I didn't respond—at least, not with words.

"I believe you are accustomed to being in control. Of yourself. Of those around you. And that perhaps, just once, you secretly wish to relinquish that control to another. I think, if I were to have you this way in my bed, you'd not only allow it..." He dropped his hand.

I would *not* mourn its loss.

Terran leaned down to whisper into my ear. "You would enjoy it. Perhaps more than you've enjoyed anything in your life."

My core clenched at his words, at his soft breath as Terran spoke to me.

I would die before confirming anything he'd said, not only out of pride but of ignorance. I'd never played the game quite like this. Taken lovers? Aye. But allowed them to do what Terran suggested? Control me? Nay.

Because he was right. I was in control. Always. It could mean the difference between life and death. And even immortals understood that line was thin.

"Turn around."

Every bit of me rebelled at his words. At Terran's commanding tone. I wasn't his to command, and yet, stupidly, I trusted him not to hurt me.

"Turn. Around."

His voice was like the sharp edge of the cliffs outside his bedchamber window.

I'd allowed him to tie my hands. If I did as he said, Terran would win much more than this one simple game.

"I will ask just one more time, Lyra. Turn. Around. Now."

His green eyes blazed.

I turned.

Anticipated.

Cursed myself for a fool.

Then, just as quickly as he'd first reached for me, Terran slipped the sash from my wrists, freeing them. I waited, but he didn't make any further move. Realizing that was all he meant to do, I turned back.

Words were unnecessary. What would I have said anyway? I hadn't known, until this very moment, that I wanted to give up control. That such a thing would inflame my senses and make me forget decades of training.

What had I been thinking?

Reaching for my sash, I grabbed it, resisted one last look at the specimen of perfection that was Prince Terran of Gyoria, and stepped toward the archway. It wasn't until I got back into his bedchamber that I breathed again.

Defeat was a bitter bedfellow, and unless I wanted to get comfortable sleeping with it, I would do well not to play that game with Terran ever again.

13

TERRAN

After dressing, I emptied the tub but didn't leave my bathing chamber just yet. She would be out there, and while I could face the fiercest immortals in Elydor, I'd prefer not to face this particular Aetherian just yet.

I leaned against the gossimite counter, its gold flecks glistening in the near-darkness. What had possessed me, I was uncertain. Taunting her, as I had, knowing Lyra was as stubborn and competitive as they came—that bit of knowledge coming from my brother—perhaps it was the outcome I'd hoped for.

Yet she'd quickly turned the tides against me. Hair spilling around her shoulders, Lyra's eyes mesmerizing as they dared me to continue, she had become the very opposite of how I knew her. No longer cool and aloof, though still very much measured, with the first tug of her silken sash, it took every bit of discipline I'd learned to remain still.

The thought had simply come to me, and before I could weigh its consequences, I'd decided there was, indeed, much more beneath the surface. If Lyra epitomized control in every mannerism and action, outwardly, would she secretly desire the very opposite? If I thought more on it before reaching for her wrists, I'd have remembered she trusted me least of nearly anyone in Elydor. Lyra shouldn't have allowed me to bind her wrists, though I was certain she could wrest free using magic. Still, it was her willingness to succumb that surprised me most.

After that, I'd nearly released the thin thread of control I'd been maintaining.

Stepping back from her had been difficult.

Inhaling, reminding myself that Lyra was no ally... that the consequences of losing this game would alter the path of my life as surely as Kael's when he chose Princess Mevlida, I pushed up and strode into my chamber.

No sign of Lyra.

But the table had been set with domes forged from thermoneutral, the Gyorian heat-holding alloy, covering trenchers of food. Thankfully, my servants were as loyal as my men. That I'd asked for a meal for two would not be questioned. Even so, Lyra could not remain here much longer.

I needed to retrieve the Stone before my father decided to wield it, contributing to the undeniable Unbalance, the cause of which he'd known and chosen to hide from me.

She sat in my leather chair, shoeless, feet curled under her, reading. It was a text I knew well: *Chronicles of the Rift Wars.*

"Hungry?"

She looked up. Hair back in place, features schooled. Aside from her bare feet, there was no other hint of the Lyra that had occupied the bathing chamber.

"Aye," she said, replacing the book.

Caught staring at her fine-looking backside, I turned and Lyra followed.

Pulling off the domes, I snuck a glance at Lyra as she surveyed the meal. I'd asked for something worthy of an honored guest, and to bring wine instead of mead.

"I'm impressed," she said as I poured two mulled Sylverwines.

"Spiced venison stew and root vegetables," I said, surveying the trenchers. "Hearth-baked bread with herbed oil and roasted stonefruit glazed in honey and thyme."

"You speak," she said, tasting the wine, "as if you prepared the meal."

I sat across from her, wondering what it might be like to be partnered with Lyra.

An absurd notion which I dismissed immediately.

"One of the palace cooks was orphaned in the Battle of Narn, and he was raised by my mother. We're still good friends, and I've spent many days learning from him."

After chewing a piece of venison, she said, "That was kind of your mother, to take him in."

"I could regale you with many similar instances."

"As I've heard. Your story does not surprise me, given her reputation. She must have been extraordinary... to be mourned with such fury."

I took a bite of bread, considering her words. I said nothing to refute the latter part. Fury was an appropriate word for the decades-long campaign my father waged against humans.

"She was."

The silence that followed as we ate by the fire should have been awkward.

"Tonight," I said, sitting back, wine in hand, "I will take the Stone."

"You've located it for certain?"

"Nay, but I know my father well. Or so I believed," I amended, realizing that wasn't entirely true. "If it's not in the Throne Vault, I will live the remainder of my days in Aetheria. He's posted an extra guard there, which alone should have raised suspicions... if anyone had known to be suspicious."

"The Throne Vault?"

Was I mad to take her along? I told myself it was a strategy, that she knew more than she let on, that I could control the risk, exposing her true plans. But maybe, also, I just didn't want to let her go.

"Few know of its existence. To the guards and all others, it's nothing more than a hidden spiral staircase built into the mountain that leads to storage and little else. But in that chamber, disguised as a part of the stone wall, the entrance to a long corridor is revealed to those who... can pass through."

The Vault was also guarded against magical interference, but I kept that bit of knowledge to myself.

"What is the plan?"

"There is an entrance near the throne room through which none would expect visitors. There are two guards to contend with, still, but I have a plan for both. It is not getting into the Vault, or retrieving the Stone, I worry about, though."

"Nay?" she asked, picking up a piece of honeyed fruit. "It would seem perhaps you should be."

I watched her place the berry delicately between her lips.

"I'm concerned more with the guards waking. And my father discovering the Stone missing."

She licked a bit of honey from her fingertip. If only I could do the same, though I'd not stop there...

"Wake? What, precisely, is your plan to get by them?"

"To knock them out, of course."

There it was. The "Aetherian Stare." All knew of it. Hated it. A reminder that the first Elydorians lived in, and established, what was now Aetheria. The keepers of our history. And with a full knowledge of the past came insights no other clan could claim.

"That is one of the many reasons we hate Aetherians," I blurted. She blinked. The Stare was gone.

"We don't need to be told you feel superior when you look at us that way."

I expected her to argue. To defend herself and her kind. Instead, she cocked her head to the side.

"I hadn't realized," she said finally. "And did not mean to condescend you."

"What were you thinking?" I asked, expecting her to lie.

"That it was foolish to use brute force against your own guards when doing so would alert them to trouble." She paused. "And that it was very Gyorian to do such a thing."

She was not wrong. Even so.

Our gazes held, and something, I could not be sure what it was, passed between us.

"The Sovaen Whisper." Her voice was barely above a whisper itself.

"Is merely a legend," I said.

"Is it?" Lyra asked, picking up her wine.

By her question, I expected not. Which meant... surely, she could not perform it? Even in the legends, very few could manipulate an Aetherian Whisper and allow the wielder to enter a subject's mind. Induce calm, a fogged memory. Or even sleep.

"If it were real, its wielder would be branded a mind-bender. A criminal offense in every clan," I reminded her.

"Indeed," she agreed. "One of the reasons it was outlawed by Aetherian scholars and twisted into legend. Its power to manipulate without consent was seen as unconscionable."

Twisted into legend.

"Only those trained," she said between sips, "as kings or queens, or Shadow Diplomats, were taught fragments of it, in secret, to be used for missions where violence could spark political fallout, or war."

"In the legends?"

"Nay, Terran. Not only in the legends. Not every war is won on the battlefield. Some are never declared at all."

"An Aetherian proverb—"

"More than simply a proverb. 'Tis a creed of Shadow Diplomats. A reminder to use magic such as the Sovaen Whisper judiciously."

It could not be.

"An Aetherian Shadow Diplomat is also naught but a myth, used by non-Aetherians to keep young ones in check."

She watched me.

My mind raced with all I knew of Shadow Diplomats. Trained in magic never seen performed, their presence never recorded and actions never acknowledged by the crown as they were purportedly trained in emotional manipulation and advanced negotiation tactics.

Shadow Diplomats were real, and Lyra—as well as her parents, I'd guess—were among their ranks.

It would explain how she could navigate royal politics, walk into enemy territory, and hold her own with kings.

Which meant, the outlawed magic they used was real too.

"The Subvocal Arts?" I asked.

"Legend."

"Wordbinding?"

"Real. Though never used. A promise that could only be obtained in such a way is useless. The ability was discovered inadvertently while developing... other skills."

Wordbinding was real. The Sovaen Whisper, real. It was no wonder Aetherians gave the rest of us such a stare. We had our secrets, but none such as this. How often throughout our history were such skills used?

Or abused?

"Who knows?"

"The king, and no other. With exception of those who whisper in the shadows, or have done so in the past. You told me of your Throne Vault. I am extending the same courtesy of a secret."

A secret, indeed. "How many are there?"

Her smile was Lyra's only response.

"You aren't worried I'll share your secret?"

"No," she said softly. "At least, as worried as you are that I will share yours. But if you were going to betray me, you'd have done so already."

On that, Lyra was right.

14

LYRA

Time passed much more quickly than I'd have expected.

After revealing my deepest secret to him, one that those closest to me didn't even suspect, I freed my mind from doubts that would serve no master except regret, which is a useless sentiment. It was done. He knew.

With luck, he might guess that the Sovaen Whisper wasn't the least invasive of the skills I'd learned from my parents, the only partnered Shadow Diplomats in Aetheria's history. Having one mentor made me part of an elite group of individuals. Having two?

"Lyra?"

Hours had passed, our meal long ago eaten. We'd nurtured a second flagon of wine while I hid in Terran's antechamber as we waited for the palace to slumber.

"I was thinking," I said, tucking my feet between my crossed legs. One advantage of chairs made for Gyorians? They were massive. I could sleep in this one, by the fire, and likely would. Certainly, if we were successful, I would need some rest before heading north.

With the Stone.

My plan was fluid, as were most missions such as these. Though it had quickly become clear Terran was my best chance at getting the stone, how I would proceed from there was less obvious.

"You were thinking?" he prompted.

Terran sat across from me, legs outstretched, wine in hand. The firelight flicked against his prominent cheekbone and jaw, both defined and broad all at once. Every feature pronounced him of royal bloodline. Or perhaps it was the way he used them. Less haughty than exceedingly confident, it was one trait both Prince Terran of Gyoria and his brother had in common.

"If I were to describe this day to someone, I'd scarcely find the words."

We spoke of the mission. Of Gyorian, and Aetherian customs. Of Kael, and even Mev, after Terran finally admitted his curiosity about the lost princess. Thankfully, one thing we didn't speak of was the incident in his bathing chamber. With luck, he passed it off as manipulation on my part. The truth was much, much, worse.

"I've known you for many years. Or thought that I had," I admitted.

"What *do* you know about me, Lyra?"

Though we could no longer see Gyoria's cliffs outside a window, there was an unexpected openness in this chamber.

"I know you were taught to hate me."

His brows raised. "As you were me."

"Nay," I argued. "I do not hate you, Terran. I hate that your father tore our clans apart. But I do not hate you."

"Some may argue it was your king that tore our clans apart when he opened the Gate."

"If it weren't meant to be opened, he'd not have been able to do so. Do you truly believe one king's will could undo centuries of peace, if that peace hadn't already been fractured beneath the surface?" I paused. "The Gate didn't break Elydor, Terran. It merely revealed the cracks your father swore never existed."

He watched me, but remained silent.

I tried another tactic.

"Your brother is no more a traitor to Elydor than I am. He didn't abandon you for the love of a woman. He merely realized if there was love in his heart for the daughter of his enemy, one with both Aetherian and human blood, perhaps there was space for others as well. Elydorians he only hated because he'd been expected to do so."

"You seem to know my brother well." He placed his empty goblet on the wooden table beside him.

"We've spent much time together since Mev came through the Gate."

"Mev," he repeated. "That's what you call her?"

"It's the name she used in the human realm," I said, taking the opportunity to share the most egregious of King Balthor's secret crimes. "When your father kidnapped the queen, he somehow erased her memory of her time in Elydor. Mev's mother returned to The Crooked Key believing she'd been drugged, and later, on discovering she was pregnant, raped."

I didn't have to wait long for his reaction. It was the first time since coming to the palace I'd seen him truly angry. Shooting up from his seat, he disappeared into a back chamber, the loud thud telling me exactly what was happening even though I couldn't see it.

In that chamber, I'd spied a well-worn Gyorian training stone, a pillar wrapped in padded hide and reinforced with bands of infused iron.

When he returned, Terran appeared visibly calmer.

"I'd wondered why you kept that in there."

He picked up his goblet, filled it, and sat as if naught had happened.

"Kael put it in there for me," was all he said, but no additional words were needed.

Though I should likely not press him, having Terran retrieve the Stone would not help open the Gate. I also needed to convince him to come with me to Aetheria. He'd never willingly give me the Stone of Mor'Vallis, and circumstances had put us together while retrieving it.

My best chance was to gain his acquiescence in using it, and Terran was turning. I was certain of it.

"Mev spent her life wanting answers. She became a museum curator specializing in ancient artifacts and was eventually led to Jon Harrow, an ocean away from where she was raised. Carrying her mother's Aetherian ring, she gained just enough knowledge of our realm that, when she accidentally came through the Gate, Mev knew only that Gyorians and Aetherians were enemies. Taken by Kael, who had just left the Summit and sensed the Gate's opening, she spent her first days in Elydor having learned of its existence just moments earlier. Neither did she have any knowledge that Mev possessed magic. As it began to manifest and she realized she and Kael were enemies, Mev attempted to escape, which was when I found the pair."

He hadn't interrupted once.

"Your brother didn't fall in love with the lost princess or King Galfrid's daughter. He fell for a scared human woman who slipped through a portal we thought was closed. He'd worked it out by the time I discovered them, and he asked that I train her."

I didn't have to tell Terran an untrained Aetherian could be dangerous, both to herself and others.

"And that's when he took her north?"

I shook my head. "Nay. He'd still planned to take her to your father, despite his feelings for her."

I managed to surprise Terran once again.

"What changed?"

"You'll have to ask your brother. I suspect he realized that hate was easy. Love... required courage."

It was as if I'd struck him. Terran's nostrils flared, though he didn't become nearly as angry as he had when I revealed the depths of his father's deception.

"Hate," he began, and then stopped.

"Is not easy?" I guessed his train of thought. "It allows us to free ourselves from blame, and looking inward is never a comfortable exercise."

He sighed. "You have all the answers, Lyra."

It wasn't meant as a compliment.

"Nay," I said, carefully considering my words. Self-deprecation was just as uncomfortable, but necessary. It would leave me open, and raw. But I could not lose sight of the mission. Nothing mattered more now than Terran trusting me.

"I have but few of them. For instance... why did I—a Shadow Diplomat supposedly more highly trained in diplomacy and strategy than any Elydorian—allow my 'enemy' to tie my hands behind my back so easily?"

Terran's expression changed.

The heaviness of our conversation lifted, his entire body relaxing. He was back in familiar territory. Standing, he took one, and then a second and third, step toward me. Leaning down, until his face was so close to my ear that I could feel its breath, he whispered, "You allowed it because you secretly—so secret, you haven't admitted it to yourself—wish, just once, you could loosen the reins on your tightly held control. And you know I would love nothing more than to see that happen. *Make* it happen. With me."

My breath caught. If I turned toward him, our lips would touch. He continued to lean down to me, clearly letting me decide.

Every nerve ending in my body fired at the thought of letting him take control again.

How could I want something so badly I'd never considered, even once? How had Terran known before I did?

Before I could decide, he stood straight, looking down at me.

"Just once," he said, "let it go."

15

TERRAN

Before she could respond, I headed into the solar to prepare for our mission. If Lyra gave any hint that she would do as I asked, the Stone would remain precisely where it was this night.

I slipped on my leather boots, still seeing her face clearly in my mind. Hearing her intake of breath in my ears. Until now, I couldn't be certain if her "interest" in me was part of her ploy.

She is a Shadow Diplomat.

Until I could talk to one of the Gyorian elders, or find a text that spoke of the supposed legends, I had to rely on my memory of how extensive Lyra's training might have been. But what I was fairly certain of. She desired me as much as I did her.

And I desired Lyra very, very much.

Finished lacing, I sat. Attempted to clear my mind, as if such a thing were possible after this eve's revelations. A memory that resurfaced about my father replayed itself.

"I heard him," my brother had said, years ago. "Speaking to Valdric. Why would Father be using Drelshade?"

"He wouldn't."

Drelshade was outlawed in Gyoria. Its king would never

access it, unless he wished to lose the faith of his people. A night-blooming vine native to the caverns beneath the palace, when distilled, its sap induced a dreamlike state. Given too much, it slowed time and perception, clouded memory, and left its recipient susceptible to suggestion. Like many of the skirmishes and battles throughout the years, Drelshade was the root of a war that led to its use being strictly forbidden, relegated to a category of similarly potent dark magic.

I might have dismissed my brother, not wanting to believe our father would use outlawed magic, but I'd done some digging, nonetheless. The moment Lyra told me Father had "somehow erased" the queen's memory, Kael's words from many years ago had slammed into my skull.

"We should hope he, of all people, does not," Kael had said. "'Tis said when combined with the power of the Stone, the effects deepen into a less temporary suppression of memory."

I had no doubt he'd used both to ensure the Queen of Aetheria never sought to return to Elydor. Which meant he realized returning, even after he closed the Gate, would be possible. Unless he did it to ensure she'd never return, even if his attempt to close it failed.

Either way, he had lied.

To me. To Kael. To his people.

"Are you ready?"

She stood at the entrance, all Aetherian warrior. Head high, wearing an expression of calm and determination, Lyra waited for my response.

Tell me. That you don't just want to ensure Elydor's balance returns. Tell me you want the Stone of Mor'Vallis for your king. For your friend, Mev. For the humans.

Say it.

"What do you intend, after I retrieve it?" I found myself asking.

She hesitated.

"I've already given my word I will not attempt to take it from you."

"That's not what I asked."

She stepped inside.

"Retrieving the Stone of Mor'Vallis is essential if balance is to be restored."

"Also not what I asked."

I closed the distance between us. I considered grabbing a fistful of Lyra's hair, holding her head in place, and crushing her lips with a kiss so consuming it would leave no doubt who in this chamber wanted the other.

Instead, I waited for her to take the next step toward me.

Say it, Lyra. Tell me why you're really here.

She either thought so little of my intelligence that Lyra had no notion I'd worked out her true purpose, or she couldn't bring herself to say it aloud.

Her gaze dipped just slightly to my mouth.

"If you mean to distract me from my question—"

"I mean nothing of the sort," she quipped. "Your closeness is simply... distracting."

Just one touch.

I reached up, brushing my knuckles along her cheek. "When I did this before, how did it make you feel?"

Her cheek was so very smooth.

Lyra swallowed.

"Tell me," I said, the question in my tone replaced by a more commanding one.

She licked her lips. "It felt like... I didn't want it to stop."

Wiping her lower lip dry with my thumb, I tugged it down until her mouth opened.

"You take orders well for someone unaccustomed to it."

Her eyes flashed. Lyra's instinct was to refute me... to deny she would ever take an order from me, a Gyorian.

"*Voren vel'kora*," I said, holding her gaze before pulling my hand away.

Lyra's mouth closed. Neither of us spoke. Or moved. Instead, we stood toe to toe, our breathing syncing.

"What does it mean?" she asked finally.

It was bad enough I'd uttered the ancient Gyorian phrase without thinking.

"When you speak your own full truth, perhaps I'll tell you."

With that, I spun from her and left the solar. Not because I wished to make a dramatic exit, but because, if I stayed a moment longer, the Stone of Mor'Vallis would remain hidden.

* * *

"A torch? So very... human of you."

Peering over my shoulder, Lyra's face illuminated by the very torch she teased me for carrying, I slowed my pace. The caverns beneath the palace were built to connect each wing but were strictly forbidden from use without explicit permission from the king.

"To walk the tunnels without decree is to tread the footsteps of traitors. Even by me. Using any sort of Gyorian magic down here would be courting destruction. These walls remember what the palace would rather forget."

"I don't understand."

Nay, she would not. I stopped and turned, once again illuminating her face.

Voren vel'kora. What had I been thinking?

"Lord Thalric, High Minister of Infrastructure during King Vornar's reign, oversaw these magical channels beneath the palace when they were still used regularly. He also used them to stage a coup against the king, believing himself more powerful. He attempted to steal the Stone of Mor'Vallis to prove his claim after King Vornar denied his request to challenge him during the Rite of Stone and Soil."

"Vornar," she mused. "The shortest reign of any Gyorian king."

"Which makes some believe Thalric may have had a legitimate claim. But he was caught and executed as a traitor so none will ever know. In the incident's wake, these caverns were seen as cursed, likely by design to keep anyone from using them in such a way again."

"Do you believe they're cursed?"

"Nay." I turned back and began to walk once again.

Pushing all thoughts of my father and Kael, of the princess and her mother... and most especially what I'd blurted to Lyra, from my mind, I concentrated on navigating us below the exit closest to the throne room. It had been many years since Kael and I used these caverns as a way to quietly defy our father when he became so overbearing even Mother couldn't placate him.

"I believe this is the exit."

"You believe?"

"As I said, these caverns are rarely used. This way."

If memory served, the rock stairs carved into the mountain which we ascended would lead to a corridor to the east of the throne room. None, by design, would lead directly inside.

"There will be a guard at the front of the throne room," I said as we reached the top. "And another now positioned at the entrance to the entranceway leading to the Vault. If something goes amiss, I will—"

"Nothing will go amiss."

She said it with the confidence of one who had performed this particular type of mission many times. It wasn't a loud, boasting confidence but one of quiet resolve. Lyra would do what was necessary to achieve her goals, and this time, our goals were one and the same.

"You mentioned that it will work best on a small number of targets. If other guards are alerted?"

"I will take care of them. You doing so risks discovery."

I was about to open the door when a bit of the Shadow Diplomat lore came back to me. A story I assumed was legend…

"Performing the rite on too many targets?" I asked.

Lyra was close enough behind me as we stood on a small landing atop the stairs that, if I leaned forward, we would be touching. Her eyes sought mine in the flicker of the torchlight, pleading with me not to ask questions.

My grandfather, who had long since faded, used their legend to keep Kael and I in line.

They are difficult to kill, but a Shadow Diplomat has one particularly gruesome method of doing so, when bested.

"Lyra. We will not move from this spot—"

"Backlash," she said, as if that would be enough of a response. I waited.

"Not unlike any Elydorian who harnesses too much magic. Weakness. Headaches."

"Eventually," I finished, already knowing my grandfather had been repeating whispers of truth, not just tales, "you will bleed out."

She appeared unconcerned. "'Tis an exceeding rare occurrence."

"But has happened?" I guessed.

"Only twice."

That was two times too many. The thought of Lyra lying on the palace floor, blood oozing from her nose, her mouth...

"If there are more than two, I will handle them."

Her chin raised.

"I will have your acquiescence on this."

"You'll find I don't take orders well. Especially from a Gyorian."

The moment the words left her lips, she wanted to recall them. I could see from her expression Lyra had remembered the bathing-chamber incident too late.

"That," she insisted, "was different."

"Was it?"

"Aye."

I moved the torch to the side, enabling me to lean closer.

"And when the deed is done, and you're back in my bedchamber, what then? Lyra of Aetheria? Will you cede control once again?"

I could feel her breath. Almost tasted her lips. The desire to consume her was nearly too great a weight to bear. Eyes wide, lips parted... Lyra treaded well outside her place of comfort now.

"We are far from a successful mission."

A non-answer. So "Lyra" of her. I tried a different tactic.

The truth.

"I would not see you killed today."

It surprised and, hopefully, disarmed her.

"Why?"

One simple word. One simple question.

The answer was neither.

16

LYRA

One of the most basic tenets of my training was clearing the mind. Ensuring it rested not on past failures, or successes. Not on future possibilities or anything but the present since naught else mattered. Allow the body to rely on training and instinct, remain focused on the mission, and the rest would follow.

It had been years since I had any problem following these tenets. There had been some difficult missions, of course, but I'd never had this much difficulty as a fully trained Shadow Diplomat remaining focused.

We were about to face at least two well-trained Gyorian guards who, if I didn't perform the Sovaen Whisper correctly, could ruin the most important mission of my lifetime.

Voren vel'kora.

How could I possibly clear my mind with near-constant thoughts of our exchange, and those words I'd pretended not to understand ringing in my ears? I'd panicked, not knowing how to respond, and feigned ignorance instead. But since Shadow Diplomats were trained with knowledge before they ever began to learn advanced magic, even ancient Gyorian was familiar to me.

When the clans split, they'd each begun to form their own language. But the Treaty of Vel'Thara marked a fragile peace and the beginning of Elydor's Unification Era which lasted for many years. With it, common Elydorian was encouraged, the clan's separate languages relegated to text alone and, eventually, ceasing to exist altogether.

Learning them had been a part of my training.

Unsurprisingly, Terran never answered my question. He likely didn't know why my life meant anything to him, or even why he'd uttered *Voren vel'kora*. We were both in unchartered territory, the lines between my mission goal and feelings for Terran blurring.

He was becoming more as Kael had described him than the stoic and ruthless Gyorian prince I'd come to know over the years. Kael insisted his brother was not simply their father's puppet.

"Are you ready?"

I wasn't.

My parents would be mortified.

"Nearly," I said, closing my eyes and flexing my fingers once, then twice, a habit from early training. The pulse points at my wrists throbbed with a quiet, rhythmic energy. I pressed my thumbs there... pressure, breath, release. Repeat.

I closed my eyes. A single breath.

I let the echo of his voice – *Voren vel'kora* – fade. Not because it meant nothing, but because it meant too much.

I opened my eyes. He was watching me.

"Aye."

Opening the door slowly, Terran peered out, looking right, then left. He pushed it open, and we both stepped into the corridor. I turned back to watch as he closed the door, set within the stonework, as its seam disappeared.

An incredible feat of architecture and concealment.

Beyond lay a narrow corridor carved from the same obsidian-hued stone as the inner palace walls. The floor beneath our feet was smoother, less worn, and the air felt cooler, untouched by the bustle of the main halls. Occasional torch brackets dotted the passage, though most sat unlit, casting deep shadows along the floor.

At the end of the corridor, we stopped. Terran pointed to the right, indicating the first guard lay just beyond that wall. I nodded and stepped in front of him, blocking out his presence. My target couldn't see me first. If he did, there was little purpose in putting him to sleep. Peering around the corner, I watched as he scanned back and forth, ensuring none entered the throne room. We stood there for some time, Terran never uttering a word. I expected him to become impatient, asking why I waited.

Instead, he trusted me to my skills.

Finally, the guard turned away from us. Without hesitating, I inched out as far as I dared and breathed in slowly, feeling the air around us, muttering, *sova enai* with a twist of my fingers.

Drawing intention from the elemental current around us, pairing it with the ancient Aetherian phrase more superstitious than practical, I held my breath, waiting.

The guard dropped to the floor.

We were clear.

I turned to my companion.

"You seem surprised," I whispered.

"Hearing of it and seeing the Sovaen Whisper performed are two very different things. Come."

Stepping out, he walked past the guard skeptically though I knew he would not wake for some time. Once inside the throne room, we moved quickly, through it and beyond a door at the back of the chamber. Another corridor, this one more well-used.

Terran pressed his finger to his lips. Passing door after door of mostly storage, according to Terran, we came to one last turn. Beyond it would be the second guard. Inclined to agree with Terran that it was an exceedingly odd place to post a guard if something important were not within these walls, I followed his lead and peered around the corner.

This time, there was less space for the guard to move. He stood like a statue, not moving, staring straight ahead. I could perform the rite from where we stood but would have preferred to be a bit closer as he was quite a way down the corridor from us. But there was no help for it.

I looked at Terran, conveying my concern without words.

He understood, and did something extraordinary.

Terran smiled.

It wasn't mocking, or jesting, or like any other of the smiles he'd given me thus far. This one was genuine and encouraging. The kind of smile a friend would give you.

Not one of an enemy.

As before, I cleared my mind and performed the rite, praying to Zephra it would work at this distance. But just as before, the guard slumped to the floor.

It wasn't until we stepped over him—Terran grabbing a wall torch since he'd abandoned his other one in the throne room—and pushed in what looked exactly like a wall beyond where the guard stood, another entranceway revealed, that either of us spoke.

"Well done," he said, holding the light to the side of us.

"Thank you."

So many other words went unspoken as he turned and said, "The stone staircase is long and narrow. Watch where you step. I will do my best to light the way."

He'd not been jesting.

We walked down, and down, and down, the air becoming cooler and damper, as we descended. If either of the guards woke... if any above were somehow alerted to our presence... there would be nowhere to escape. Terran and I would be well and properly caught.

"If we are somehow discovered, what will you say?" I asked, finally too curious not to know his plan. I'd executed my part, and the rest depended on him. Had I been foolish to lay my life at the feet of a Gyorian prince? That there had been little choice didn't make my racing heart slow, despite the methods I'd been taught to slow it in situations such as these.

Slow breath in, Lyra. Hold it, remind yourself there is no past, no future, and that at present, you are alive and breathing, and another slow breath out.

"That you forced my hand."

I froze. Terran turned up to me, smiling once again.

"Or that I was gathering intelligence. Technically true." He shrugged. "I haven't decided yet."

Humor. From Terran of Gyoria.

Fascinating.

Finally, after what seemed like hours, though had likely been just minutes, we arrived at the bottom. The stone-carved chamber was small, and bare, except for a single stone chest lying on a stone pillar.

"You Gyorians do love your stone."

He huffed a quiet laugh. "It endures."

The chest was carved from obsidian-veined granite, its surface etched with ancient runes that shimmered faintly in the torchlight, which he handed to me.

Without pause, Terran stepped forward and pressed his palm to the lid. With a low, grinding sound, the runes pulsed once... and then it opened.

I rushed forward and peered inside.

17

TERRAN

My father's crown.

Though Lyra gasped, I wasn't surprised to find it inside. So many secrets, and yet my father was predictable in many ways as well.

Forged from a fusion of obsidian and silver, the Stone of Mor'Vallis at its center shimmered with a dark iridescence, shifting in hue from midnight to, when used, a deep crimson. Along the band, ancient runes pulsed faintly even now with aetheric energy, a reminder of the pact once shared between Gyorians and the elemental forces of the land.

"I've seen it many times on his head. But here, like this..."

I understood what Lyra meant. There was something dark, almost sinister, about it. Perhaps knowing what he'd used the Stone to do?

I had no intention of taking the crown. It was my father's, earned by being the strongest land-wielder in Elydor. But the Stone... it belonged to Gyoria, even if Father was the only one who it responded to while he was king.

Stepping back and placing the crown on the floor, I placed

both hands near it. When the floor hummed faintly, I pressed my palm over the Stone, feeling for the weave of my father's warding spell. The metal of his crown warmed and then softened like clay.

I lifted the Stone free, but as expected, it didn't respond to my power.

Standing and replacing the crown, I closed the lid and turned to Lyra.

"I've always known he closed the Gate, but for as many times as Kael and I asked Father to explain how he'd done it, precisely... I did not know he erased her memory. In her state, 'twas a cruelty."

"Separating mothers from their children, stranding visitors in a realm they only even thought to visit, forcing them to make it their home... closing the Gate as he did? It was always a cruelty, Terran."

They never belonged in Elydor.

It was a refrain Kael and I heard from him, one I repeated many times over the years. If not for the humans, my mother—the kindest, most gentle Gyorian who ever lived—would still be alive. Babes were a rarity in our immortal world. When she was blessed, a word our mother had used often, with twins, her "world had been complete." Only to have been taken from her by a disease that didn't belong in our realm.

"You pressed your palm to it," Lyra said, ever-observant, nodding to the chest.

The fog of past thoughts lifted. We were not in the clear yet.

"Only those with royal blood running through their veins can open it."

Her eyes widened. I was beginning to know her, understand Lyra's way of thinking.

"You could never have retrieved it without me."

"I'd not have tried."

Like my father, Lyra blatantly lied.

"Aye," I said, resigned. "You would have."

The bigger question was, what would Lyra do now? I'd find out soon enough.

Slipping the Stone in the pouch I'd brought for this purpose, I took the torch from Lyra.

Noticing she did not refute my words, I led us back up the winding stone stairs. Up and up we climbed, silent. My own thoughts tumbled from the Stone in my pouch, to my father's secrets to, most often, the woman following beyond me. As we approached the top, I also carefully considered, once again, what might happen if our guards were discovered. What I would do, and say, to my father.

I'd crossed a line, taking Lyra with me. Or maybe I'd crossed it when I allowed Kael to pass our men and I on the road as he and Princess Mevlida escaped to Aetheria. An action I'd not have taken had he not lied about so many details of the Gate's closing. Or stealing the Wind Crystal and tossing it into the Depths. Or the current elemental unrest.

We reached the top. Taking a deep breath, I pushed open the door. Having prepared for the worst, I was pleasantly surprised to see the guard lying precisely as we'd left him.

"Dren was right," she murmured.

I'd mentioned to Lyra that my right hand had verified the guard's changing times.

"Dren is always right," I said.

We made our way back to the first guard who was, somewhat surprisingly, also lying undisturbed on the floor, as if he'd simply fallen asleep.

As if Terranor himself wished for our successful mission, we encountered no others on the way back.

Lyra hadn't argued when I told her to walk in front of me, though she had shot me a look that said, *This isn't necessary*.

But it was.

I'd taken her, expecting an attack. Expecting her fingers to twitch. Expecting a battle. Anticipating that Lyra might attempt to use magic to take the Stone, and me being forced to stop her. The thought of how far I might have had to go to stop her was somehow worse than the one of us being discovered.

Instead, she simply sauntered back to my chambers as if she'd gone there many times before.

"Satisfied?" she asked as I closed my chamber door behind us.

"Not even a little," I said, purposely mistaking her meaning. "Are you offering to attempt to rectify that?"

Her laugh filled my bedchamber in a way nothing had for some time.

"Attempt? I can assure you, my prince, if I chose to rectify that situation for you, it would be more than an *attempt*."

The prize in my leather pouch momentarily forgotten, as was perhaps Lyra's goal, I took a step toward her.

"So I am your prince now? How very... deferential of you."

The air had shifted. My senses heightened from what we'd just done, and from the dance Lyra and I had been playing all night, I moved even closer to her.

Lyra held her ground, not moving, but also not dropping her Aetherian air of indifference.

"You clearly missed my tone, if not my words. I have no prince, or king, but Galfrid and his daughter."

"I do not doubt your loyalty to them. Your willingness to serve is on display." I purposefully lowered my gaze to her ample bosom. "Even now."

"You think I meant to seduce you into securing the Stone of

Mor'Vallis? And then, pray tell, what was my plan? To attack you, steal it, and flee north?"

"Precisely."

"I'd have done so by now."

I had always found Lyra's overabundance of confidence irritating. Aetherian. Yet at this moment, it was just the opposite.

"How would you have done so?" I challenged.

I watched Lyra's fingers closely. They barely moved. And yet, a soft current of air, like an intimate whisper, brushed along my ear. Her fingers did move then, just slightly, as every candle in the chamber dimmed. A maneuver I'd seen much less often than the first one, requiring a high measure of control over the air.

In response, I planted my feet, channeling the stone beneath the floorboards to anchor myself. When the blast of air came, pressing against my chest, my stance held. Behind Lyra, a floor tile cracked with a small ridge of stone jutting up behind Lyra to trip her if she backed up.

In response, she didn't back up. But Lyra did take a step forward toward me as she used a thin whip of pressurized air to flick a nearby candle's flame sideways, the heat catching my attention. Any stronger of a gust, it could have burned me.

"You've made your point," I said, resting the tile back down with a flick of my fingers. "We've established your skills are more advanced than most." I closed the gap between us, itching to grab a fistful of that silvery hair and make Lyra beg for me. Instead, I placed one finger beneath her chin, forcing it upward until she was looking directly into my eyes.

My finger remained there, but I didn't move otherwise.

"But so are mine."

She didn't move. Or push my hand away.

"I don't doubt it, but surely you realize by now I have no intention of attempting to take that Stone from you."

I stroked my thumb across her chin, and then upwards, along the outline of her cheek, as I did before. Though her eyes blazed, Lyra gave no other indication she felt anything at all, as if my touch didn't affect her.

"Then what do you intend, Lyra?"

"To convince you to come with me."

I brought my thumb back down, this time, running it along the bottom of her lower lip.

To come with me.

"You know I will do no such thing."

Lyra allowed my touch but made no move of her own.

"I know you no longer trust your father, nor should you, after what he kept from you. From Kael."

My hand froze, though it remained in place.

"I know you feel trapped between your allegiance to him and your duty to those who follow you, expecting you to do what's best for Gyoria. I'm only asking you come with me. Speak to your brother. Hear the truth and decide for yourself on the best path forward."

I know you no longer trust your father.

He wasn't the only one I no longer trusted.

"Open your mouth, Lyra."

Finally, a reaction. Her eyes widened. At my command? Or her body's reaction to it? The second, more likely. Even immortals could learn something new about themselves.

She paused.

Then parted her lips.

I slipped my finger inside. This time, she didn't have to be told. Lyra closed her lips around me as I pulled gently and then pushed it back into the sweet warmth of her mouth. Hardening immediately at the sight of her, the feel of her mouth on me as I imagined so much more... pulling from her, I used my finger to trace her lips.

"Is your mouth the only thing wet, Lyra?"

Her shoulders rose and fell.

"Tell me," I said, in the last tone I'd expect Lyra to respond to, but one I'd learned she would.

For me.

"No."

That one simple word was all it took for my control to snap. Done imagining her hair between my fingers, I reached out and made it happen. Fisting it and pulling her toward me, our mouths crashed together and neither of us hesitated.

Whimpering as I held her head firmly in place, Lyra grabbed the material of my tunic on both arms, holding tight. Slanting for better access, I thrust my tongue inside her mouth, demanding without words she do the same.

Melding together perfectly, I forgot to demand, taking what I wanted instead. Lyra gave it freely, our tongues tangling in a kiss that ensured I'd never be the same. When I tightened my grip on her hair, the sound deep in Lyra's throat threatened to make me lose control.

No longer the icy Aetherian Shadow Diplomat, Lyra gave herself to the kiss with an abandon only hinted at, but one that made me want to consume her.

And I might have if the knock at my door hadn't interrupted us.

I pulled away, somehow shocked at the sight of her. One I'd never forget.

The always assured, collected Lyra, her lips swollen from our kiss, hair tangled from my grip, didn't appear repentant, sorry for the mistake of kissing me.

Submitting to me.

Instead, she stood before me, head high, daring me to...

To go with her.

I'd spent centuries letting others decide what loyalty meant. Maybe it was time I did, too.

"Terran."

It was Dren.

"Stay aside until I'm assured he's alone," I said, making my way, regrettably, toward the door.

She did immediately, her warrior's training taking precedence over everything. Including that kiss.

"Did it work?" Dren asked, stepping into my chamber.

I patted the pouch at my side. "It did."

Dren let out a low whistle. Of surprise. Respect. I wasn't certain.

"Lyra?" I called.

She stepped forward.

"You've met my right hand? Dren, Lady Lyra."

She held her fisted hand to her heart in greeting. Dren did the same. Both cordial. As if they were not enemies.

"I have," she said. "You accompanied Terran and Kael to the treaty of Arlyn Cross." She smiled. "Though I recall you were less diplomatic then."

Dren smiled back. "And you were more effusive than usual. A side effect of too much wine, if I remember correctly."

"I'd hoped you had forgotten that."

As if it were possible. It was the first time, in many meetings, I'd seen a hint of her true self. The Lyra that, just moments ago, had melted into my arms. That kiss...

"I risked my neck bribing a steward and disabling the north tower scrying spell." Dren interrupted my thoughts. "So unless you mean for her to get caught, it's time for me to take her."

My eyes met Lyra's.

"I arranged for Dren to escort you safely from the palace," I explained.

This would be the true test. If Lyra came here to ensure the Stone was safely away from my father, to prevent any further Unbalance, there was no reason for her to stay.

"You will not come with me? To speak to my king? To your brother?"

I could see Dren watching us both carefully.

"No. I won't."

Though her eyes didn't dart to the Stone, I sensed they wanted to.

Your move, Lyra.

"Very well." Heading deeper into the chamber, she gathered her satchel, slinging it over her shoulder, and stood beside Dren. "I'm ready."

She's ready? Lyra would simply... leave?

Impossible.

"If you change your mind," she said, "I will wait at Grimharbor, at The Siren's Rest, until the new moon."

"Grimharbor is no place for a—"

Her eyes widened, challenging.

I remembered her treatment of the guards. This was no ordinary Aetherian, and I'd do well to remember that.

"It has been a pleasure, Lady Lyra," I said instead, hand to my heart.

She did the same. "I do hope you reconsider."

With that, she strode to the door, forcing Dren to follow. He looked back at me.

I nodded.

No other words of parting. No mention of our kiss. No regret, it seemed, on Lyra's part, for she swept past Dren as if there might not be someone waiting in the corridor, as confident as ever.

Thankfully, there didn't seem to be anyone out there. All went quiet and stayed that way for some time. No alarm raised. Nothing unusual except the emptiness of my bedchamber.

Perhaps I'd been wrong about her intentions. Surely, if Lyra had truly come to retrieve the Stone, she would not have left with Dren so willingly, knowing she'd not be admitted re-entry into the palace walls after my father had banished her.

If that were true, my retrieval of the Stone was warranted. What, precisely, had my father been using it for without telling me? How was he contributing—and I had no doubt, now, he had been—to the recent Unbalance we'd been experiencing?

Most of all, how was I possibly going to get that kiss out of my mind?

There seemed to be just one answer.

I wasn't.

18

LYRA

"He's the one sitting alone in the corner."

Ilyas Rho had proven to be more resourceful than Marek had suggested.

"Elvric's memory is a library. His mind, unfortunately, is a storm. Most think him mad, but those who know respect his knowledge on relics and inter-realm leyline equilibrium. He will, no doubt, be useful to your mission."

"Thank you. Elydor owes you a debt that cannot be repaid," I said, watching the former Royal Naturalist and elemental historian as he stirred his steaming mug of kavess.

"Contact me in the usual way if you have further need of my services."

Useful, but he still made his living as a smuggler. No coin would do as payment.

"Thank you," I repeated, relaying information I overheard from two guards in the palace. "There's a breach in the Emberwatch patrol grid near the western cliffs. For now, it's unguarded."

His eyes widened. Such information would be invaluable to him. With a fist to the heart, Ilyas disappeared toward the market, leaving me in the entranceway of The Siren's Rest, the sailors and smugglers surrounding it little concerned with my presence.

"Elvric Fenlor?" I asked, approaching.

The thaloran stood. He'd seen at least five hundred years, as evidenced not only by the lines on his face and the graying around the temples, but by the way his eyes watched me with the kind of knowledge that comes with so long a life.

"I've heard of you, Lady Lyra," he said, fist to the heart, which I mimicked. "But never expected we would meet."

I sat, the scent of his kavess stronger as the thick, spiced brew sat in front of me.

"Thank you for doing so," I said, nodding to his mug. "It is the one Gyorian staple I've never become accustomed to."

He lifted the mug. "Strong enough to jolt a stone-wielder awake and bitter enough to match their mood, as they say."

I laughed as he took a sip. "You are not at all what I expected."

Unbidden, a memory of Terran's kiss flashed before me as it had so many times in the days since I left the palace. There was no time to dwell on such a memory. My mission here was still unfilled.

"You expected me to be crazed, no doubt?"

I was ashamed to admit it. "The king worked hard to rewrite your narrative."

A tall, wiry Gyorian with sleeves rolled to his elbows and a permanent scowl approached the table. His apron bore the stain of too many rushed mornings, and he didn't bother hiding the inked rune coiling up one forearm. Ordering quickly, I picked up my conversation with Elvric as our server walked away. "I will admit, even I haven't fully understood the depths of Balthor's desperation to ensure his people remained in the dark until now."

Elvric's eyes, wise but faded, their light having gone out long ago, peered into his mug.

"I served him well. And his predecessor, too. The queen's death changed him."

As I'd heard many times. "The fact remains, the queen is dead. Has been for many years. His reasons, even though they may be valid, matter less now than his politics."

I thought of Terran's bathing chamber. The way he spoke of his mother. And could understand how such a woman softened the Gyorian king. Without her, he'd become lost.

"More Gyorians would agree with you than most think." His voice gruff, Elvric took a swig as my own drink was placed before me. I thanked the server and took a sip, waiting for the ousted historian to continue. "There is a growing faction who can see with their own eyes what Balthor's isolationist policies have cost us."

I listened as he outlined the current state of Gyorian affairs, in his opinion, which was in line with our own assessment. But I wasn't here to discuss inter-Elydorian sentiment.

My mind wandered.

Voren vel'kora.

You are bound to me by choice.

It wasn't a phrase a Gyorian would typically utter lightly. Its true meaning would be lost by most, but I'd been trained to understand such nuances. Spoken aloud, it carried weight... far more than the simple translation would suggest. Its origins traced back to the earliest blood-pacts of the elemental clans when Elydor was one kingdom. Back then, it was used in sacred vows... between bonded warriors, lovers who chose devotion over duty, and even rulers who swore allegiance not by blood, but by will.

To say it now? To me?

It signified dominance, but not control. It was a declaration. A surrender of trust.

Most wouldn't understand the difference. But I knew its etymology.

And so did Terran.

Snapped back to the present, I waited for a break in his story.

"Will you tell me about the Stone?" I asked. "And its possible role in the current Unbalance?"

It was a loaded question, and my companion knew it. Some would consider this conversation treason on his part, between a former Royal Naturalist and an Aetherian.

"The Stone of Mor'Vallis is semi-sentient," he said quietly, his eyes darting from me to the other Siren's Rest patrons. "More relic than raw magic. It is common knowledge that each of the three relics—the Stone, the Wind Crystal, and the Tidal Pearl—can only be used by the most powerful in each clan. What most misunderstand is that it does not align with strength alone, but with the balance of the wielder's elemental heart. Balthor could wield it because he was the most powerful in Gyoria, aye, but also because he was more balanced, before his descent into hatred."

He leaned in. "There's more. Something most scholars don't write down. The relics are not just bound to bloodlines. They are listeners. Observers. Each carries a core memory... a living imprint shaped by every hand it has touched. The Stone of Mor'-Vallis remembers more than power. It remembers the kind of power it served."

I stared at him. "You're saying it judges?"

"No," he said, voice low and steady. "It remembers. And it protects itself from being used by those it deems unworthy. There is an old saying among elemental historians. *Velar ith'morra.* The relic remembers the wound."

I'd never heard such a saying before.

"If you do not believe me," he said, likely sensing my skepticism, "ask Salvia of Zephros. She will verify the same of your Wind Crystal."

No Keeper of Artifacts in Elydor's history knew more of such things than Salvia.

"Why would she not have mentioned it to King Galfrid?"

"Because Salvia suspects, as all who have studied elemental relic history, as I do. These relics are chosen based on more than just elemental strength. Disclosing too much could tip the balance by revealing as much to those who would challenge the current rulers. How would most Elydorians react if they learned their relics were "remembering wounds" from the First Crossing, for instance?"

I understood his points, but was still surprised such knowledge had been kept hidden for so long. By all three clans. Which reminded me of Estmere.

"What of the humans? How do they play into this knowledge?" I asked, working through his revelations aloud.

He sipped his drink, considering. "That depends on which humans you mean. Most were collateral in the First Crossing. But not all. The Harrow bloodline was different. Chosen, some say. Marked." Elvric's gaze narrowed. "There's a reason some of us still say, 'Where blood lingers, memory wakes.' Most have forgotten the phrase. Fewer still know it refers to the relics."

"Thank you," I said simply, unsure how else to repay Elvric for his knowledge.

"I tried from within for many years but failed. Perhaps you will have better luck. I fear for Gyoria, for Elydor, if you do not." He stood with a fist to the heart. "It has been a pleasure, Lady Lyra."

The historian was gone before I could even offer my own parting.

I sat back, taking in everything he'd said.

There was much to consider. The relics. The balance. The Gate.

And Terran.

None of what I'd learned would matter if he didn't join me in Grimharbor.

I'd spent a lifetime learning to read people, bending their weaknesses to my advantage. But he was not simply a mark. The way I responded to him... my body responded to him... that was a warning.

One that made me dangerous.

Still, no one else stood a better chance of securing the Stone. If Terran came, the plan could still work, especially with my newfound knowledge of the relics.

If he didn't...

I would find another way.

19

TERRAN

It had flickered.

Not once, but three times. Three more than the Stone should have given. I wasn't the most powerful land-wielder in Gyoria.

"It happened again."

Dren stopped what he was doing, showing a young one how to harness the core of Elydor well beneath his feet, and sent the girl back to her trainers. Partnered but childless, like most Elydorians, he would have been a good father.

"When?"

"Just now."

Dren looked at the leather pouch. "You have it on you? Have you gone mad? And how do you know it happened again if it's in there?"

I gestured for him to leave the training field with me.

"The same grumbling, when the land beneath our feet has been disturbed... it's something like that." I shrugged. "I just... felt it. When I looked inside, it flicked as it had done before."

Neither of us wished to discuss its implications.

Dren was more concerned with the fact that, as of yet, the

Stone hadn't been discovered as missing. As for my thoughts, they were frequently, since last eve, on a silver-haired Aetherian whose body responded to my command. Whose lips tasted like a cross between the sweetest Thalassarian fruit and... and danger.

A deadly combination.

Every instinct I possessed screamed to keep my distance. She was a weapon wrapped in silk, deception cloaked in desire. And yet I'd tasted her, let her see more of me than I had anyone in years.

Fool.

"Even now," I said, "it pulses as if waiting."

Like her, in Grimharbor.

"You need to speak to Kael."

It wasn't the first time Dren had said it. After a fitful sleep, I woke to the same feeling as I experienced now from the previously sleeping relic.

"If only he was here."

We passed the outer rim of the training grounds where thistles grew wild and sharp... useless for healing, excellent for teaching pain. I remembered scraping my palms on them during my first trial run, bloodied but proud. That was the Gyorian way: bleed first, ask questions later.

I'd once believed in that.

Now I carried a stolen relic in my belt and couldn't stop thinking about an Aetherian who made me forget the rules I'd been raised on.

"You could—"

"No."

It was becoming a tired argument.

Dren stopped walking. Sighing loud enough for my father clear across the palace to hear, I did the same.

"Pride will be a useless defense when he discovers it missing."

"Pride? I have no notion—"

"Aye." Dren cut me off as if he were the Prince of Gyoria and I was his right hand. "You do. After raging against your brother for months, you refuse to admit his actions may have held some merit."

I hated how well he knew me.

"She lied to me," I said, not for the first time.

"Aye," Dren agreed. "But perhaps the Stone serves a dual purpose."

Whether he meant it could both restore balance and open the Gate, or something else, it mattered naught.

"I will confront him," I said, more determined than ever. For answers. For clarity.

"And I will give you his response, if you wish to hear it. His rants have become predictable as of late."

"As have yours," I said, considering tossing Dren into the thistles.

We both froze then, the ground rumbling under our feet.

I knelt down, closed my eyes, and connected to its source. Sighing, my worst fears confirmed, I stood.

Dren's brows raised in question.

"He's discovered it missing."

"Are you certain?"

"His energy is unmistakable," I said. "Sharp. Furious. Like when he shattered the basalt pillars after the treaty was signed."

"What will you do?"

I stood. Resigned.

"Speak to him. Father has gone unchecked for too long. His lies were the tipping point."

At least, that was the plan. I was no coward, to run as my brother had. Neither was I a traitor to Gyoria.

Kael is neither.

Attempting to reconcile my brother's actions had taken a toll. One that appeared to pale in comparison to what was about to be a confrontation for the ages.

My father's guards.

They marched toward us with purpose.

They marched toward me.

Their formation split the training field like a blade, boots pounding against sun-baked earth as if they meant to shake the land itself. Gyorian elite, armed and unyielding. Not a patrol. Not a warning.

A retrieval.

"Do not engage," I warned Dren, already unfastening the pouch at my side and slipping the Stone beneath my tunic, against my skin.

"It's too late for that," Dren warned.

The captain raised a fist. "Prince Terran, by order of the king, you are to be detained for questioning."

Dren dropped down, slamming his palm to the ground.

The field responded instantly.

A ripple surged through the hardened soil, cracking the surface in a jagged line that raced toward the oncoming guards. The first two stumbled, the earth shifting beneath their boots. One fell. The other righted himself just in time to catch a face full of grit as the ground kicked upward like a beast bucking its rider.

I didn't wait.

I dropped to one knee, fingers splayed, and sent my focus deep. The pulse of Elydor thrummed beneath the surface... restless, awake. It knew me. It listened.

Shift, I commanded silently.

A stone barrier erupted between us and the front line, not tall enough to last but enough to break formation.

Dren grabbed my arm, hauling me to my feet.

"They'll go around it," I muttered.

"They'll try."

Another rumble echoed as I slammed my heel into the ground, eyes narrowed. The air around us shimmered with residual energy... thin threads of power flickering up from the soil like steam after rain. It was the old magic, the kind most had forgotten. But not me.

Not the king's blood.

A low-frequency vibration rolled beneath my feet, subtle, but growing. The Stone at my chest pulsed in time with it.

Behind us, one of my loyalists dropped to the ground, hands pressed flat as he whispered a command. Another followed, and then another. A chorus of intention. We weren't soldiers now. We were sons of Gyoria, bending its body to our will.

The terrain shifted again, this time more violently. Thin fissures broke through the clay, forming a pattern we'd trained for, a spiral disruption meant to confuse pursuit.

"Now," Dren hissed. "Before they anchor."

We ran.

The ground opened in our wake, not enough to kill, but enough to warn. The guards slowed, unsure where to place their feet as the field betrayed them.

"We can't keep this up," I said, breath ragged as we sprinted toward the ridge path.

"No," Dren agreed, "but we only need to make it to the outpost."

"To her," I corrected.

He glanced sideways. "Took you long enough."

One last command before I did the very thing I swore I'd never do: flee my land, my people, as Kael had done.

"You will not be branded as a traitor. Go to the Hollow. Find those still loyal to Kael. My men will meet you there."

I'd hoped my father would not do this, but I'd prepared just in case he did.

"What do I tell them?"

We panted, running away from the very place that had kept me safe.

"Tell them the tides are shifting. That Gyorian blood still flows with purpose, and we'll need every ounce of it before this ends."

Dren stared at me for a breath too long. "You sound like him."

My brother. The one I'd been railing against since the Gate responded to Princess Mevlida.

"No," I panted, focusing on the trail. "Kael ran from Gyoria. I'm taking it back."

20

LYRA

He wasn't coming.

Which meant I needed to return to the palace in disguise. At least this time, I knew the Stone's location, even if taking it by force from Terran no longer sat well. It wouldn't be the first time my personal feelings about a mission threatened to interfere with its execution, but this one was unique in more ways than one.

Nestled into the side of a cliff overlooking the churning sea below, The Siren's Rest was located at the edge of Grimharbor. I sat in its hall, listening to the crash of the waves below as the sound mingled with the low murmur of travelers and smugglers, Gyorians mostly.

Out of nowhere, a hand appeared on the table in front of me. Before I could react, a small piece of parchment was left behind. I spun in my seat, the hooded figure already heading deeper into the inn.

I reached for the parchment.

Room thirty-six. Don't make me come get you.

Terran.

I should have recognized his assured gait. Why I wasn't appalled at his tone—just the opposite—was something that could be explored at a later time. It seemed as if a disguise wouldn't be needed after all.

Leaving a coin on the table, I stood and made my way to the third floor. Before I could even knock, the door opened, as if Terran knew I would follow. And quickly.

"Your flair for dramatics is most unexpected," I said, Terran only pulling down his hood after the door was closed. Ignoring the flutter in my chest at seeing him again, I waited for Terran to explain himself.

"When you're fleeing your father's men, and said father is the king, one tends to be overly cautious."

My eyes widened. "He knows it was you?"

"Suspects, I suppose. He sent his men to 'detain me for questioning.' I thought it prudent to leave."

It was worse than I'd imagined, though not surprising. The moment he'd taken the Stone, the wards on the crown would have told Balthor exactly who had breached them. Terran had spoken of hiding the relic, confronting his father, teasing out the truth. Noble, but naïve. The only question had been how quickly he would act. Now I had my answer.

"How did you get away?"

Terran's expression nearly made me laugh, despite the situation we found ourselves in. Exasperated, as if to say, *How do you think?* he declined to actually answer.

The king's guards were the most well-trained of all Gyorian warriors. Terran, it seemed, was even more so. Kael had warned me of the fact, though I thought his words were exaggerated. I had never seen Terran's display of skills personally to verify their strength myself.

Despite the urgency of our situation, the air suddenly shifted between us. This wasn't just about the Stone. Terran knew it. I knew it. But the stakes were too high to allow the way he looked at me now to affect our plans.

"We don't have time for games," I said, confident he'd been about to say something inflammatory.

"Then perhaps don't look at me as if you missed the feeling of my fingers wrapped through your hair."

The effect of his words was instantaneous.

"I looked at you in no such way."

"Mm, I could disprove it easily."

"How?" The question was out of my mouth, Terran provoked, before I thought better of it.

"By tearing off every layer of your clothing, and defenses. Your body doesn't lie."

No, it doesn't.

"I think we have more important matters to discuss."

Sighing, as if reluctantly resigning himself to the truth of my words, he wandered toward the window, looking out at the very rocks below I'd been staring at when he first approached.

"You've set off a chain of events that can't be undone by coming here, Lyra."

Although that was the entire point of this mission, I refrained from saying as much.

"You'd have preferred to allow your father to descend into a madness that would cause a war? Already, he's isolated Gyoria, angered even his strongest allies, and destabilized Elydor in a way that hasn't been seen since—"

He turned to me. "Your king opened the Gate?"

"With permission from all three clans," I reminded him.

"None expected the humans to be given land to settle here. That was Galfrid's doing."

"I won't argue this with you. 'Tis clear we have different views on the matter."

"You think?"

His scowl made me smile. "Like a trexan that guards its den as fiercely as it hunts."

"Call me soft again, Lyra. I will enjoy proving you wrong."

His words sent a tingle from my toes to my very core. I would enjoy it as well but had to stop allowing Terran to know that.

"So sensitive, for a Gyorian."

I goaded him, and Terran knew it. Instead of taking the bait, he turned back to the window.

"I'll go with you, to speak to my brother."

My heart leaped at the victory, one more hollow than it should be. I hated lying to Terran about the true purpose of my mission. But that, I reconciled, was a matter between brothers. I'd been tasked with bringing the Stone of Mor'Vallis to Aetheria. That it was carried by one of the most fearsome Gyorian warriors of our time was a matter for Kael and Galfrid to reconcile.

"And my king?"

"I imagine speaking to him will be unavoidable."

A victory, to be certain. But we needed to get there first.

"I assume your father's men are searching for you?"

"Aye."

"My presence hasn't gone unnoticed here," I said, joining him at the window.

Terran glanced sideways at me. "No. I imagine it hasn't."

There was something in the way he said it… "That sounded suspiciously like a compliment."

"It was."

Even his compliments were gruff. I laughed aloud then. "You are a strange one, Prince Terran."

"And you are not at all what I expected, Lady Lyra."

I wasn't certain what to make of that.

"I've made arrangements for us to travel by boat. My father's land trackers are too skilled to avoid for long. You have a disguise, I assume?"

I hid my surprise. "I do."

"Wear it. Meet me at the eastern quay, beside the fisherman's shrine."

It was time to return to Aetheria. Without further comment, I turned from the peaceful, yet violent, scene below as wave after wave crashed against the Gyorian shore.

Terran grabbed my wrist, stopping me.

"And Lyra."

I looked up into a pair of bright-green eyes, as turbulent as the sea but still somehow as grounded as their owner's clan.

"When we reach Aetheria..." His gaze dipped to my mouth, lingering. "We finish what we started."

21

TERRAN

The ship's captain had trained in Thalassaria many moons ago, before the Gate's opening. Though Gyorians were still welcome in Elydor's southernmost kingdom, they were becoming less and less so as my father's policies discouraged everything from trade to knowledge sharing. The old queen, though no lover of humans, refused to take a stand against Galfrid, angering my father. How he and the new queen, Nerys, would fare was still unknown.

But I had more pressing problems.

Namely, being stuck on a small ship with only its captain, one more reticent than even the most stalwart Gyorians, and Lyra. I'd paid him handsomely to ensure no others sailed with us, but as the morning dragged on, unless I wished to remain in a cabin so small, I couldn't do much more than sleep in it, it was evident we couldn't avoid each other.

"He talks less than you," Lyra said.

We stood at the bow of the ship, scanning the horizon.

"Chaleo is a vaelith whose Fading time has come."

"You obviously trust him. Most would not wish to smuggle their prince away from its king."

"He bears no love for my father. With Thalassari deep in his lineage, an expert sailor, he once refused my father's bid to serve him."

We fell into an easy silence.

Too easy.

"Did you sleep well?"

"Have you thought much on the topic?"

"Of you sleeping?"

"Aye. Or in my bed. Though I will admit, the cabins are smaller than I'd like—"

"Terran," she warned.

A warning I didn't heed.

"But since you've been given the captain's quarters, perhaps I can visit you this eve instead?"

Lyra tugged her hair to the side and began to braid it.

"Don't," I said, the word coming out more like a command. There was a time and a place for that, and this was neither. "Or rather, I'd prefer you not braid your hair."

"Why?" she asked, Lyra's question without censure.

"I like to watch it catch in the wind."

The admission did not put me at ease. Though Lyra and I were bound together until Aetheria, we were far from allies. I would do well to remember that.

"You once told me my hair reminded you of the river mist at Elydor's edge."

She remembered.

Lyra had attended the Rite of Stone and Soil with her parents. They had been given a seat of honor in the hall after her father negotiated safe passage for Aetherian travelers. I'd caught her looking at me, but instead of acknowledging it, she lifted her chin and refused to glance my way for the remainder of the meal. Her haughtiness had irritated me, hence the insult.

"I lied."

"A particular habit of yours?"

"Of mine?" Ironic, Lyra asking such a question.

"You lied also, insisting you weren't watching me during negotiations. Do you remember that?"

"I remember everything, as I told you. Including the way your body responded to me in my bedchamber." My gaze dropped to her lips. "How your mouth fit perfectly with mine. Even now, they part, begging me to slip my tongue between them."

I was warming to the topic.

The sea breeze. Open ocean and calm waters lulling us into forgetting, if just temporarily, the chaos we'd left behind and one we sailed toward.

"I don't beg."

It was the gauntlet I hoped she'd throw down.

"Do you remember me telling you that you would? Beg for me?"

"Aye." She breathed in the salty air, ignoring my presence and looking out to the horizon as if completely unaffected.

I knew otherwise.

"You said, 'I don't have a deferential bone in my body.' Do you remember that?"

She could pretend all she wanted.

"I remember something of the sort."

"Then you will also remember obeying me when I told you to turn around. Or does that not meet your definition of deferential?"

I tried not to smile as Lyra rolled her eyes.

"An innocuous enough command."

I had no doubt Lyra goaded me on purpose.

"It will be less innocuous when you're kneeling naked in bed, with me behind you, and I demand you on all fours before I lick you from behind from front to back."

There was no time to relish in her expression. I wasn't quite finished.

"And when you do beg me to make you come with my tongue, I'll bring you to the threshold and remind you who decides."

I leaned forward, whispering into her ear.

"I do, Lyra. I decide when you come. How hard you come. And maybe, just maybe, if you beg loud enough, I'll allow it."

Being hard enough that it was painful was little price to pay to watch the ice lady thaw.

"When I do turn you over." I swung my body in front of hers, planting a hand on each side of the rail, trapping her. "Dripping wet and calling my name, I plan to ride you so hard that every time you take a step the next day, you think of me."

Our bodies were touching.

Our mouths so close that I only had to lean forward and claim her lips. Lyra would melt into my arms. But we couldn't finish it. Not here. Not on this ship.

"Do you want that, Lyra?" I asked, my gaze holding her. "Do you want me?"

Her nostrils flared. She alternatively hated that I asked and craved to let someone else take the reins for once.

"Say it. Tell me you want me as much as I want you, Lyra."

So proud.

This time, when I whispered into her ear, it was accompanied by the feeling of our bodies being flush together, her breasts pressing against my chest. No doubt she could easily feel the evidence of my desire.

Pinned against the railing, flush against me, Lyra could easily summon a wind gust with her fingers that could toss me over the side of the ship. Instead, she tilted her head, giving me better access to that pretty neck of hers. I took advantage, flicking my tongue first and then trailing a kiss toward her ear once again.

"Say. It."

"I want you."

I smiled against her ear. "*Voren vel'kora*," I whispered. This time, it neither slipped out nor was spoken unintentionally.

This... thing... between us. It was more than lust. I'd desired women before. But this?

"Don't mean to disturb," Chaleo said behind us, "but we're being approached."

I didn't jump back right away. Wouldn't have at all, Chaleo be damned, but if we were being approached, it was likely my father's men.

"We'll finish this later," I whispered finally, taking a step from Lyra and addressing the captain.

"*Vel'kora dra'ven.*"

I froze. Turned. The approaching ship forgotten.

Our eyes met.

"You know ancient Gyorian?"

"Of course." A slow smile curved her lips. "You're not the only one with dangerous secrets, *my* prince."

22

LYRA

They were, indeed, King Balthor's men. But they didn't seem to be following us, as unlikely as it seemed. We watched, and waited, as the distant ship kept our course. Every so often, the captain grunted a few words, mostly unintelligible.

With him by our side, there was no more talk of ancient Gyorian, though I'd clearly surprised Terran earlier. It was almost worth knowing, with each discussion, we ventured down an unreturnable path.

Voren vel'kora.

When he first said it, I'd been too surprised to respond. This time, I had been ready with another phrase, one I'd had to pull from the recesses of my training.

Vel'kora dra'ven.

Bound by choice, if you can keep me.

It should have been a game. Words traded in an ancient tongue, nothing more than verbal sparring.

But I knew better.

Terran wasn't the sort of man to speak carelessly, and I wasn't the sort to yield without calculating the cost. Already the lines I'd drawn in the sand were blurring.

The relic. The Gate. The balance of Elydor.

Those were the reasons I boarded this ship.

And yet, the more time I spent in Terran's shadow, the more I wondered if I could truly separate the Gyorian from the mission... or if I even wanted to.

"Not for us, after all."

I had been so deep in thought, I hadn't even noticed the ship sailing away.

"A temporary stay."

Terran gripped the railing in front of him with both hands. I tried not to imagine those hands gripping me.

"I thought Kael had taken a momentary leave of his senses. When we learned he'd changed course," Terran said, "none could understand it. Until he uttered the words, 'I will die for her, brother,' I thought he would return with me. But Kael would not make such a claim unless he meant it." He pushed back from the railing. "I thought him weak. A traitor." His gaze found mine, sharp enough to pin me in place. "Now I'm not so sure."

For a breath, there was no wind, no creak of the ship, only the press of Terran's look, heavy with things unsaid.

It was not for me to convince him. Terran had to come to the same realization—that his father was well beyond saving—on his own.

"Mev was the catalyst," I said instead. "Kael had been long-tortured by his role as a prince of Gyoria. When he served on the Gate Council, he learned tolerance of humans. But after the Gate closed, he reverted back to his old ways of thinking."

"My father's ways."

He could, at least, recognize as much. "Aye. Yet Kael acknowledged the human's place in his opening speech at the Summit. It was as if... he had to remind himself he hated them. Mev opened his eyes, aye. And I'm not discounting his love for her. But simply saying..."

What was I saying? Could Terran even understand it?

"Have you ever been in love?"

"No."

His answer was so immediate, I knew it to be true.

"Then I cannot possibly explain what it makes someone do. Or how it might change their thinking," I said quietly.

His jaw flexed, but he didn't look away.

"I'm learning," he murmured.

My heart thudded, the conversation quickly becoming personal as I ignored the implications of that comment.

"I watched it happen," I tried again to explain. "The more he cared for Mev, it wasn't as if Kael suddenly changed his thinking completely. But his love for her exposed your father's prejudices in a way that became harder and harder to ignore. Does that make sense?"

"No."

He was impossible.

I tried again.

"Did your mother hate humans?"

His expression sharp, Terran's jaw flexed once more as he warned me not to go there.

Too late. I had and would not relent.

"I know the answer already, of course. As do you. Elydor welcomed them for a reason. Estmere has been a boon in so many ways, their Sight a magic all of its own. If not for your mother's death, think of how an Elydor with four clans, all equal, could prosper."

He looked about ready to murder me. And yet... the Terran of a few days past would have cut me off before I'd even finished.

"The Accord of Estmere wasn't just politics, Terran. Your historians recorded it themselves, that the Sight strengthened the Council's decisions for two centuries. Even the Gyorian crown acknowledged its worth... until fear rotted what they'd built."

He sighed, his expression softening.

For a Gyorian.

"It's back."

He'd gone completely rigid, standing erect and peering at something I couldn't see. It took me a moment, and the captain's shout behind us confirmed it.

"Four of them," Terran grumbled. "It was a scouting ship."

We ran to the captain, who was already adjusting the rigging.

"They'll have Fayette on board," Terran told Chaleo.

A Thalassari defector who, after challenging and losing to his queen, denounced his clan. I'd never met or encountered him, but his sailing abilities were renowned.

Chaleo grumbled something, though I could only make out "scourge" and "sea." As he cut a sharper line to put distance between us, I shook my head while the two men plotted how best to lose the small fleet of ships that were attempting to intercept us.

Hundreds... *thousands* of years and still they underestimated us.

Instead of explaining that Fayette might be a skilled Thalassari sailor but my own companions failed to remember I was, indeed, Aetherian, I calmly made my way to the front of the ship.

I braced myself at the prow, the wind sharp in my lungs. Closing my eyes, I found the currents above us, the invisible rivers threading through the sky. I coaxed them down, wrapping them around our sails until the canvas snapped taut and the mast groaned with the sudden burst of force. The deck lurched underfoot as our bow cut harder through the waves.

Then I reached farther, past the edges of our own wind, to where the fleet bore down on us. I twisted the currents at their backs, letting them fracture and scatter until their sails sagged. What wind they caught turned unpredictable, slipping between their masts instead of driving them forward. The nearest ship tilted awkwardly as the helmsman fought the wheel, momentum bleeding away.

Voices shouted behind me, Terran and Chaleo startled by the sudden change, but I held my focus. The air answered, bending to my will as easily as if I were still a girl racing storms along the cliffs. Our ship surged ahead while the enemy dwindled in the haze.

When I opened my eyes, Terran was there.

"Impressive."

"Thank you."

"I underestimated you, Lyra of Aetheria."

"You did," I agreed. "But I am accustomed to it, especially by—"

"Don't."

He knew I'd been about to say *"Gyorians."*

"How can we heal a divide we continually name?"

He was right.

We couldn't.

Our gazes held, the captain no doubt watching our every move. This wasn't the time. Or place. But with the Aetherian coast fast approaching, it would be soon.

The thought was both thrilling, and terrifying.

"If the wind holds, we will be there by morn," I said, stating the obvious.

"*If* it holds?" There was laughter behind his eyes. Terran in this state was without doubt the most attractive man I'd ever encountered.

"You should smile more," I said softly.

"Continue to give me reasons to," he answered, breaking eye contact and looking out to where the ships had been, "and I just may."

23

LYRA

Our journey to the Aetherian shores, after initially being followed, was uneventful. Terran's first use of the Ascension Gate, unimpressive... according to him. I almost could have fooled myself into believing the reunion between brothers would go smoothly.

The others were gathered, we were told, in the Celestial Hall, waiting for us. Even though he'd never been inside said hall before with its ceiling that fooled most into believing it was truly an open-aired sky, Terran hadn't seemed to see anything around him.

Not the palace. Not the king. Or even Mev, who most people were enthralled to meet for the first time.

He marched directly up to Kael and, without a word, punched him in the face. Chaos erupted as Mev rushed forward, bending down to Kael, who was kneeled over. The king hadn't reacted, aside from a set of raised bushy white eyebrows, but I certainly did.

"What in the skies was that?" I yelled, running forward.

Terran looked at me as if he'd merely said hello to his brother.

Kael stood up, assuring Mev he was fine.

"I deserved that for not sending word to you before changing course. But not for anything else. So that shot will be your last."

Although they were twins, Kael and Terran were easy to tell apart, at least for me. Terran was slightly bigger, though most might miss that detail. It was his expression, perpetually scowling, that differentiated them. Kael was no ray of sunshine, but compared to his brother...

"You abandoned us."

"I did what was necessary."

For the first time since we entered the chamber, Terran seemed to realize we weren't alone. He glanced from his brother, to Mev, and then the king.

"I must say." Galfrid glided toward us. Both commanding and elegant, his white hair matching his robes, the Aetherian king looked like a cross between a grandfather who'd taken hundreds of years to age and the most powerful person in Elydor, as most believed him to be. "I never expected you to come here, Prince Terran. But you are most welcome."

"Not at all the greeting I received," Kael mumbled.

King Galfrid smiled kindly. "You've done much to change my thinking, and for that, I'm grateful," he said, defusing Kael's words effectively.

"I'm here to speak to my brother," Terran said as gruffly as when I'd first come to Gyoria.

"You've not met the princess," I reminded him.

Mev was glaring at Terran. He obviously hadn't ingrained himself to her by punching her partner, Kael's left cheek showing the evidence of the strike already.

"That wasn't nice."

Terran startled at her speech. It was an accent we hadn't heard in some time. Once, when humans flowed freely into Elydor, occasionally those from outside England would find their way to York and through the Gate. It happened enough that Elydorians became accustomed to a variety of different accents from the human realm. But it had been nearly thirty years since the Gate was open, and those who remained had eventually learned Elydorian.

"He deserved it." Terran was less than apologetic. "As he admitted."

Mev crossed her arms, unconvinced.

"I watched the two of you battle. At any time, you could have stopped to listen to your brother's side of the story. But nooooo, you blasted him first and asked questions later. Oh wait"— she snapped her fingers, as if remembering something—"that's right. You never asked any questions, just laid into him for—"

"Mev."

She spun her head toward Kael.

"What? I was just getting started."

"I know. That's why I stopped you."

The king tried, and failed, not to smile. I was accustomed to their bantering and used the opportunity to actually introduce the two.

"Prince Kael, this is your brother's partner, and now your family," I reminded him. "Princess Mevlida."

"He hit you," Mev repeated as Kael gave her a *don't do it* look. She clearly wanted to continue her well-earned tirade against Terran.

"And I did abandon him, even if it was justified."

She looked as ready to hit Terran as he had just before he struck his brother. I'd seen Mev angry before, with Kael especially, when they'd first met. But the fury she directed toward Terran was unlike anything I had seen from her.

This was not going well.

"Perhaps we should allow them to speak. Your Majesties," I said to both the king and Mev, "I have much to relay. 'Tis pressing." I caught Terran's eye. "And we should, perhaps, prepare for battle."

Terran didn't disagree.

"Were you followed here?" Kael asked, concern etched in every feature.

"Since Father has likely guessed I took the Stone of Mor'Vallis? And four of his ships were spotted just off the Blackshore Coast."

Everyone had stopped listening at *took the Stone of Mor'Vallis*. I willed them not to say any more. Thankfully, the king seemed to sense my rising panic and gestured for Mev to follow us.

"Come," he said to Mev and me, graciously leaving his own hall. King Galfrid rarely used his throne room, except for formal and official events. Though I followed my king, it was imperative I caught Kael's attention. When he finally glanced my way, I shook my head ever so slightly.

No, he doesn't know we want to use the Stone to open the Aetherian Gate.

Kael understood. I was certain of it. Before we even left the chamber, he'd already begun to question Terran.

"What does she mean, prepare for battle?"

It was the same question King Galfrid asked as we entered his solar chamber. It was as different as Terran's as could be. Windows and light made it seem like part of the sky, as it was with so many of Aethralis's chambers. There were no regular windows, though. Each one an enchanted, and impenetrable, pane of crystal that shifted hue with the light, mirroring the skies beyond.

"As Terran said, he has the Stone. Balthor suspects it was he who took it."

I started at the beginning, regaling my time in Gyoria and leaving out some of the... grittier details.

"So he has it," Mev summarized, "but hasn't agreed for us to use it? And it's very likely either Balthor, or at least his men, are on their way here to retrieve it."

I nodded. "It was a gamble, leaving the Gyorian palace. But without Terran's aid, I'd not have been able to retrieve it."

"A bloodline seal?" Galfrid guessed.

"Aye."

"What's that?" Mev asked.

"It's an elemental binding woven into the royal line," Galfrid explained to his daughter. "The crown's wards recognize the magic in our veins... wind and sky, the gifts of Aetheria. Land and all beneath it, gifts of Gyoria. And the sea, Thalassari's gift. Without it, the seal stays shut, no matter the key or spell."

"It's a good thing you recruited Terran."

"'Recruit' is not the word I'd use. He agreed to retrieve it having seen the beginnings of an Unbalance himself. That Balthor lied about seeing such evidence, and much more, planted seeds of mistrust—"

"Which you took advantage of. Lyra." The king sighed. "You have exceeded all expectations."

Why, then, did I feel like a failure?

The Stone was within our reach, yet... I'd deceived Terran, just as his father had done.

"He knows nothing of the Gate."

Galfrid sat, so Mev and I did the same. I'd always loved this chamber, its chairs carved of pale ashwood and cushioned in clouds of silk. Elegant, ethereal... like sitting in a wisp of sky. Yet as I settled, my thoughts strayed to Terran's chair in his own solar: deep-cushioned, worn to the shape of him and warm from the ever-burning hearth.

"Nothing at all?" Mev's question was a good one.

"He is smart, and likely suspects."

"But has not asked you directly?" Galfrid appeared thoughtful.

"Nay."

"You care for him."

I'd been looking at the ring my mother gave me, not unlike the one Mev wore. My head snapped up.

"Your majesty—"

"Galfrid in these quarters, as I've told you many times, Lyra."

He had, but it was difficult not to see him as my liege. I still saw myself as I did the day my parents left their positions, and I officially began to serve the crown: a young Aetherian, eager to serve her king. Certainly not an equal, as he suggested with permission to use his given name.

"Galfrid." It felt... unnatural.

"I have many years on you, and Shadow Diplomat you may be"—his smile was warm—"remember who trained you."

He did. Among others.

"Shadow... what now?" Mev's expression was as open and honest as always.

"I will explain later," I said, having meant to tell her for some time now. There was no purpose denying the truth. "I've come to..."

Care for him? Desire him? Want to be near him every waking moment? How could I possibly put into words my tumultuous feelings for Terran?

"It doesn't surprise me," he said. "Both Terran and Kael"—

Galfrid looked at his daughter—"were raised by two strong, intelligent Gyorians."

He had never spoken of King Balthor in such a way.

"Father... you're talking about the guy who kidnapped Mom and sent her pregnant through the portal. I mean, Gate."

"I am aware," he said in that calm, soothing tone that was Galfrid's signature. "But that does not negate the fact that Balthor is one of the strongest of his clan in many generations. His sons were trained by the best, and their mother one of the kindest and most caring I knew. She balanced him, keeping Balthor in check in ways that became evident after her death. You've seen evidence of this through Kael. It does not surprise me Lyra sees the same in Terran."

"But even Kael says his brother is more like their father. That he's harder... more unforgiving."

"Both true." I could testify to it easily. "But with many redeeming qualities. None of which will help our cause if he can't be convinced to help us."

Galfrid sighed deeply. "First, we deal with Balthor's imminent threat. Once I can be assured our people are safe." He looked me straight in the eyes. A kind king, aye. But not a weak one, as evidenced by Galfrid's expression now. "We open the Gate. With Terran's permission to use the Stone." He sighed heavily. Regretfully. "Or without it."

24

TERRAN

How I could feel trapped in a bedchamber with so many windows it felt as if I was perched outside, on the top of this damn mountain, I wasn't sure. The door was unlocked. Kael insisted I could come and go as I pleased. Yet every time I'd peered out, the guard was still at the end of the hall. When I asked my brother, who'd come to fetch me for a meal I had no wish to eat, he said it was "standard practice" for "guests such as you."

For enemies of Aetheria.

I listened as the meal Kael sent, without asking, was cleared away behind me. I'd eaten, not because I was hungry, but because I needed sustenance and wasn't stupid enough to think otherwise. But every bite had tasted bitter, Kael's words from our argument still fresh.

"You didn't trust me."

"Do you intend to push everyone away, including me?"

"Your stubbornness aids no one, including Gyoria."

Kael's accusations stung, not because they were leveled relentlessly against me or because they were untrue, but because they came from the only person who had stood beside me when our father had begun to turn his back on the ideals he'd taught us. If Kael could doubt me...

Would I truly rather burn every bridge than bend, as he'd accused?

And if every bridge was ash, what harm was there in letting one person cross the wreckage? Even if she was the last woman I should trust. Even if Lyra had already proven she could wound me in ways no enemy blade ever had.

Tomorrow, we prepared for battle. Even now, as I sat in this damned chamber, Aetheria was arming itself against Gyorian forces that were more than likely to have followed me here.

Would Father be with them?

How could our clan survive this?

"Lady Lyra," the attendant exclaimed.

Turning, I watched as she floated into the chamber, smiling at the young woman as she wheeled away the cart. "Leave the wine," Lyra said. "And bring another glass, if you would."

"I don't want it."

If my tone was gruff, there was a good reason for it. I'd come for answers, and Kael gave me none. I'd stopped short of asking him why Lyra had truly been sent to retrieve the Stone, already knowing the answer, and waited for Kael to admit it on his own.

He hadn't.

Talk of battle, of Gyoria lost, of The Unbalance... everything except the real reason I was here. The real reason was that the guard was watching my movements. I had no doubt if I asked, Kael would admit it. My brother had betrayed me, though Kael saw it differently, but he'd never lied to me.

And he never would.

Lyra, on the other hand...

"You're angry."

She moved to the narrow table that stood between two of the windows which framed the darkening sky, a sheer drop visible from every angle. Lifting the decanter the attendant left behind, she filled the goblet with my untouched wine. A moment later, that same attendant returned, skirted the massive bed, its frame carved of dark Aetherian oak, its headboard worked with a relief of mountains and storm clouds. She handed Lyra the second goblet and left the chamber as I scanned it, watching firelight from the hearth catch glints of silver on the coverlet. Each stitch was precise, too fine for a warrior's chamber.

It was a bed meant for display as much as rest, a reminder of power and wealth, not comfort. Just as the hearth was less for warmth, Aetheria's climate cooler than the south but never uncomfortably so, as it was for ambience.

Lyra belonged here, in the chamber.

I did not.

"Take it," she said, handing me the second goblet. "It will remove the edge that you've had since we stepped foot on Aetherian land."

I didn't disagree and took it begrudgingly as Lyra joined me at the window.

"You smell like... something."

I couldn't place the scent. It was fresh, and clean. Yet subtly enticing.

"Is that supposed to be a compliment?"

"No."

If I wanted to compliment her, I'd mention Lyra's simple, but elegant, white gown. Its flowing sleeves moving like the air every time she lifted her arm to take a sip. Unlike Thalassari, whose clothing was often spun from fabric so sheer, it left little to the imagination, the Aetherians favored a similar fluid drape in thicker, more substantial weaves... warm enough to cut the mountain chill, yet light enough to move as if carried by the wind.

I never cared for their style. Until now. Every curve of Lyra's was highlighted as she moved. The cut showed just enough of the curve of her breasts to leave a man wanting more, but not so much he was given an ample view.

Everything about her was elegant.

And deceptive.

"Talk to me, Terran. Tell me why you are so angry."

I was jolted from my perusal by her words. Different than the ones my mother often spoke to my father, but similar too.

I'd always resented that he needed to be coaxed into smiling, or relaxing, by her. Always wondered why he didn't have the skills to do so on his own.

You are becoming our father.

How many times had Kael accused me of as much?

As many as I'd denied it.

"Because my brother is right."

That was one thing I could do that my father hadn't. Tell the truth.

"About?"

I downed the wine and headed back for more. Filling my goblet, I rejoined Lyra as she patiently waited for me to finish.

"All of it," I said, unable to put the truth into words.

We stood in silence for some time as I replayed the argument, the time since Mev had come through the Gate, again and again in my mind. I wanted to forget it all, but couldn't. A battle was coming, and I had to choose a side.

Surprised that Lyra asked no more questions, I finally turned to her.

"Why did you come here tonight?"

She simply looked at me.

I took her goblet and placed it, along with my own, on the table, asking her again, "Why did you come?"

Lyra forgot the game.

Her chin raised defiantly.

"In here," I said, waving toward my bedchamber, "I am in charge. Answer the question, Lyra."

A switch had been flicked.

Ahh, she hadn't forgotten the game. Lyra was playing it. Hard.

I could play harder.

I spun her to me so that we were nearly touching. I waited. Her eyes, ever so slightly more open than before, were all the answers I needed.

"I will ask just once more. Tell me why you're here."

"And if I do not?"

No more words.

I grabbed the hem of her gown, pulling it up to her waist. There was no barrier under the gown, though I'd have torn it off if there were. I didn't pause, or hesitate. With the only permission I needed—Lyra not raising a hand to stop me—I held her gown up with one hand and cupped her with the other. Slipping a finger inside to confirm my suspicions, and then another, discovering her as wet as I assumed, I watched her face as I worked Lyra.

Hard.

Not thrusting, but easing in and out. Circling her with my thumb. Ignoring my own body's response to being inside her, even if it were just my fingers.

For now.

I wanted to kiss her. But I wanted to watch Lyra's expression more. Her lips parted, tempting me beyond measure.

"You will tell me why you came to this chamber tonight, Lyra," I said, not softening the edge of my voice.

She held firm, pressing against my fingers... Her breath came more quickly. I could help Lyra find her release, just a small adjustment of my thumb...

"Terran," she breathed, nearly tearing me apart. I wanted to be inside her. Claim her. But I also knew what Lyra needed, and it was to let herself completely lose control.

Which meant, I needed to take it for her.

"Tell me."

With that final command, my fingers stilled, just before her walls began to clench.

"No," she said, finally realizing my intention. "Terran, please."

My hand remained still. "I do love hearing you beg for me to continue. As I said you would," I reminded her.

Lyra's eyes flashed. She'd evidently forgotten that. I hadn't. Not even for a moment.

"But that wasn't my request."

"Request?" She panted, a sweet sound if I'd ever heard one. "Command, you mean."

I moved, just slightly. Not enough, but just as a reminder. She pressed against my hand, urging me on without words.

"Command," I confirmed. "And I won't ask again."

She was going to come just as we were. I could feel it. Sense it. And so I pulled my fingers from her completely.

"No!"

Smiling, I left my hand where it was. But said nothing.

"I came here... for this," she said finally.

I thrust my fingers into her, relentless in my pursuit of her release.

"*Voren vel'kora*," I whispered, before claiming her lips, mimicking the movement of my fingers with my tongue and knowing it would not be long.

When it came, Lyra's release was as powerful as her magic.

She cried out as the involuntary pulses around my dripping-wet fingers verified what I knew already.

Aetherians prided themselves on control of themselves. With me, she'd been able to let go in spectacular fashion.

But I wanted more.

Pulling my hand from her and dropping Lyra's gown, I waited for her to refocus on me.

"Did you come to my chamber," I said, running a single finger down her cheek, "to find release by my hands? Or did you come here to be thoroughly, and completely, claimed? If the latter, I've a mind to tear that gown from your body, toss you on my bed, and bury myself so deep inside you that neither of us will leave this chamber the same as before you entered it."

Lyra's chest rose and fell, her cheeks still flush and her breathing not quite back to normal.

"I came for all of you," she said more readily than I'd have expected.

My thumb brushed her lower lip.

"Then that's exactly what you shall get."

25

LYRA

Why hadn't I expected Terran to make good on his promise?

It was only when one of my favorite gowns lay on the floor, the fastenings unusable after he quite literally ripped it from my body, that I understood the intensity of what was about to happen.

And I welcomed it. Every moment.

Perhaps I shouldn't. Terran was a Gyorian prince. And I was a woman who had trained for multiple lifetimes, in human terms, to overcome the will of warriors. Men who would subjugate me, or attempt it. The very idea of obeying a command from anyone but my king or queen, and now Aetheria's princess, should have appalled me.

Instead, I'd had the most glorious orgasm of my long life. One that would certainly be impossible to match.

Or perhaps not.

"You've stripped me bare," I said as Terran removed my corset. "But stand before me, fully clothed."

"If you want something Lyra, ask."

That tone. One Terran never used in our regular speech but

had reserved for the bedchamber. At least with me. I was certain the commandment in his voice was learned from years of practice leading his men.

"I want you," I said, knowing anything other than full honesty would only lead to me being deprived.

A half-moan, half-growl escaped him as Terran did exactly as I asked. First, his boots. And then one by one, he shed his clothing, leaving me to stare at what could only be described as the most perfect specimen of immortal I'd ever seen.

Every bit of him. Including his extremely hard evidence that I wasn't the only one aroused.

"Now get into my bed, on your hands and knees."

Brought out of my stupor by his words, I began to argue them.

"It's one thing too—"

My words were cut off as he finished undressing and lunged for me. Grasping the back of my hair, Terran pulled me into him for a brutally delicious kiss, one I hadn't expected. His tongue explored as it had done earlier, deep and sensual, a dance that could make me forget everything, including things I should not.

His hold on me was firm, though not overly so.

But just as quickly as he'd grabbed me, Terran let go.

"Get into my bed, on your hands and knees. Now."

It was a command meant to be obeyed, and I did. Scrambling to the bed, unusually shier than I'd even been with a man before, my timidness having been shed many moons ago, I positioned myself as he'd asked.

Remaining there, vulnerable and more than a bit aroused, I heard no sounds behind me. Turning my head, I wished I hadn't. Terran stalked to the bed as if I was his prey. He was in full command, and I shuddered at the sight of him, whipping my head back.

The bed sank under his weight. Though I could sense him

behind me, Terran didn't touch me. I thought of how he'd stilled his fingers, and then removed them.

Please don't torture me like that again.

He didn't hear my silent pleas, of course. Just as I was about to peek back at him, his hand connected on my right ass cheek. A slap, for certain. One that startled more than pained me, though there was no doubt a red mark would remain, at least temporarily.

I did look back at him then. Terran knelt at my feet, dominant.

Glorious.

"Was that for any particular reason?"

"Next time, when I ask you to get into the bed, do it. The first time."

Another shudder.

My heart thudded as I dropped my head down just as Terran's hand covered both ass cheeks. He used them, and his thumbs, to spread me wide. And that's when I felt his tongue. At first, just one long lick, Terran reaching my pussy more easily than he should have for such a large man, at that angle. Another lick, but this time, instead of removing his mouth, he circled his tongue. Teasing. Taunting.

Playing with me.

I grabbed the coverlet in sweet anguish, crying out his name.

In response, Terran seemed to redouble his efforts, as if nothing in Elydor mattered more than what he was doing. The response he attempted to elicit.

And then his hand joined in.

I lifted myself as he fingered me. Licked me.

Destroyed any resistance I had to hold on. When I came this time, I didn't think to hold anything back. I screamed his name, thankful there were no others nearby.

"By the Winds," I cried as wave after wave of pleasure took over.

When he pulled away, I thought Terran was taunting me again. Instead, he flipped me over and positioned himself between me.

"I'm still—"

"I know," he said, holding himself with one hand and me open with the other. I wanted him inside me with an intensity that was beyond frightening. When he entered me, the final ebbs of my orgasm mixing with the fullness of him, I grabbed both arms.

Pulled Terran into me.

Thrust my hips to meet him.

It was as if something had taken possession of my body which was frantic with the desire to have him release as powerfully as I just had. Arching my back and giving him a full display of my breasts, I smiled when he groaned and began to pump into me harder.

In and out, we rode the new wave together.

Our bodies were made to be joined.

"Lyra," he bellowed. "I need you to—"

When he tried to put his hand between us, I pulled him onto me. While it was true, if he played with me now, it would be easier to come. But I didn't care about that. Or anything other than Terran experiencing what I just had.

He kissed me, thrusting hard. I was so wet, he was easy to take, even at this pace. I bucked my hips to meet him, the bed rattling under our weight.

My nails dug into his flesh. Terran buried himself so deeply, it was a wonder I didn't split into two. And then he pulled away from our kiss, looked at me and made a sound so guttural, so... Gyorian, that I might have come again.

It was difficult to tell when one of us ended and the other began. He held me, and I clung back. Breathing as heavily as him. We stayed that way for a long time. So long, that it became almost more... intimate, than our joining.

When he did pull away, lifting his weight that Terran had carefully controlled with his arm, otherwise I might have easily been crushed, it wasn't far. His face was inches from my own.

"Lyra." His tone could not have been more different than before. No longer commanding, but just the opposite. His jaw was set, the muscles in his jaw flexing nearly as hard as the one in his arm that supported him.

"Say it."

This time, it was me who commanded.

I knew what he would say. But this time was different. Not a phrase tossed out in the heat of passion or a way to reward me for obeying him.

His struggle to get the words out, after what we'd just shared, told me it was much, much more.

Terran looked into my eyes.

"*Voren vel'kora.*" His voice was as gentle as it had ever been toward me.

I lifted my head and kissed him. It was a kiss unlike the others, underscoring his words.

Pulling back, I laid my head back on the bed.

"*Vel'kora dra'ven.*"

26

TERRAN

I couldn't trust her.

And yet, I wanted her to stay.

It was madness. Insanity, as the humans might say. But something had shifted between us this night. Those words which began as a game, a tool of dominance, were no longer either.

They were real.

"You are more perfectly formed than any in Elydor," I said, watching her dress. When Lyra had risen, I considered asking her back to bed. There was nothing I wanted more than to continue to caress her soft skin. Learn every curve.

But *wanting* had led me to bed a woman who should be my enemy. One who deceives... withholds... even if she had let me see a secret part of her.

"Training," she said, adjusting her gown. I'd attempted to assist her until Lyra shot me a look that had me chuckling and lying back down to watch instead. "Though I'm certain it pales in comparison to yours."

Fully dressed, she turned to me, unabashedly scanning me

from head to toe. I hadn't bothered to cover myself in any way. Gyorians were not known for modesty.

"Keep looking at me like that if you care to find yourself disrobed and pinned beneath me once again." This after I told myself not to ask her to remain...

"Don't tempt me."

I was up from the bed and before her before Lyra could utter another word.

"Me"—I reached for her neck, pulling it toward me—"tempt *you*?"

I kissed her. Claimed her with my mouth, wanting more even knowing I should not.

When she reached down between us and grasped me, I was lost. Her fingers slight, her movement as easy and graceful as the wind, she stroked me.

And then knelt down at my feet.

The sight of her... "Lyra, no."

It was more insane to attempt to stop her than it was to want Lyra to stay the night. But as she wrapped her hands around me, guiding me into her mouth, I had no more thoughts of distancing myself from her in any way.

In fact, as I reached for the back of her head and pulled her toward me, I did the very opposite. Clutching two fistfuls of hair in my hands, I matched her pace as Lyra took me in... and out. If Lyra's goal was to ensure I'd have no coherent thoughts left in my head before she left, she'd accomplished it already.

"The love of Terranor," I said, evoking our god and considering evoking hers too. There weren't enough Elydorian deities to pray to, the feeling of her full lips around me. When I warned her, sooner than I'd reached a climax in memory, Lyra simply took me in more deeply.

She meant to keep me there.

I had no notion to pull away, releasing every bit into her sweet mouth, the suckling sounds she made, combined with the sight of her at my feet, making every spasm intensify tenfold. If there was something to hold onto, I would have, for fear of toppling over.

"That was..."

No words could do it justice.

As she licked the last drops and pulled away, the look Lyra gave me then couldn't possibly have been any sexier. Sitting back on her feet, her lips wet, Lyra's eyes wide with anticipation as if... as if she'd wanted to please me...

"Do you mean to kill me?" I asked, only partly in jest.

She wiped her mouth and stood.

"Why?"

It was a simple enough question but Lyra had no ready answer. What happened between us earlier? We'd been building toward it for some time.

But this, 'twas for my pleasure alone.

She blinked. Lyra didn't know why she'd done it. She had planned to leave. But instead... My eyes widened.

Of course.

I reached for her. Pulled Lyra into me. Cupping her cheeks between my hands, I summoned my most commanding tone, and I looked down, into her eyes.

"The bedroom will be my domain. In there, you are *mine*, Lyra. Do you understand?"

She nodded. "Aye."

"Out of it? 'Tis yet to be seen. But if I ask for you to drop to your knees, you'll do it."

Her lips parted. If this aroused her, I would gladly give Lyra what she wanted.

"But know this," I added, "there will always be pleasure, for us both, in here. Never pain." And the next part would be important. "Never deceive. If we cannot be honest about what we want, this will not work. Do you understand?"

"I do," she said.

I released her wrist. It seemed to snap Lyra out of the trance she'd been in since I started my speech.

"I have to speak to Mev before the morrow."

I was certain she'd done so already, but I offered no argument.

"Until we meet again, then," I said. "Tomorrow should prove an interesting day."

"Until then," she said, fleeing the bedchamber as if she wasn't certain what had just happened. But I knew.

Whether I liked it or nay, it mattered not.

And I most certainly did not like being bound to a woman who continued to actively deceive me. But we were bound, despite it, in a way that would be difficult to walk away from.

But she was Aetherian.

And war was coming to our clans. The air was too still... The breath before the break. I'd fought battles before, but never one that would carve the fate of realms. If we fell today, Elydor would fracture, and every sacrifice we'd made would turn to ash.

I told myself I was ready. But readiness and peace were not the same thing, and peace had abandoned us long ago.

"There's no sign of them," Mev said, joining me in my favorite spot in all of Elydor: the king's outdoor platform.

Located between his solar and throne room, an outdoor space jutted out from the mountain, poised high enough to see what seemed like all of Aethralis below. Many who were not Aetherian, comfortable in high spaces that seemed to almost touch the clouds, refused to come to this spot.

Gyorians, especially.

"Have all reports come in?" I asked.

Last I'd heard, there had been no whispers from our scouts at the foot of the Ascension Gate. We'd been receiving whispers from every corner of Aetheria—from the coastal towns to our borders with Estmere and Gyoria—but thus far, nothing from one of our closest outposts, which was concerning.

"Yep. Nothing. Not land. Or water. Balthor's men are nowhere to be found. Yet."

We were certain they had followed us.

"Perhaps they retreated to Balthor and are amassing an army."

"That's what my father thinks too. His generals are continuing to prepare for full-scale war."

Full-scale war. In Elydor, it could mean utter destruction. When immortals who've been training for hundreds, sometimes thousands, of years to weaponize elemental magic, even a minor skirmish could be catastrophic.

I shivered.

"Any word from the men?"

Mev shook her head. "Nope. Nothing."

Terran and Kael had been gone since morn. No one, not even Mev, knew precisely where.

I twirled my fingers absently, playing the wind. Swirling it. Practicing. Preparing.

Trying not to think of last night.

"Rowan and the queen?" I asked.

"Being escorted north as we speak."

"Both of them?"

With the Wind Crystal in our possession, the Stone as close to it as we could get at the moment, King Galfrid had sent word via whispers to Thalassari. We assumed someone, likely Sir Rowan, would bring the Tidal Pearl north. But I'd not have expected Queen Nerys to accompany him.

"I guess so. Marek and Issa are bringing them."

"Of course," I murmured. Few could navigate the waters quite like Marek.

"I can't believe this is really happening. When they get here, if Aethralis is still standing... holy shit." Mev paced back and forth, though never approaching the platform's rails. Sometimes, her human side showed more than others. For the most part, I typically forgot Mev was not Aetherian born and trained. Until she spoke, of course.

"It will stand," I said, confident of it. "And your father will open the Gate. The question is, what will you do then?"

Mev stopped.

"Go through it, I guess. What else?"

"Alone?"

"No." She shook her head. "Kael already said we can't chance it. He'll go through with me. Just in case."

Just in case it somehow closed back up again.

So Kael was prepared to give up immortality for Mev. It both surprised me, and didn't.

"And your father?" I asked.

"Will stay. If for some reason, things go badly on the other side, as much as he wants to reunite with my mother, he's afraid of what Balthor might do if he never returned."

I resisted the urge to shudder again. "A disconcerting thought, if I ever had one."

"We've heard from them," Eirion said, approaching.

The Council enforcer, when the Gate was open, and Galfrid's former general of Aetherian forces, he served as a military advisor to the king.

"Is all well?" I asked, suspecting his response. Eirion appeared overly calm for there to be anything amiss.

"Aye. No sign of any Gyorian forces."

"From any direction?" Mev asked.

Eirion shook his white-haired head. "None."

We let the news sink in. "I'm meeting with your father shortly. Will you be joining us?" he asked Mev.

For Eirion to defer to the princess showed how far Mev had come since arriving.

"I will," she said, "but must speak to Lyra for a moment first."

He nodded and left.

"If Balthor does not plan to follow, or attack, imminently... when Nerys gets here..."

She trailed off, but no explanation was needed.

"Let me do it."

"With luck, it won't be necessary and he will volunteer our use of the Stone without having to be persuaded. Maybe after talking to Kael, hearing another perspective..."

"I would be surprised," I admitted. "Terran isn't Balthor, but neither is he Kael. He truly blames the humans for his mother's death."

"Kael did too."

"He is." I thought back to last eve. "Different."

Harder. More domineering. In more ways than one.

"Lyra?"

My head snapped up. By Mev's narrowed eyes, I could see my momentary lapse of control over my emotions had cost me.

She knew.

"Oh. My. God. Are you serious?"

I schooled my expression back to neutrality.

"We have important things to discuss—"

"Yeah. Like you and *Terran*. Holy shit. How did I miss it? When did this happen? I can't even believe it. You guys are like... I don't know. Oil and water." At my expression, she continued. "Air and stone."

"We are very different," I acknowledged.

"Different? That's the understatement of the year. He is..." She stopped abruptly as the object of our discussion joined us, along with his brother.

At the sight of him, in daylight, my body confirmed what my mind already knew. I was falling for the Gyorian warrior—a prince—like no one I'd been with before.

Heart hammering, his presence ignited every nerve in my

body as I imagined him coming over to me, as Kael joined Mev, and claiming a kiss.

Claiming.

It's what Terran had done, and not only had I let him... I encouraged it.

"Eirion meets with your father," Kael said to Mev. "Will you join them?"

"Aye." She tugged on Kael's hand. "Come with me."

Though he appeared momentarily confused, Kael did go with her, leaving Terran and I alone, precisely as Mev planned. What she truly thought of us, I couldn't be sure. But one thing was for certain.

In the dawn before what would likely be a time written about in history scrolls, Balthor's response to his son absconding with the Stone of Mor'Vallis, the possible reopening of the Aetherian Gate, I had only one thought.

And as Terran stalked toward me, it wasn't about the fate of Elydor.

I wasn't *falling* for him.

I'd already fallen, and there was no way back.

TERRAN

"You look as if you're preparing for battle," she said.

"Perhaps I am." I stopped just before reaching her.

"Something Kael said upset you?"

I wanted to kiss her. Turn from her. Make love to her. Walk away.

That was precisely the problem. What I wanted when Lyra was near was not at all the same as what was prudent. Especially after speaking to my brother.

"Not what he said," I explained. "But what he did not."

The care Kael took, as Lyra had, not to ask me for use of the Stone, as if it were mine to offer, angered me more than anything. My brother was not one to speak in riddles, but he'd done precisely that. When I accused him of being unduly influenced by Aetherian ways, Kael became angry, said I was inflexible. But the brother I knew would have simply told me what he wanted. Why Lyra had been sent to Gyoria.

Instead, he spoke of unity and Unbalance and the fate of Elydor. And, of course, our father's increasing proclivity to guard Gyoria from all outside influence.

"You are angry."

"Aye." I looked into her eyes. They revealed nothing.

"What did Kael say?"

She was back to the calm, collected Shadow Diplomat that gathered information without offering it.

"Not nearly enough."

I reached for her. Pulled Lyra into my arms.

She didn't resist, though part of me wished she would.

My hand snaked behind her neck, Lyra looking up with the same measured expression that would have me think she continued to be unaffected.

But I knew better now.

Her eyes reminded me of starlight storms. They happened rarely—every century or so—though I was fortunate to catch more than one.

"I asked a question, the day you arrived." Threading my fingers through her hair, I made no other move to bring us closer. For her part, Lyra slowly raised her hand, placing it delicately on my forearm. Not to push me away, but neither to encourage any further connection.

A simple, neutral movement. Very... Lyra.

"What game do you play?" I asked, reminding her of that question.

"I could ask you the same," she responded. "Clearly, something Kael said upset you, though you refuse to tell me about your meeting."

"He's been too long with the princess. Too long in Aetheria."

"Mevlida. She is your family now. Perhaps you should begin to use her name."

"Perhaps you should attempt honesty with me." I tugged her closer. "Or better, with yourself."

Her nails dug into my arm, the only indication I had any effect.

"You have no shame. To use my weakness against me."

"Weakness? Wanting is not a weakness, Lyra." To prove it, I leaned forward to kiss her. Not claim, but kiss. A slow, methodical response to her accusation. She gave herself fully, and I did the same. Our bodies pressed together, and if not for the weight of this day... the impending war... I'd have happily lost myself in the kiss.

Instead, I pulled back, hoping to have proved my point.

"I lose myself every bit as much, if not more, every time we're near. 'Tis not a weakness but a sign of trust. One I want to return."

That startled her.

"What did he say?" she pressed.

I let go and stepped back.

"Kael said much and nothing at all. My brother bides his time. Waits for me to come to the same conclusion as you."

Her shoulders rose and fell as Lyra watched, and waited. Calculated and understood.

"Terran—"

"If you thought it would be possible to seduce me into obtaining the Stone of Mor'Vallis and using it to open the Aetherian Gate, you were half-right."

I wanted to be wrong. But as I turned from her, attempting not to hear the pain in her voice as she called me back to her, two things became clear.

Lyra had been playing a dangerous game with me.

And I'd let her.

* * *

The ivory-colored structure rose above the western edge of the palace grounds as I approached. Though smaller than the palace, the Temple was no less imposing. Its white stone columns were etched with golden filigree that caught rays of sunlight from every angle. I hadn't meant to come here, to the ancient building that housed the Gate, but with every step closer, the Stone that had gone silent began to pulse with a now-familiar faint vibration from the pouch at my side.

A pair of Aetherian guards crossed their halberds before the entrance, blocking my way.

I stiffened, expecting as much, but before I could summon either excuse or defiance, a familiar voice cut through the stillness behind me.

"He's with me."

Kael's figure emerged from the shadows, his tone allowing for no argument. The guards returned to an at-ease position but said nothing as we silently climbed the marble staircase together, making our way through the towering glass-and-gold doors into the chamber.

Inside, the Gate loomed at the far end, a vast arch of cream-colored stone, its surface carved with constellations and sigils that seemed almost to breathe with their own faint light.

"My only other memory of being here never felt like my own."

Kael knew me well enough to understand I didn't expect a response.

I'd been little more than my father's shadow then, another blade at King Balthor's command. Though it was so long ago, my memory of the relics flaring was vivid.

"I understand the runes carved into that arch as little as I do the power that thrummed it for so long."

Kael approached, pointing to one. "Aetheria's mark, the

breath of sky, running through a current that carries life. And this one," he said, "you know it as Elydor's crowned arch, but its center is hollow since it's meant to hold the symbol of all clans. Without unity, Elydor is empty."

I didn't remember that particular rune glowing that night my father closed the Gate, only the crushing certainty that whatever light burned in all of them, collectively, would never shine again.

The weight of that day suddenly pressed hard against my chest as I was unable to look away. Whether that arch opened once again, or remained locked, my fate, all of Elydor's, was bound to it.

"We didn't know."

Those whispered words from Kael carried more weight than anything he'd ever said.

"We knew enough."

He didn't disagree.

I turned from the Gate's ominous presence, concentrating instead on what I could control.

"You sent her under false pretenses, at best. I never knew you as a coward, Kael."

Part of me wanted a fight. Expected one. Surprisingly, my brother didn't accommodate. His hand didn't twitch. His temper didn't flare. Instead, he stood before me, as calm and collected as Lyra might.

"If I'd come, I would have been locked up as a traitor before I even stepped foot on Gyorian soil."

I resented the implication. "I would not have allowed it."

"You wouldn't have had a choice. He's lost, Terran. He's been lost for some time. We just didn't see it."

Anger welled within me. Unlike my brother, my fingers did twitch. My fist balled. Kael noticed, but said nothing. I wanted to disagree with his words, but even I wasn't that much of a fool.

"She lied about her purpose for being there. Worse, I allowed it."

Kael's brows rose. "Did she? You've not felt The Unbalance?"

I snorted, an unprincely sound and one I fully welcomed. We were no princes but two outlawed brothers with less true power than anyone in Elydor.

"Does it matter? Our father is king. What are you proposing, Kael? Short of killing our own father, he will remain so. None are more powerful than he, even in his current state."

Kael's eyes darkened. "I never proposed to kill him, or aid another to do so. But I disagree that we are powerless. Taking a stand is power. Defiance is power. Truth, unity, refusal, hope... these are power. And they are weapons Father cannot strip from us."

"You sent her. *Her.* To prove a point."

Except, he didn't. Kael had no notion what I was talking about. No idea how I'd felt about Lyra, before. And certainly not now.

At least he'd not stooped that low.

Before my brother could ask any questions, I forged ahead. On a different topic.

"What do you propose we do?"

But I knew the answer already, of course.

Kael waited for me to confirm it.

Turning back to the Gate, I considered, as I had every moment since realizing Lyra's true purpose in Gyoria, the implications of reopening the Gate.

Of my father's response.

Or more importantly, of my mother's.

Squeezing my eyes shut, I envisioned her standing here with us. Of the last moments we spent with her before she left us, forever.

Opening them, I wiped away the single tear that had formed, proving they were still possible. Kael, thankfully, said nothing. He waited. Watched.

I could feel him next to me.

"It is good to have you back," I said.

"I never left. You just stopped seeing me."

Trust Kael to turn comfort into rebuke. Still, the words lodged somewhere deeper than I wanted to admit.

"Then maybe I see you now," I said, though the admission tasted like surrender.

Kael's mouth curved, not in triumph but in something quieter. Something I didn't have the strength to name.

I would stand beside her at the Gate. I would help them try to open it.

But not for her. Or for Kael. Or even Mother.

For a kingdom that deserved better than Father's hate.

"You've been avoiding me."

It had been two days since he'd touched me. Kissed me. Sought me out.

I thought to go to him last eve, but Terran knew where I was located since I'd shown him. And my pride kept me in my own bedchamber.

After the second restless night following the big revelation—Terran would allow us to use the Stone of Mor'Vallis to open the Gate—I should be celebrating with the others. Instead, I broke my fast in my own chamber and headed toward Galindre's instead. King Galfrid's high steward, also a healer, would know as well as anyone how to calm my restless mind.

As always, his door was wide open.

Galindre's long silver hair was tied at the back of his head. Though his back was to me, he would know I'd entered. Somehow, Galindre knew... everything.

"Good morn, Lady Lyra."

I headed to his long table of herbs and potions. Most air-wielders left such things to their Gyorian counterparts, masters of all things grown from the land, but since relations had soured with Balthor, he had become quite skilled.

"Good morn." I watched as his slender fingers moved quickly, reaching into glass vials as he measured precise amounts of each.

When he finished, Galindre looked knowingly at me.

"What troubles you?"

A laugh escaped me. Where to begin?

"There is much that troubles me, but the remedy is less more elusive than its causes."

"You worry it will not work?"

So Galfrid had told him about the Gate. With still no sign of Balthor's men, we had agreed yesterday to attempt its opening the moment Nerys and Rowan arrived, which could be as soon as this day. He'd kept his circle tight but planned to loosen it with the Gate's imminent opening.

"Aye," I admitted. "And of Balthor's response."

"It would not be the first battle we've fought with him. Aetheria is well prepared."

He waited, but what else could I say? The fate of Elydor rested in the events of these next few days, but the reason I came to him—the true reason—was not because of the Gate. Or an impending battle.

"It is not the Gate, or the battle, that keeps you up at night?"

I wasn't surprised he guessed, but neither would I admit it. Either of those should be cause for concern... but both? Aetheria faced an imminent inflection point, and I wrestled with the affairs of my heart.

I should not have come.

Before I could respond, Galindre turned back to his table, bringing together three herbs and a liquid I didn't recognize.

"Here," he said, handing the concoction to me. "It will quiet the storm, for a time. But storms return, unless you face them."

"Thank you," I said, taking the vial from him. "What do you believe will happen?" I asked, curious. Galindre was vaelith, even older than the king. He'd seen all there was to see of Elydor and offered wise counsel, always.

The smile he offered reflected his knowledge, a wisdom that could only come from the varied experiences the high steward had lived through.

"Power alone never opens what is sealed. Balance does. Remember this, Lady Lyra."

Unfortunately, he was as Aetherian as they came. I imagined Terran standing beside me. His response to Galindre would be blunt, and perhaps even rude. The thought made me smile in return, until I remembered Terran was angry with me.

Perhaps I should have told him earlier what he'd currently guessed. But my loyalty was to Aetheria, the Gate's opening for its inner council alone to ponder. I could never have returned to King Galfrid, to Kael and Mev, if I'd shared too much, costing them the possibility of seeing the Gate reopened.

"I will do so," I promised. "Thank you, Master Galindre."

"The thanks are mine. You've been resourceful and brave, Lyra. And have done your fellow Shadow Diplomats proud."

My eyes widened. "You...?"

"Nay. Though I was there when they were first formed. Even trained a few in my day, many, many centuries ago."

Riddles and secrets, Terran would say. And he would be right, the accusation accurate.

"You will never cease to amaze me," I said, before turning to leave.

"When the four winds meet, what is sealed shall stir. Until then, even kings grasp at shadows."

I'd have asked Galindre what he meant by that but a familiar voice stopped me.

"There you are," Terran said, standing in the doorway, my body's reaction to his appearance telling me all I needed to know about how deeply I'd fallen.

But he was not alone. Both Kael and Mev stood at his side. Which could only mean one thing.

"They're here," Mev said. "It's time."

30

TERRAN

For the second time since arriving in Aethralis, I climbed the stairs to the Temple, built to house the Aetherian Gate. Though Kael was accustomed to being here, having served on the Council which regulated entry into Elydor from The Crooked Key on the other side, I was most certainly not.

It was a symbol of death, and hate, and the beginning of an instability that had lasted since the first human came to our realm. Even before Mother had died, there was much disagreement about who, if anyone, should be allowed entry. My father fought Galfrid every step of the way, exacerbated when the Aetherian king carved out land for what became the Kingdom of Estmere for the humans too.

And now, we were betraying him to reopen the portal to the human world once again.

"You've been quiet today."

Lyra.

She hung back, presumably, to speak to me. Since the Thalassari queen and her king had arrived, Lyra and I had been mostly separated. Meetings and hushed conversations, a meal during which I said little and now, as dusk fell, the reason we were all assembled. Two of the three most powerful Elydorians, a princess and two princes... a delegation that had everyone who wasn't previously aware of what was about to happen speculating.

Or so Kael had told me.

"There is much to distract me."

I'd not stopped thinking of her for even a moment these past days. But giving into temptation—reaching for her, touching her, getting close to her—would serve only to make it more difficult when we parted.

"Much that does not," she said as the others disappeared into the Temple. "Including me."

"This is hardly the time to discuss... us."

As I expected, my words angered her. Though it would have been difficult to tell before, I understood the nuances of Lyra's expressions even as most would have thought her features unchanged.

"Of course," she said, taking a step away from me, toward the others.

Grabbing her wrist, cursing myself for doing so, I stopped her.

"You lied to me. From the start."

She didn't attempt to pull away, though I did resist the order to tug her closer.

"I never lied," she began, but I stopped her.

"Half-truths are lies still," I clarified. "At least, in Gyoria. Here—"

"I thought we agreed that maligning each other's clans would further neither of our causes?"

I wanted to kiss her. Make love to her.

Make Lyra mine, fully and completely. The ancient words I'd spoken to her, more than once, weren't given lightly. But there was still much between us making such a thing impossible.

"You stand before me and claim no mistruths between us?"

Deny it. Go ahead, Lyra. Deny it and push us even further apart.

"I could not tell you."

Could not. It was marginally better than denying she'd lied.

"You thought me dense enough not to suspect?"

She did pull her wrist away then.

"Perhaps you two," Kael called to us from the Temple's entrance where the others had disappeared, "might continue your conversation after we open the Gate to the human world?"

He said it with so much sarcasm in his voice that Lyra smiled. I nearly did as well but remembered that the woman beside me had come to Gyoria and stolen my heart under false pretenses. So instead, I followed Kael inside.

With the sun setting outside the Temple, it was awash in a glow that seemed to underpin the weight of this moment. Kael and I spoke at length about what was about to happen: the repercussions of allowing the Stone to be used in this way, without our father's permission... against his will.

But I'd not look back.

Having been introduced to Nerys and Rowan, as we made our way toward the Gate, I watched them interact. All three couples —my brother and Mev, along with the two Thalassari and human couples, the queen with her partner and their escorts— appeared very much in love.

And then there was Lyra and I, at opposite ends of the chamber.

King Galfrid stood before the Gate, every inch the king he

had always been, his silver hair gleaming as the last rays of sun filtered through the high-arched windows of the Temple. The carved runes pulsed faintly, as though stirred from centuries of slumber, and the chamber seemed to hold its breath.

"Bring them forth," Galfrid commanded.

At his word, the relics were carried forward one by one. The Tidal Pearl, shimmering with a light that rolled like waves across its surface, placed reverently into a shallow basin that hadn't been there earlier. The Wind Crystal, catching even the smallest draft of air, spun with a soft hum as though recognizing the Temple's vaulted heights.

I closed my hand over the Stone of Mor'Vallis, its weight far heavier than the leather pouch that concealed it. For days, it had whispered to me... but now, in this place, it was utterly silent.

A murmur swept through the gathered delegation. Kael caught my eye beside me and nodded. I took the Stone from its pouch, said a silent apology to the king who had raised us, though not the one who currently ruled Gyoria, and stepped forward.

Reaching Galfrid, about to take Kael's label of "traitor to Gyoria" a large leap forward in branding myself the same, I handed it over.

Taking it, the Aetherian King Galfrid lifted his hands.

"By the blood of kings and queens, with the artifacts of each clan and the memory of the first sealing, I call balance once more. Let the Gate be opened, that Elydor and the world of humans might be joined."

The relics answered first. Light sparking from crystal to pearl, pearl to stone, threads of energy weaving a lattice that climbed the arch of the Gate itself. The runes ignited, one after the other, until the ancient doorway blazed with firelight.

My breath caught, though not with awe. The wrongness in my chest grew.

The human, Sir Rowan watched me. He knew something the rest of us did not. What I felt but could not put into words. Something was... amiss.

The chamber filled with light, and then with sound, an unearthly keening, as if the Gate itself cried out against being forced awake, the glow faltered. Stuttered. Sparks leaped from the runes and seared across the floor, scattering the delegation into panicked shouts.

"Hold!" Galfrid roared, straining to keep his hands raised, though the backlash drove him nearly to his knees. "Hold!"

But the Gate would not.

The lattice collapsed in a shiver of sparks, the relics dimmed and silence slammed into the chamber. The door to the human world remained shut, its arch of runes now nothing more than cold marble.

Galfrid lowered his hands, his breath ragged. "It should have worked."

His eyes swept the assembly, searching for answers.

But none were offered.

I had only questions, but was not the only one. Everyone began to speak at once, asking Galfrid what he had done differently this time. He insisted the ritual was exactly the same. But then his gaze rested on me.

"Your father offered an imitation when he returned the stolen Wind Crystal to Aetheria."

Anger coursed through me at the unveiled accusation, but Kael moved before I could respond. He stood at my side, his hand on my wrist, steadying it.

"My brother did not bring an imitation Stone. I can verify that it is the real one."

Galfrid's eyes softened, though slightly. "He fooled you once."

While it was true our father had sent Kael on a mission to return the Crystal with a fake, my brother not knowing it at the time, his accusation resonated as another insult.

"You malign us both—"

This time, it was Lyra who interrupted.

"I was with him," she said on the other side of me. "When he retried it. That is the real Stone."

Yet there was a time we were not together.

I could have swapped the real one for a fake before reuniting with Lyra on the coast. She knew it, and took the chance I had not. That alone should have abated at least some of my anger—toward her, toward Galfrid—but it did not.

"I betray my own father," I ground out, "to be accused of treachery?"

The Aetherian king's shoulders sagged. "I should not have done so."

My eyes widened in surprise. My father would never admit wrongdoing.

Ever.

"I could see her," he said to his daughter. "I could see her, and nearly touch her, so sure I was that it would work precisely as it had done before."

Her.

His queen. Mevlida's mother.

When I thought of her in the past, I had never let myself feel sorry. She had been taken from the king just as our mother had been.

Nay. Not just the same.

Father's actions were deliberate. More brutal in their intentions, and with the queen enceinte.

"What could have happened?" Marek, the sea captain, asked.

None had any answers.

One by one, we stepped forward. I took the Stone. Queen Nerys took the Pearl. But Galfrid hung back, clearly as devastated as his daughter, who was now in tears in my brother's arms.

It had not worked.

The Aetherian Gate and portal to the human world remained closed.

31

LYRA

After the chaos of the Gate's continued closure, the Starfall Glade was precisely what I needed.

A hidden meadow deep in the forest on the edge of Aethralis, some said the veil between realms shimmered in this place at night. At the mountain's foothills, it was often empty. Aetherians liked to be higher up most often, closer to the sky. As did I, before him...

It only occurred to me that this spot was one of a few on the same elevation as much of Gyoria, as I looked up. The Glade, glowing faintly with falling motes of starfire, remnants of Aetherian energy bleeding into the world, was recreated in the palace. But no recreation could compare to this. The real thing.

"It was not easy to find you."

I whipped around, not expecting another's presence. Certainly not his.

I left the Temple first, feeling oddly out of place. As Mev broke down, her hope of returning home, even if temporarily, ensuring her mother knew she was alive and well, dashed, I left word with Issa in case I was needed.

"I told Issa where I was headed."

He followed my gaze, and though Terran would never admit it, I could tell he was as impressed by the Glade as all those who entered it.

"Elydor's magic is strong here."

His tone lacked the edge of anger it had at the Temple.

"There is a history in this place that, any other time, I would share."

"But not now?"

"There are other matters to discuss. The Gate. The Stone and Galfrid's—"

As he was inclined to do, Terran reached for my wrist. One moment, we were separated by years of anger and hate. The next, I was in his arms, kissing him.

So much to discuss... and yet the only thing that mattered was him. It wasn't until my back was against the very tree rumored to root through both realms that I realized the Glade itself was responding. Starfire spiraled around us, clinging to us like sparks. His mouth claimed mine, fierce and furious.

With my hands against his chest, I could almost hear the Stone's echo. Power— his? Mine?— leaped between us, so unbridled that I almost pulled away. Instead, I leaned into it, realizing this was Terran's land magic, one I'd only felt as an antagonistic force. It was like the opposite of a wisp of air, an Aetherian lover's caress.

Arching into him, moaning, I let the Glade's magic fuse our fury with desire. When he lifted the hem of my gown, I welcomed it.

When Terran pressed his fingers into me, warming me for what was to come, I welcomed it.

And when he finally unleashed himself and buried himself deep within me, I welcomed it with every part of me. This was a different kind of claiming. A shared one with no pretense, and one we'd likely never be able to retreat from.

Not that I cared.

"Your back," he said, breaking the contact of our kiss mid-thrust.

"Is fine," I assured him. The bit of rubbing might leave a mark, but it would be the most welcomed "battle scar" I'd ever earned. I understood his concern.

Terran wasn't gentle, and I met every thrust, my legs wrapped around his waist now, by pressing as deeply into him as possible.

"No other will have you again," he said, in typical Terran fashion. His voice was rough, ragged. That particular thrust, deeper than all the others.

I wanted it.

I wanted *him*.

"Nor you," I said. "I do not share well."

"I do not share at all," he said, his eyes searing into me, both a promise and warning. One I had no need of.

"Take me, Terran," I said. "All of me."

With a roar worthy only of a Gyorian, he buried himself inside me and remained there. Jaw clenching as my back continued to rub against the ancient tree, Terran pressed his hips against me. Circled. But never withdrew.

I grabbed his tunic on both shoulders, as if holding on would matter. As the pulses began, I screamed his name. The Glade seemed to understand and responded.

"Lyra." He claimed my mouth again, his kiss almost bruising in its intensity as we floated together. Everything fell away but us... not an Aetherian and Gyorian who hated the other but two Elydorians who left just enough of themselves exposed, trusting the other when trust should not have existed.

With one final thrust, he came into me, spilling a seed

unlikely to bear any fruit. But I welcomed it, him, still. And welcomed the relief of my back no longer against the tree as he carried me, still joined, deeper into the Glade. Placing me onto my feet, he didn't bother adjusting his breeches or righting my dress.

Instead, he held me against his chest where I could hear the rampant beating of his heart. With Terran's arms around me, eventually, it settled into a steady rhythm.

"How could I have fallen in love with an Aetherian?" he asked finally.

Fallen in love.

As undeniable, and incredible, a claim as it was... hearing the words had me taking his jaw in my hands as I looked up.

"The same way I, somehow, fell in love with a Gyorian prince."

He leaned down, giving me the gentlest kiss we'd ever shared. I returned it gladly.

"I will never lie, or mislead you, again. The circumstances—"

He pressed a finger onto my lips.

"I wish to remember this moment for what it is."

What did that mean?

That he loved me but... our love would be fleeting? That it was impossible to be together? My mind wandered as he pressed my head once again to his chest, to the situation we found ourselves in.

The Gate, still closed.

Terran, now a traitor to his people.

To his king.

A mistrust between us that continued to linger.

What is it, precisely?

Though I wanted to ask, I allowed the question to float away. Afraid of its answer.

32

TERRAN

"She is magnificent, is she not?"

The human watched his partner, Queen Nerys, below. She, Lyra, and Mev stood below on a platform, still higher than any Gyorian would feel comfortable standing with no guards around it.

Aye, Lyra was magnificent.

Pulled apart again last eve after the Glade, I hadn't spoken to her yet. The aftermath of the Gate had sent the palace into a frenzy of activity. With no sign of my father or his men yet, I was left to my own devices after declining to meet with the king and Kael this morn.

Heading back to my chamber, I stopped in the open corridor, spying the women.

"I've not seen anyone do that before," I responded as the queen channeled sea water from further away than was typical. As they spoke, each of them performed some sort of magic. We all did it, absently at times, as an outlet for our extreme emotions.

In their case, sadness. Frustration. And not a small measure of confusion.

"Some say Nerys is the most powerful water-wielder in Thalassaria's history."

I looked at Sir Rowan with more than a small measure of skepticism.

"More powerful than King Thalos the Tidebreaker?"

An entire fleet was named after him, so powerful was the water-wielder who was said to summon waters without use of his hands, though I knew no one who had actually seen him do it.

"I suppose power is subjective and a case could be made for them both."

"A human Thalassari king. A first. Do they accept you, Sir Rowan?"

"Rowan," he said. "Some do. Some do not. It is Nerys who rules her people, and those who realize it take me for my role."

"Which is?"

"Supporting her. And my own people, however I'm able."

Something about the way he spoke... it was impolite to ask, but I was not known for subtlety.

"What is your human ability?"

He smiled.

An odd reaction to a question many would see as offensive.

"I've more than one," he said. "Why do you ask?"

A non-answer, but I'd not expected one.

"It seems to me, supporting a Thalassari queen would take a human of exceptional skill."

My brother had told me little of Sir Rowan, though it was clear he held the man in high regard. Especially for a human.

"From what I've been told, you have little regard, much less admiration, for any human."

"You are not one to mince words. My brother mentioned as much."

We watched the women pace, practicing their skills like caged trexan having been cornered. How could the failure of an action I never intended to aid weigh so heavily?

Lyra.

She'd not stormed into my life but slipped in as gently as any Aetherian. I'd seen her coming, but it mattered not. And the repercussions would be many, perhaps lasting for centuries.

But 'twas done. I'd no sooner see any other touch her than—

"They've breached the palace defenses."

Those five words, impossible as they seemed, had to be true. Shouted by a guard nearby, and supported by evidence of chaos surrounding us— from the women below, who all began running at the same time— to Rowan's expression, they were a catalyst like any other.

We both took off in the same direction: toward Nerys and Lyra and Mev.

The alarm bells clanged in my skull, and Rowan and I sprinted toward the platform. The air vibrated with the queen's water magic, waves surging through the stone channels as she tried to fortify the walls.

"How in the hell did they breach undetected?" Rowan yelled.

"Cloaked ships," I called to him, somehow knowing even though I hadn't detected as much before now. "The Aetherian whispers can't pierce iron and shadow. Someone inside must have helped them."

The first wave of my father's men crashed into the courtyard like a tide, shields raised, eyes gleaming with the kind of hate only bred in Gyoria. I met them head-on, magic pulsing through my fingertips and then flagstones. Buckling the ground beneath their boots as a tidal wave washed an entire contingency away. When a fissure formed, I knew without seeing him it was my brother. Only Kael, and my father, could create one so precise as that.

One Gyorian warrior fell screaming into the fissure. Another staggered as a strike of wind from the north side of the courtyard saw him join his comrade.

This was my clan Father was destroying.

A roar of frustration at my father for forcing such a clash followed another fissure, this one circular in pattern.

Lyra darted forward, my heart sticking in my throat watching her enter the fray. Wind magic lashing into a cyclone that threw two soldiers back against the wall. Even in the chaos, I felt her fury tethered to mine. But then another joined it, one so powerful, I knew it must have come from King Galfrid.

Except, when the wind subsided, it was his daughter who stood amid the carnage.

"Terran!" Kael's voice thundered from behind me, my brother now at my side.

Cries of pain rose as our warriors moved with purpose. Gyorians in obsidian leathers met Aetherian power in bursts of wind and stone. Archers filled the terraces above, their volleys vanishing into a storm of magic. Queen Nerys's water had begun to flood stone channels as she attempted to hold fires at bay. Palace guards tried to drive a wedge through the Gyorian flank and failed.

This was not a skirmish at a border post. This was the kind of fight that rewrote songs.

And then I felt it. His presence.

My father.

King Balthor pushed through the chaos as though the battle parted for him, his great black ax in hand. He had little use for it, but cherished the weapon. The world seemed to hold its breath as he advanced. Magic rippled out from him... dark, heavy, ancient, as if the mountain itself remembered what it was to fear a king. Lightning flickered through the clouds, turning the palace spires into jagged silhouettes. Below, hundreds clashed as stone and screaming wind unleashed immortals' power.

I'd faced monsters, traitors, and gods. None of them compared to this. Balthor's very presence bent the world around him, his will a storm that sought to break us all. The power that sealed a gate between worlds was within him.

He wasn't just a king. He wasn't just my father.

He was the wound Elydor never healed from.

"Balthor, call them off."

The king of Aetheria, now stood beside his daughter. Bodies all around us. The ground split in more places than I could count. Buildings around us, demolished. But it would be just the beginning. All knew what a battle between the three most powerful rulers of Elydor meant.

The palace would be destroyed.

Balthor's gaze, as hard and unforgiving as ever, found mine. Kael's.

"You stand between me and our enemy. You've chosen your sides, and now you will fall with the rest of them."

I tightened my grip, heart hammering. Whatever fate awaited, it was coming for me now.

It was coming for all of us. Just when I'd found her. Lyra could not get to me, nor I her, from across the deep chasm, but she was there. Standing beside the princess and her father with Queen Nerys looking on.

"I chose you. He"—I gestured to Kael—"chose you. For decades. But you chose hate over both of us."

My hand twitched. Another explosion of magic like the one that had accompanied our clan would end tragically for too many.

The air thickened. This wasn't just another battle... it was the reckoning of bloodlines. Kael's power pulsed beside mine, answering our father's and cracking the stones beneath our feet. The fire around us seemed to hesitate, caught between thunder and silence, as if waiting to see which of us would fall first.

Kael moved closer to me. So close, we were nearly touching. It wasn't difficult to sense the unease, seeing us united in this way, among our warriors. It was them I spoke to.

"Well done," I shouted. "A surprise attack against Aethralis has never been executed before in Elydor's history. To what end, Father?"

"He will not listen to reason," Kael said, loud enough for me, and no one else, to hear.

No. He would not. It had been some time since he'd done so. I'd been blinded by memories of the father he once was to have overlooked the fact.

My chest constricted as Father flexed his fingers, the gesture small but noticeable enough since it was one we'd seen many, many times before.

Apparently, the Aetherian king had as well, and he would take no chances with his daughter's safety, having seen what our father was capable of. He didn't move his hand, but Galfrid was close enough to us that his expression was not difficult to interpret.

I cannot do this.

It was a silent plea to Kael, but somehow, he heard it, nonetheless. He grabbed my right hand—something he'd not done since we were young ones —leaving my most powerful weapon, my left hand, free.

"Blood answers blood." The words, if not the crack in his voice, were my brother's. No one could do it but us.

I squeezed Kael's hand, and at the same time as the King of Gyoria made a fist, Kael and I dealt the killing blow. He anchored the fissure as I kept it so tight, none but our father fell through.

I heard the gasps. Knew they weren't for the death of the Gyorian king but for the kind of precision magic that had likely never been seen before. I certainly had no notion such a thing were possible.

It would not have been. Not without my brother by my side.

We released each other's hand as deafening silence settled on all those gathered.

The Stone, at times restless and others, silent, released an energy impossible to ignore. With the shock of our father's death having not yet registered, I reached for it, almost without thinking.

This time, there was no mistake.

It glowed as I'd only seen it do before for my father.

Every Gyorian warrior, including my brother, fell to their knees. They could be killed in such vulnerable positions as that. But would not be, of course. Neither Galfrid nor Mevlida nor Nerys would interfere now. They were mine to command.

And probably, I'd known it for some time. It had just been easier to deny it rather than admit my father's days had been numbered.

"We killed him," I whispered, pulling Kael to his feet. "We killed our father."

I stared at the crack that had swallowed him in disbelief.

"We killed him."

"We didn't kill our father," Kael said. "He died many years ago."

I didn't see her coming, but I felt Lyra at my side. Pulling her into me, I wiped a tear from her cheek. Words escaped me, but thankfully, they weren't necessary. King Galfrid's voice boomed through the courtyard.

"I know the pain of your loss well," he said, addressing our clan.

Addressing me.

"May Balthor rest in peace as a new dawn for our clans, for Elydor, arises. I recognize his son Terran as the most powerful among you, and the new King of Gyoria, as does the Stone he holds in his hand."

"As do I," Queen Nerys added. "May we unite in the coming days. Forge a new path forward. End an unwarranted hate among those who wish only to live peacefully among us."

She looked first at Kael and I, and then her partner, Sir Rowan.

Lyra tugged on my tunic, which is when I realized I was expected to speak. Gazing at my brother, who nodded, I said the only thing there was left to say.

The silence was suffocating, and I was expected to break it.

Raising the Stone high into the air, I took a deep breath, buffeted by Lyra on my left and Kael on my right, and called out, "I am Terran of Gyoria." Lyra was amplifying my voice. How many hidden skills did she have?

I would enjoy finding out.

"The Stone has chosen. I vow to lead not with hate, but with the courage and strength to end it. Rise and do the same. Your king commands it."

And they did.

One by one, they rose.

I was King of Gyoria. The price for such a title, heavy. But it was mine, now, and I would not see it wasted as our father had.

Terranor take him.

Reunite him with Mother and let him find peace in the after-life that he was unable to find among us here gathered.

33

LYRA

As we picked up the pieces of yesterday's battle, its aftermath had only begun to reveal itself. Terran led his father's warriors from Aethralis to the forest outside our capital where towering trees with silvery bark began to give way to small, rocky outcrops, hinting at a sturdier terrain across the border in Gyoria. From there, they would return under the command of a Gyorian I'd never met. A thaloran Terran trusted to send word to Dren, now the second most important in all of Gyoria—aside from Kael. He, along with Terran's other most trusted warriors, had been sent to Hawthorne Manor along Estmere's western border to supposedly deal with Adren, now Lord of Hawthorne, in a cleverly executed diversion.

From ironclad transports which blocked Aetherian whispers, to a traitor within the palace's ranks, a lesser noble Balthor had been apparently blackmailing for years, the now deceased king had planned his attack well. And according to one of Lord Valdric's men whom Terran summarily exiled, along with his master, it had been long in the making.

But for now, Terran had Aethralis. The moment he stepped

into the Council chamber, a silence descended among those gathered. Those who had fought at what was being called, "The First Breach."

"Leave us," King Galfrid said to Eirion and the two generals who sat on either side of him. "Summon Galindre, if you would," he added. "Have him anoint the courtyard with a calming draft, cleansing it of the breach's violence."

"Will that work?" Mev asked.

"In as much as it is believed to? Aye."

A symbolic cleansing more than a practical one. Tensions had run high in Aetheria, higher among those who lived and worked in the palace, since the attack.

I wish to remember this moment for what it is.

Even suspecting what Terran meant, there still had to be hope.

How could I have fallen in love with an Aetherian?

He loved me. As I loved him. But I'd fallen for a prince. Terran was now king.

My heart raced as he approached, standing beside me.

"All is secure. None remain in Aetheria and a new second in command has been named. Courtesy of your Whispers," he said to Galfrid, "I've been able to communicate with him, though my imminent return to Gyoria is still necessary. Some of the worst who colluded with my father—"

"Our father," Kael interjected. "You need not bear that weight alone."

Mev placed her hand atop Kael's, a silent act of support.

"Our father," Terran amended. "Some have already been brought to justice, though I suspect many more will follow."

I imagined Terran placing his hand on my left shoulder in a similar gesture as Kael's. But it remained bereft of any touch. The air shifted suddenly as his scent and presence were replaced by an absence.

Galfrid had gestured to Eirion's empty seat at the round table the king was so fond of. I looked from one to the next at a sight none, in Elydor's history, had ever seen.

An Aetherian king, his daughter and her Gyorian partner.

A Thalassaria queen and a human, now proxy king, sitting beside her.

Myself, a noblewoman, honored to be sitting among such a group. To my right, Lady Issa and her Thalassari corsair.

"You are always welcome at this table," Galfrid said as Terran sat. "I have no doubt what you and your brother did to save our city was extremely difficult and I am saddened it was necessary."

"To save us all," Terran said. "Not Aetherians alone." He inhaled deeply. I wanted to comfort him, but couldn't. He looked... sad. Tired. But also resolute.

"We've been offered a new beginning," Nerys said. "Thanks to King Terran and Prince Kael's sacrifice, for the first time in many years, an opportunity for true peace is possible."

King Terran.

Would I ever become accustomed to hearing it?

"I wish that same peace"—Galfrid looked at Mev—"for my daughter."

Mev, who had been holding her head high since we attempted to reopen the Gate, now dropped it in defeat.

In response, Terran took the satchel he'd not removed since coming to Aethralis, and lifted it over his head. Standing, he walked to Kael, handing the Stone of Mor'Vallis to his brother.

"I leave this with him," he said. "Along with my blessing, Princess, to use it to reopen the Gate."

Kael placed the satchel in front of him on the table, staring at it as if the Stone would roll from the leather pouch and attack him.

"If only we could," she said, her voice barely above a whisper.

It hadn't worked. None understood the reason. Admittedly, we'd been preoccupied since that night. But when order was restored in Aethralis once again, I had no doubt we would attempt to discover it.

"Our father," Terran boomed, his voice as deep and commanding as it had always been, though it was now tinged with... kingship, "has sown seeds of dissent between us." He addressed Galfrid and Mev. "And us." He gave his attention to Rowan. Then Issa. "But blame does not lie at his feet alone. I allowed myself to be led astray, my mother's memory a beacon of hate rather than love, as it should have been."

A beacon of love?

It seemed I wasn't the only one surprised to hear Terran speak this way. Kael's expression bordered on comical, his brows drawn and nose widened in unconcealed astonishment.

"I suspect it will take many years for that new path you mentioned." He addressed Nerys. "Neither will it be unlittered with the bodies of those who still believe we are stronger separate than we are united."

"Divisions are easily sown," she said, "but so is hope." Nerys turned to Mev. "Do not give up hope. You will be reunited with your mother as Rowan and Issa," she added, "will be with their ancestors. I've no doubt."

Optimism? Or something more? Was I the only one to see the quick glance exchanged between Nerys and Rowan?

"Thank you," Mev said finally. "To all of you. For accepting me. For attempting to open the Gate." She looked at Terran who sat down at the table. "For saving us. I will forever be grateful and, as my father said, you are welcome at this table, in Aethralis, as an honored guest until the end of your days."

Terran's half-smile did little to make me forget our time together.

"Careful, princess. You forget how long an invitation you extend in a realm of immortals."

Mev grinned. "Sometimes, I do forget. But not today."

Around the table we went, each speaking, conjecturing about the Gate, sharing intelligence we'd individually gathered about the attack, making predictions about its fallout.

Personally, I found it difficult to sustain my attention to admittedly important matters. When I caught Terran's gaze, and neither of us turned away for a heartbeat too long, the only thing that seemed to remain in my brain was the memory of our joining in the Glade.

I wish to remember this moment for what it is.

A moment I would remember, fondly, for all of my days.

34

TERRAN

"I would stay the night if I could..."

Lyra had just opened her bedchamber door when I blurted that out. For someone taught never to apologize, the words sounded foreign to my own ears. It *was* an apology. One I gave freely since it was true.

"I didn't expect you so soon."

After we'd left the meeting, Kael and I walked, alone, through the palace and into the decimated courtyard. I'd told Lyra I would come to her as soon as I was able. Eventually, he'd encouraged me to come here, knowing we had very little time.

"I'd have come sooner."

The door had barely closed behind me before Lyra was in my arms. Through her devices, or my own, I knew not. It was the first time I'd held her since the Glade. Seeing her in danger...

I kissed her, wanting more but knowing there was no time. My rule was a tenuous one. Dissent could easily give way to revolt, even though those in the courtyard accepted me. Lyra gave herself so willingly, and freely, our tongues tangling and arms pulling the other inward, but not close enough.

Do not, Terran.

I vowed, my hand on the handle of her door, not to do the thing I most wanted above all, with one exception... making Lyra mine completely. In ceremony. By blood. A partner for all time.

Making love to her will do little to relieve the ever-present ache when we're apart.

I had too many memories with her already.

"When I saw you," I said, reluctantly breaking the kiss, "across that courtyard."

"I was never in real danger," she said. A blatant lie, and Lyra knew it well. "But you..." She tipped her chin up to me. "I am sorry, Terran."

Sorry my father was dead? Sorry I killed him? I wasn't sure which, but it hardly mattered.

"As am I."

She reached her hand to my cheek. "It was the bravest thing I've ever seen."

I'd have laughed if Lyra didn't appear so serious. My Aetherian Shadow Diplomat had likely seen, and participated, in many brave acts in her days.

"I'm not certain," I began, the admission eating at me, "I could have done it without Kael by my side."

"The precision? I've never seen anything like it." The corners of her lips raised. "From a Gyorian."

With that, the tension in the air around it, one rife with unspoken goodbyes, broke.

"I thought we were no longer focusing on our differences."

"You are right. I forget myself."

"A rare admission of a misstep." My own lips mimicked hers. "Coming from an Aetherian. Forgetting yourself is coming easier to you these days, is it not?"

Her eyes, wide with a mixture of mirth and sadness, suddenly hooded, if but slightly. I should not have made the quip. Thinking about how she opened to me, allowed me to see her desires, was not helpful.

"Courtesy of a certain Gyorian king, aye."

I stood back as if burned, too many memories flooding my mind at once.

"If I stay..." Saying the words aloud would be akin to making them true.

"I understand," she said. "A king with duties to his clan."

"My father's hatred of the humans broke Elydor's balance, I realize now, more than any blade. So aye, I've much to repair if it is to be restored. And you have your own duties as well."

I wanted to ease the strain from her shoulders. Make her worries disappear.

"Why did it not open?"

The question had been asked many times. I had no answer.

"A Gyorian scholar—"

She grinned. But held back the comment.

"Once wrote that Galfrid was able to open the Gate because he bore not just the relics, but the will of Elydor's people united. Without harmony, the Gate remains deaf."

"Ours hint at the same," Lyra said, likely not noticing she'd begun to pace the chamber. "Which does not explain how Balthor was able to close it, without the will of... any."

Ignoring the tightening of my chest at the mention of my father, I speculated. "Opening it, allowing humans to enter our world, and closing it... two very different things."

"True," she said. "Perhaps the relics wait for a voice that has not yet spoken."

"Meaning?"

Her shoulders sagged. "I do not know. But coming to you with claims of an Unbalance were not unwarranted." Her expression became un-Lyra like. Sheepish. "If not entirely my mission."

"No?" I teased, pulling her back to me, against my better judgment. "Was your mission to find yourself in my bed, Lady Lyra?"

"Aye, precisely that. How have you guessed?"

I said aloud what we both knew already. "Because you've been attracted to me... nearly as long as I've been attracted to you."

"Debatable."

"Liar."

I kissed her. It was to be the last kiss... for now. Forever? I did not know. Tenderly, her lips moved across mine. It was goodbye.

"Be safe," I said, when the kiss ended, too soon.

"I am not the one attempting to lead a clan of angry Gyorians."

"We are not all angry."

Her brows shot up, skeptical.

"Not all of the time."

One last kiss.

And then, before seeds of dissension and revolt could be sown back home, I pulled back. Rested my hand on her cheek, my thumb memorizing every curve and warmth of her skin, as if that single touch might hold me together when everything else threatened to break.

* * *

In that space between sleep and wake, I could almost feel her.

Tossing aside the memory of more than a fortnight ago when I last saw Lyra, I rose and began my day. Not as the son of King Balthor, but as the ruler of Gyoria. A role I never expected, but one I was determined would negate, if not erase, some of my father's worst offenses.

Of which there were many, I'd learned.

Kael and I had long known he trafficked in shadows and secrets, but the full breadth of his treacheries still staggered us.

"Good day, your majesty," Dren said as I stepped into the solar. The look I gave him only made him smile more broadly.

He relished my new role. Excelled in his own. And without Kael, I could not imagine having stepped into it without him. But he could be damned annoying.

"Just practicing," he quipped.

"We are alone," I reminded him.

A feat not easily accomplished. It had taken days to clear my mornings in such a way.

"Not for long. I've asked the envoy from Thalassaria to break our fast with us."

When a knock at the door was followed by Dren's hushed conversation, I thought nothing of it, until he returned to the table and informed me of a visitor.

When Dell walked in, my chest constricted at the sight of him.

No longer blending in with our clan, muted browns and greens were replaced with the colors of Aetheria, his pale-blue tunic delicately ornate. The sight was oddly startling.

It brought me immediately back to her.

He approached, and began to bow, but I stopped him.

"There are no formalities in this chamber," I said. "Come and break your fast with me."

He sat down, looking different than usual, though I could not explain the reason.

With a smirk, Dell reached for a crust of bread.

"Can you inform the envoy," I asked Dren, "I am unable this

morn but will meet them instead at the midday meal? Have something special, distinctly Thalassari, prepared?"

"Of course," Dren said, leaving us, clearly still pleased with his jest.

"If I could bring him back, I would."

It needed to be said. Addressed.

Dell startled, which is when I remembered he wasn't privy to my thoughts. Immediately on seeing him, I was brought back to Seryn's death.

I had been so far down the wrong path, it was a wonder I'd not fallen into the same abyss as the father I'd so admired.

"Seryn," I clarified, realizing he thought I had been speaking of my father.

Though I would not say it aloud, my immediate horror at what Kael and I had done had been replaced with another: the realization that I would do it again.

"As would I," he said somberly. "Though we both knew the risks."

Dell sat up straighter. Looked me in the eyes.

"I was a spy for Aetheria, embedded here for many years. By rights, you could send me to the same fate as my fallen comrade."

"And yet." I snagged a piece of warm bread. "You have returned and sit before me. Knowing the risks of doing so."

"Knowing you," he said, not hesitating, "you would not have killed Seryn."

If not ordered to do so.

The silent words hung between us. Bold for him to come here. To make that claim. But it was also true.

"Nay," I agreed, "I would not."

"I chanced coming back for that reason. And also to offer my services."

I finished chewing, watching him carefully as Dell took a sip of centuria from his clay cup.

"Your services?"

"I have become accustomed to living here. When the speech you gave the day you returned as king was recounted in Aethralis, I decided to come. If you truly do wish to usher in a new era of Gyorian and Aetherian relations—"

The decision was an easy one.

"I would welcome you onto my Council."

Dell froze. "Your..."

"Council. Two spots remain. I can think of no better bridge between our clans than you." I drummed my fingers against the table. "Although you proved quite competent at it, your spying days must come to an end. You will be expected to swear your allegiance to our clan as a resident and member of the Gyorian Council."

"There would be no reason to undermine one whose goal is to work with Aetherians. We have the same vision for our lands and people."

I waited.

"And aye, I would gladly swear allegiance to one who has ended a centuries-long feud."

I laughed, unable to keep the bitterness from my tone. "Ended? Every day, we root out my father's loyalists who attempt to undermine my rule."

Dell leaned forward. "Another reason I am here," he said, voice lowering. "Your father's reach did not end with his death. Some still answer to the memory of him, as you know. One group, in particular, meet under the guise of trade in the southern quarter, using the same signs I once did myself, only clumsier."

I studied him carefully. "And you know this because..."

"Because I was trained to be unseen," he said with a smile. "And because I once often sat in the same shadows they now occupy. You should know, their eyes linger on the Stone and on you. If left unchecked, that rot spreads."

"The Stone?"

"There have long been rumors, among these warriors, that it was used to close the Aetherian Gate."

Ones which needed to remain only that: rumors.

"It seems I will be visiting the southern quarter."

Dell's eyes widened. "Yourself? You will not send others?"

"This is my clan," I said, resolute, as Dren returned. "Change of plans," I told him. "I will meet with the Thalassari envoy now."

Dell laughed at Dren's expression.

My clan. My problem. One that would get taken care of immediately.

If only the same could be said of the one problem I could not resolve through pure strength... of the Aetherian woman who had claimed my heart.

35

LYRA

"I've enjoyed our time here," Nerys said as she and Mev and I finished our daily training. We'd taken to doing so together near the rocky outcropping of the northernmost shores near the palace. While the queen showed us how she'd managed some of the maneuvers she'd utilized against Queen Lirael in their battle for the throne, Mev and I marveled her with advanced air magic that the princess had become more than proficient with. Mastery over the breeze using naught but breath was no easy skill for someone who not long ago had little notion her abilities even existed.

Mev, as she had these past days, looked defeated. We both knew what the queen was prepared to say.

"Marek and Issa will be back in the next two days," Mev added.

The iridescent wings of a flock of glintwing finches whizzing past held our attention for a moment. I remembered another time, long ago, Terran had been in Aethralis when a similar flock flew past our congregation of delegates. He'd glared at them so fiercely, for reasons unknown, I nearly laughed. Perhaps he had seen me smile, because I'd been the next victim of his menacing stare. One that could turn easily, I knew now, into a grin.

"And when they do—" Nerys began.

"You will be returning," Mev finished.

They'd left for an unknown destination for an unknown reason—not atypical for the pair—but would be back soon... to escort Rowan and Nerys home.

"As I can do it easily, back here, the moment I am needed."

Of course she had to return, as Terran had, to rule her clan.

Why did even the briefest thoughts of him feel more painful than any cut in battle ever had? Once, a Gyorian tossed a boulder at my head—a border skirmish I'd been tasked with quelling— that an easily summoned gust of wind rerouted. When it hit behind me, however, it shattered into a million stones, one of which left a scar on my shoulder blade where it had projected at me too quickly to maneuver away from. I often said a blade slice was preferable to that stone, but I would take it any day over this kind of pain.

"She's done it again."

I'd been staring at the ground.

Nerys and Mev knew, though both wouldn't dare speak of it when I'd refused to do so before. With all that was happening around us... the clean-up and aftermath of the breach, the failed Gate attempt... me falling in love with a Gyorian was of little consequence.

"Two days. This simply means," I said, deflecting, "we must redouble our efforts."

Mev's shoulders sank. "We've talked to every sage. Scoured the Luminara. The last time I dug this deeply, researching a topic so thoroughly..."

Mev stopped. And looked down at her ring.

She did this often, but something about the way she stared at it was different.

"When I was looking for something I didn't even know existed." She lifted her chin. "Elydor."

Nerys and I exchanged a glance, neither understanding the princess's meaning.

"We're looking for an answer without knowing the question."

Nerys cleared her throat as a large wave crashed against the shore. Just as its droplets were about to wet us, she flipped her hand, gathered them into one and sent it back into the sea.

"Isn't the question," I asked the obvious, "how do we reopen the Gate?"

"Yes, but... when I was a curator, I learned that artifacts rarely spoke their truths alone. A ring in a case was just a trinket... until set beside the crown it belonged to, or the tomb it was pulled from. Meaning lives in context. What if we've been treating the relics as singular, when their answer is only revealed together?"

"The artifacts were all needed to open it in the first place," Nerys mused.

"And to close it," I added.

But this was not new information.

"There's something here." Mev jumped across the rocks as if she'd grown up doing it.

We followed her back to the palace.

"Do you remember," Mev asked me, "when I asked you why some relics resonated while others lay dormant here? You told me that Elydor required balance for its magic to thrive. And that it also depended on the hand that wields them."

Though I didn't yet understand her line of thinking, another memory came back to me. It wasn't a pleasant one, but the conversation with the historian Elvric. He had mentioned, offhand, that relics remember wounds.

Why did that feel important?

"Elydor requires balance," I said aloud, so the others could hear my thinking. "The hand that wields them can alter their power. Elydorian artifacts remember wounds."

"Their answer is only revealed together," Nerys added, echoing Mev's earlier thought. She stopped, so we did too. "You speak of relics and wounds, of balance and memory. But Elydor has always demanded more than relics. It demands those willing to bear the weight of its memory. That is why even immortals fade when their time has passed. Perhaps the Gate waits not for power, but for the one it deems ready to carry that memory forward."

"You think Mev, maybe?" I asked Nerys.

Mev, who was intently examining the rock she stood on, was oblivious.

I understood the question and had had the thought many times. Clearly, the princess had no notion of what we meant. She'd not like it. Not until she could be reunited with her mother first. There was no reason to speak the thought aloud until we were certain.

Could Mev be the preordained next ruler of Aetheria? Maybe she, and not Galfrid, should have attempted to reopen the Gate? Even that didn't feel right. It missed something... something we were close to piecing together.

"I think we are close," I said, silently telling Nerys not to speak her thoughts aloud. Not yet. We'd had one new king in as many days, and I knew from being, even briefly, with Terran, how heavily it weighed on him. Mev wasn't ready, even if that was to be her future here.

She was certainly powerful enough. Though not more powerful than her father.

"Let's go talk to Eirion some more. Maybe tell him what we're thinking." I turned to Nerys. "If that's alright with you? I don't want your last two days here to be taken up with this every waking moment."

"I do," Nerys said, her tone not leaving any room for discussion. "There is naught more important. For you, but also for my partner and his people, too."

It was easy to forget that she was partnered with a full human. Unlike Mev, not a demi-immortal, but one just like Issa, even if he was more intuitive.

And I had no doubt he was. From all I knew of Rowan, he was more in tune with his abilities than any other human.

"Two days then," Mev said, rejoining us. Resolute. "We will figure this out and try again before you leave. And if it doesn't work, we'll keep looking for the answer."

"And when you find it, I will return with the Pearl. We cannot fail if we do not give up, aye?"

"Aye," Mev and I said in unison.

With luck, I sounded more confident than I felt. Having been at Galfrid's side for many years as he attempted to reopen the Gate, I knew first-hand this was no easy task we attempted. But what else could we do before Nerys left but try?

At least it kept my mind, or nearly kept my mind, from wandering back to *him*.

36

TERRAN

Chaos erupted around me. It was no less than I expected.

It was the first time using the throne room and would be my last. If any other chamber in the palace held so many at once, I'd have utilized that instead. Having informed the palace staff—those who remained—I would not be moving my residence, work had begun to renovate much of the space back to its original state. Less ornate. More... Gyorian.

"This cannot stand."

I watched reactions carefully, as did Dren and Dell. Collectively known as "The D's," both had become instrumental to me these past weeks. Working together well, and with a similar vision for our clan, the latter also served me well in another respect.

But the near-daily whispers with Lyra could not be my focus at the moment. Against King Galfrid and my own Council's wishes, I had just informed the gathered nobles of the Aetherian king's thus-far defunct plan.

He would reopen the Aetherian Gate. If possible. And he would do so with my blessing.

"Balthor would—"

I stood from the throne, hearing my father's name evoked. Shouting over the crowd, I took advantage of the chamber's acoustics to say what had been on my mind.

"My father taught you fear. Fear of what lies beyond our borders. Fear of Aetherians. Fear of humans. That fear built walls so high, we forgot what it was to look past them. But fear does not protect people... it cages them.

"I will not lead you from behind walls. We are strong, yes, but strength is not in isolation. Strength is in standing in truth, even when it is hard to hear.

"So let me speak the truth... the humans are not what my father claimed. They are flawed, as we are flawed, but they are capable of loyalty, of love, of sacrifice. To deny them is to deny ourselves the chance for a future greater than what Balthor's rule left us. The Gate may open again. Not as a threat, but as a bridge. And when it does, we will not meet it with fear. We will meet it with the knowledge that Gyoria does not cower from change.

"Transparency is not a weakness. It is the bond between ruler and ruled. And if I expect your loyalty, you must have my truth. So know this... I stand with King Galfrid's vision. And if you stand with me, then Gyoria will not merely survive its past; we will rise from it."

Silence.

Better they understood where I stood and revolted than I continued my father's recent tradition of leading under a mountain of lies.

The D's clapped. My Council clapped. One by one, enough joined in to drown out the voices of dissent. It was not a rousing victory... too many still thought as my father had, as I had, and it would take time to mend those divisions. But we had no choice but to try.

Eventually, the hall emptied. My Council congratulated me on a successful day. And only Dren and Dell remained.

"Finally," Dren said as I stood. "Dell has been receiving an urgent whisper for some time."

Dell's expression confirmed it.

"Why did you not tell me?"

"This was not a day to be rushed. Seeing me this way, and as an advisor, is... overwhelming for some to handle."

"What is it?"

He shrugged. "I do not know. Lyra asked only to let her know when you are available."

"I am available," I said impatiently. "Quickly, reach her. I wish to know if she is well."

Dell smiled. "Well enough. I am whispering with her already," he said, putting his finger to his lips. It was torture, to communicate with Lyra this way. Never to be able to ask the questions I most wanted to, though I should have been grateful for this connection to her.

I knew from Dell they'd attempted once again to open the Gate with Mev presiding instead of her father, to no avail. I learned that Queen Nerys and Rowan had returned to Thalassaria, and that the courtyard had finally been fully restored. I knew she and Mev spent their days searching for answers, to no avail.

What I didn't know was if she missed me. If Lyra still loved me. If she thought of us, wondered if there was a future for us together, and had as many sleepless nights as I did.

The Aetherian's eyes widened. Even Dren seemed to notice that whatever Lyra said, it was significant.

"Tell me," I said as Dell waved a hand for me to remain silent. With a sound of frustration, not knowing if she was well, I considered what in the throne room needed to be demolished first so that I could potentially speed up its demise.

"Terran." Dren brought my attention back to Dell.

"She said they know how to open it. That she understands your position here is tenuous but if there is a way that you're able to travel there... to come as quickly as you are able. They are going to try again and are hopeful it might work. And..." He stopped.

I urged him to continue.

"That Kael would like to speak to you before he goes through."

Head in my hand, I rubbed my temples, attempting unsuccessfully to remain calm. He'd warned me last time of his intentions, but the Gate was so unstable, allowing Mev through but none other... If they could open it, there was a chance, and Kael knew it, he may never return.

Dren looked at me.

"What do you think?"

"There is unrest, aye. But you must go. I can handle it."

I had no doubt he, and my other men, could do just that. Many of the worst of my father's sympathizers had been dealt with by now. There would be grumblings, especially after today, but more Gyorians wanted to openly trade with the other clans than were pure isolationists.

Considering how long it would take me to get to the coast, I did a quick calculation.

"Ready my mount and the smallest of contingencies you will allow," I told Dren. I'd go alone, but he'd have my hide for it. "Ensure they are fast riders."

"Right away," Dren said, his back to me already as he sped from the throne room.

"Tell her I am coming."

Dell nodded.

"And tell her... *Voren vel'kora*."

He clearly did not know the meaning. But I did.

And this time, I meant it. Not for one evening. But for eternity.

I was not leaving Aethralis without her by my side.

Ever again.

He would be here any moment.

Although the others were gathered in the Celestial Hall for a private meal—Nerys, Rowan, Issa, and Marek having arrived the day before—I could not wait for him there.

Our reunion would not be public. There was little chance I could restrain myself from embracing him, these weeks apart telling me more than even the days we were together.

I would live without him if I must, but if Terran willed it, I would prefer otherwise.

With him, I could be myself. He made me feel as no one ever had before him. I loved him, and he loved me, though we both recognized that might not be enough. Taking an Aetherian partner, while he attempted to convince his clan decades of strife between Gyoria and the other clans should now be reversed... it would be no small matter. Which is likely why he'd not suggested it.

But I'd not have Terran leave, once again, without at least discussing the possibility.

When the sound of hooves, not an unusual one in the palace

courtyard, reached me, I knew it was him. There was something about the urgency behind their steady clapping... and just as I suspected, he appeared over the ridge.

Rising like one of Nerys's great waves she summons, his form seemed to fill the entire landscape, Aethralis's mountain and building peaks behind him not nearly as magnificent as the Gyorian warrior racing toward me.

There were few in the courtyard during mealtime, but enough to bear witness. Indeed, as Terran's great mount skidded to a stop beside me, his companions began to appear, though in not as spectacular a fashion.

Dismounting with surprising nimbleness, Terran wasted little time in grabbing me—as was his custom—and pulling me toward him. There, with his contingency as witness, Terran kissed me with little reserve. His hand clamped down on the back of my neck, not that I'd planned on going anywhere. I wanted this kiss as much as him.

When he tore his lips from mine, his small smile disarmed any parts of me that remained reserved. I smiled back broadly.

"Welcome to Aethralis."

"Do you welcome every honored guest in such a way?" he teased.

"Only Gyorian kings," I teased back.

"Hmm. Then I will be certain to hold onto my title."

"Your men are watching us," I whispered.

"Let them watch. Lyra, we—"

"What took you so long?"

I jumped back at Kael's voice from behind us.

Terran chuckled... actually chuckled. I stared at him, trying to imagine such a sound from him at any other time from the Terran I once knew.

"You know well," Terran said, embracing his brother, "I could not have come any faster. They"—he waved to indicate his companions—"were little pleased with our pace."

"They will recover," Kael said. Taking charge, he delegated Terran's companions and their mounts to be taken care of before leading Terran into the palace.

"Lyra can tell you what she discovered."

"It was not me alone," I insisted, "but Mev and I together."

It wasn't until we entered the Celestial Hall that Kael picked back up the conversation, not wanting the details to be overheard. Meanwhile, I said little, allowing the brothers to catch up as we made our way through the palace.

After a proper welcome which included Galfrid insisting Terran drop his title, a rare honor that marked Terran as part of the inner circle here in Aethralis, Kael asked me to tell the story. Terran sat in the only empty chair, beside his brother, so I leaned in toward the table to share what had happened.

"Mev"—I gestured to the princess who sat next to me, on Kael's left—"and I spent days staring at scraps of parchment with all we knew of the Gate's opening. Repeating words and phrases, under Galfrid's oversight."

"They were tenacious," the king said proudly.

Our Thalassari guests, and their human companions, Rowan and Issa, remained silent. They'd heard the story the evening before.

"It was something you said that wasn't on those parchments that became an important clue for us."

"Me?" Terran was clearly surprised.

"My father's hatred of the humans broke Elydor's balance more than any blade."

Terran glanced at Kael. "A truth I should have realized sooner."

"*We* should have realized sooner." Kael would not let Terran carry the burden of their father's legacy alone, and from his expression, I could sense Terran appreciated it.

"When I put it into context with all the others, and Mev's persistence in having us remember that relics remember wounds, it came to me."

Heart hammering, praying the revelation was our missing piece, I continued. "Humans are the key."

At Terran's confused look, I added, "To opening the Gate. There were three clans the first time he"—I waved a hand toward the king—"opened the portal to the human realm. All three relics were needed as a way to signal the clan's acceptance of such an act. But there are no longer three clans."

"There are four," Issa finished. "Something we've continued to remind even those who accept us."

"Full acceptance," Rowan said, "means recognizing Estmere not just as a kingdom of Elydor, but as one of its clans."

The distinction wasn't lost on anyone present in the chamber.

"Estmere," Terran said. "One of Elydor's four clans."

I held my breath. Terran was the last to accept the humans. To let go of his hate toward them.

"We need their artifact."

He understood. Even more, seemed to accept it. Accept *them*.

All eyes turned to Rowan.

"Of course," I added, "this was merely speculation. Until we whispered to Queen Nerys and were able to communicate with Rowan."

"How does he factor into this? And what is Estmere's artifact? Do they even have one?"

Terran was the only one in the chamber who didn't know yet. But he was about to find out.

"Aye," Rowan said. "It's me."

Obviously, I misheard him.

"What in the stones did you say?"

"I am the human artifact."

I shook my head. Knocked one side of it, hoping to clear whatever I'd gotten inside. Maybe this morn, stopping briefly to clean in an Aetherian stream, their water got inside and poisoned my mind.

"Listen to him," Lyra said beside me.

I glanced from her, to my brother, to the others gathered around the table. And then the king. Looking up, the ceiling now a night sky filled with twinkling stars, I said a silent prayer to my mother to give me strength for this discussion which had gone off a cliff, and then attempted to do as Lyra suggested.

"You," I repeated, "are the human artifact? The equivalent of the Tidal Pearl—"

"Aye."

"Or the Wind Crystal."

"Aye."

"You don't have to keep going," Kael mumbled.

"Or the Stone of Mor'Vallis."

"Also, aye."

The man was daft. I'd come here for this?

"Not daft. The relics are pieces of Elydor's balance. But every scholar's record, everything those around this table have uncovered... or failed attempt we've made—"

"Rowan," I said, stopping him, "I didn't say you were daft." But then added, "Not aloud."

"I am a seer. And my abilities are stronger than most."

The fact didn't surprise me. But most seers gather information in snippets, often without context. This was something altogether different. He'd heard what was inside my head.

"I do not do that often," he quickly added, "but only wish to illustrate my words."

"What do you mean, stronger than most?"

"Perhaps if you let him speak, Terran," my brother said, "he will tell you."

I ignored Kael, waiting for Rowan to continue.

"Terran, you yourself said opening and closing the Gate are not the same. Galfrid opened it because he carried the relics and the will of a people united. Balthor closed it because hatred wounds more deeply than steel... and relics remember wounds. And I..." Rowan hesitated, his hand brushing his chest. "I am Harrow's blood. Keeper born. Every time I touched the relics, they stirred, not because of power, but because I was the piece never counted. The fourth relic, hidden in flesh instead of stone."

Rowan looked around the table, his voice quiet but unflinching. "It was never only the jewels of Elydor. It was always the jewels and the hand that wielded them which provided power. And my hand... my bloodline... is the one the Gate has been waiting for."

Harrow's blood. Keeper born.

"What does that mean? Keeper born."

He appeared distinctly uncomfortable now. Darting a glance at Nerys, who nodded, Rowan spoke, though reluctantly.

"I was never meant to say this. Keepers are sworn to silence, to pass their charge in whispers from one generation to the next. My grandfather warned me... our role was to watch, to wait, and never reveal. To do otherwise was to risk unbalancing the very order we swore to guard. But silence has brought us here. To a Gate that will not open, and a world unraveling."

As the surprise of his earlier revelation wore off, his words made sense. There had been something about him... Kael agreed, knowing the man better than I.

Rowan's voice had softened but did not falter. "My bloodline is that missing hand. If I remain silent, Elydor remains broken. So I break my vow, not for myself, but for all of us."

I had many questions, and likely always would. A man who kept such a secret would not reveal himself completely. But one was more important than the others.

"How do you know it will work?"

Rowan went silent suddenly, as if he didn't hear the question.

"He has visions." Nerys spoke for him. "As he's doing now. They are more clear than most seers', due to his bloodline and role as the Keeper of Memories for the humans, but still always not fully formed. As he told the others—"

"Apologies," Rowan said. "I have the ability to block out such visions but do not dare now. Not with so much at stake."

"Anything important?" Nerys asked.

Rowan's gaze clouded, distant. "I see a crown resting in the dust. A hand sets it down, not in defeat, but in peace. And another takes it up. The Gate is not the only thing that opens when balance is restored."

Silence fell.

He blinked hard, as if pulling himself back. "Perhaps nothing. Perhaps everything."

Everyone had stopped eating. Stopped drinking. We hardly even moved, the gravity of his words, and implications for them, understood.

"Terran's new reign?" Galfrid asked.

Kael responded. "The hand set it down in peace, not defeat." In other words, not our father.

"As I told the others," Rowan picked up where Nerys had left off, "I knew the Gate would reopen."

He'd seen it. "Since?" I asked, unable to keep the accusation from my voice.

"For some time. I've been trained, as are all of Harrow's bloodline, as Keepers. Interfering with future events is strictly forbidden. Even so, if I knew how it was done, how the Gate would reopen—"

He looked at Nerys. Clearly, this was something Rowan had been struggling with. Lyra's look of warning to me was not needed.

I silently vowed to remember Rowan was friend, not a foe.

"Thankfully, it is a decision I never had to make. The details on its reopening continued to allude me. But when Mev and Lyra whispered to us that they'd uncovered what they believed was the key, the necessity of a human artifact." He shivered. "It would be difficult to explain, but I *knew* at that moment. The human artifact was needed, and that 'artifact' was me. Perhaps it was the reason I was sent to Thalassaria in the first place."

"Not to meet Nerys and fall in love," Issa teased.

"That too." He smiled at his partner, the Thalassari queen.

"When do we attempt it?" I asked. As monumental as it

would be, getting Lyra alone was just as important to me. We had much to discuss.

I had a question to ask of her.

"Now."

For a moment, I thought the response had come from King Galfrid. It was so forcefully and deeply spoken. But in fact, it had come from Mev.

"If it pleases you all," she added, her tone just slightly softened.

She was her father's daughter. Of that, there was no doubt.

"Terran, you did not eat," Lyra began as each of those gathered began to rise.

"I will eat when this is done," I said. And then for her ears alone: "A feast long desired and worth the wait."

She slapped my upper arm, seemingly uncaring the playful gesture was noticed by more than one. As they filtered out of the room, I grabbed her wrist, holding Lyra back. I added, "The moment we are alone, you will strip out of those garments, lie on my bed, and spread your legs for such a feast. Do you understand me, Lyra?"

As always, her expression, a mixture of defiance and budding lust, displayed the internal war she waged. But thankfully, I knew which side would win. To ensure it, I added, "And this time, if you do not cry my name so loud those in The Crooked Key can hear it, I will not allow you up from my bed until that happens."

Her lips were too enticing not to kiss, and so I did. Quickly, a taste that did nothing more than inflame my already engorged appetite for her.

She attempted to leave the chamber.

Not so quickly, my slippery Shadow Diplomat.

I held her wrist firm.

"Do you understand?"

"We are about to—"

"Lyra?"

"I understand."

I let her go. Reluctantly.

But not for long.

39

LYRA

We'd been here before. But would this time be different?

Even with the new information we'd gathered—and Rowan's revelation—the mood inside the Temple was as somber as after the last failed attempt, as if none expected it to work.

There were other differences, though.

Mev and Galfrid had once again switched places. And this time, Mev's attire was distinctly... human. As was Kael's, as if they both dressed expecting success.

Terran stood beside me, glaring at his brother. The sight of him in such attire was, I was certain, jarring. It was possible, if this worked, it could be the last time he would see Kael. If it opened, none could predict the Gate's stability.

The arch, and its runes, remained cold and silent.

"Bring them forth," Mev called, her voice strong.

As before, the artifacts were brought to her and placed in the shallow basin. When Galfrid, Nerys, and Terran stood back, only one remained.

Rowan stepped forward, briefly squeezing the decidedly worried-looking queen's hand.

Taking Mev's outstretched one, Rowan faced the artifacts with her.

Without hesitation, she began.

"By the blood of kings and queens, with the artifacts of each clan, including Estmere's Keeper, and the memory of the first sealing, I call balance once more. Let the Gate be opened, that Elydor and the world of humans might be joined."

For a moment, nothing. But then, as if the slumbering giant needed time to wake, one by one, the runes began to glow. My heart raced, the outcome already ordained. I'd spent many years on the Gate's Council and knew how it appeared when opened.

Its runes, glowing shades of blue and deep green and turquoise. Within the archway, a swirling veil unfurled, its surface alive with stars that belonged not to the Elydorian sky, or the human one, but a combination of both.

This was how it appeared for many years, while the Gate remained open. But with one difference. As we watched, a new rune etched itself into the marble Gate. A key, distinctly of human origin.

Mev had dropped to her knees, surrounded by her father and partner. The king stared, as if not believing what he was seeing. Nerys embraced Rowan, whose eyes glistened with unshed tears that were unlikely to remain so. Issa and Marek, neither of whom had ever seen the Aetherian Gate this way, inspected it, fascinated.

"It worked," Terran said beside me, as if he too could not believe it.

"Will it remain this way? We still don't know," I reminded him, "how Mev was able to slip through."

"No," he said, "but perhaps we never will. Perhaps she was simply... meant to do so."

My next words were cut short as Kael walked toward us. Mev

was in her father's arms, crying openly, unknowing if this would be a temporary parting, or a permanent one.

"Brother," was all he said as the two embraced.

I stepped aside, or attempted to, in order to give them a moment. But as Terran let Kael go, he pulled me toward his side.

"Thank you for showing me the path from hate," he said. "Be well, Kael."

"And you, Terran. I'm proud of the king you've become. When you meet resistance, remember how difficult it was for me. For you. Perhaps she can help you."

"Me?" I asked.

"You will do well in Gyoria, Lyra."

I looked between the brothers just before I was nearly knocked to the ground by Mev. She hugged me as only a human could, without reserve or restraint. "Thank you. A thousand times, thank you. I have no idea what I would have done here without you, Lyra."

Smiling, I hugged her back and pulled away, looking into the eyes of a princess.

"You've exceeded all of my expectations. With luck, this is a temporary goodbye."

She nodded. "I'm going to bring her back."

There was no need to ask who she meant. Mev's plans had always been to reunite her parents.

"I look forward to that day."

With more goodbyes, and a forlorn king standing witness, Mev and Kael finally stepped up to the Gate. Another step, and they were gone.

Silence.

Everyone looked to Galfrid, who watched the Gate.

"A celebration for some, but this will not bode well in Gyoria," he said, turning to Terran.

"I've begun to prepare my clan for this possibility. My hope is that with more transparency, I can begin the slow march back to an Elydor before my mother's death."

"A good start," Rowan said. "We have been accepted by some, but let those outside this Temple know Estmere has been welcomed by Elydor itself." He motioned to the rune. "I will do my part as well. A meeting with my fellow Keepers, and leaders of Estmere, is in order. Perhaps it's time for all secrets, including those of the Harrows, to be revealed."

"There is a reason for them," Nerys reminded him.

"Aye, and there will always be those who seek to exploit others. Seek to increase their own power or worse, abuse it. But we cannot let fear be our only guide. Secrets may protect for a time, yet they also fester in the dark. If Elydor is to heal, if our people are to truly unite, then light must be shed on what was hidden. Even the truths that wound."

"Much is about to change in Elydor," Marek said. He'd been mostly quiet—unusual for him, according to Kael. Grinning, the Navarch added, "I look forward to letting you all sort it out."

"You are impossible," Issa said beside him.

One by one, the group began to splinter. Issa and Marek agreed to escort Rowan to Estmere and Nerys to Thalassaria where they would speak, respectively, to both clans. Agreeing to wait a few days to determine if the Gate would remain open, they filed one by one out of the chamber.

"I will wait here," Galfrid said. "With time moving differently between realms, she may return sooner than we expect. If she finds the courage to step back through, I will see her the moment she does."

I nodded, going to him. "She will be back. The Gate is as it should be."

As of yet, there was no indication it would close without some sort of intervention. And with Balthor dead, that seemed unlikely.

Galfrid took my hands. The gesture was so unexpected, I stood motionless. Waiting.

"You have served me, my court, and my daughter well, Lyra. I regret only that your parents were not here to witness first-hand what a fine Aetherian warrior you've become."

My parents had long since retired to the Haven Isles, a place for Aetherians weary of courts and wars.

"I whisper with them—keeping them informed, gaining advice—often," I said. "Thank you for your kind words, my king."

Squeezing my hands, he released them, looking over my shoulder, but Terran was gone.

"There are many ways to serve. Perhaps the time will come that you might do so by bridging a gap between our clans?"

"I know not what the future might bring," I admitted.

"Perhaps." He nodded toward the Temple's antechamber. "You should usher it in yourself rather than waiting for it to unfurl before you."

Wise words.

Perhaps I would.

"She will be back," I said again, with a final glance at the now-opened Gate.

"They must," Galfrid said. His voice barely a whisper.

40

LYRA

"He'll go through if they don't return," Terran said as I walked into the antechamber, a circular room, its walls lined with floor-to-ceiling arched windows that revealed the breathtaking landscape of Aethralis. I sat after finding Terran on one of the three plush cream couches, so named by the humans who'd come through so many years ago. Throughout the years, they—along with much of the furniture in this chamber and items in Estmere —had been called many things. It was the ever-evolving nature of their language, their ways, that those who valued permanence most cared for. And stability.

Like the Gyorians.

"I suspect you're right."

"And then?" I asked, not having been able to voice the question to the king.

"And then Aetheria holds a Trial of the Tempest to find your next leader."

"Just"—I snapped my fingers in the air—"as easy as that? Will we replace him?"

"If you have no king, aye."

I shook my head. "We said no more quips, but it does seem to me at times Gyorians are truly made of stone."

"And you." He moved closer. "Of starlight. Elusive. Beautiful. As opposite of me as possible."

"I would like to think if I vanished, you might pause for a wisp of time before replacing me."

He took my hand, making circular motions on my wrist with his thumb.

"You cannot be replaced."

He said it with the same matter-of-fact stoicism as he spoke of getting a new king. To Terran, they were more than merely words. He said very little, if anything, he did not mean.

"I found it difficult, when you left," I admitted, Galfrid's advice fresh in my mind.

"I found it intolerable."

Terran pulled me into him, his arm wrapping around me. Laying my head on his chest, I stared out the window, watching the night sky and marveling at how easy it was to sit in silence with him. Thoughts of our future swirled in my head, but for a time, I left them unasked.

The Gate was open. Our world was about to change once again.

Yet, for the first time since my parents left Aetheria, a calm—a safety—enveloped me. I could stay this way forever. As to that...

I sat up. "Can a Gyorian king partner with an Aetherian so soon after—"

"You ask the wrong question," he said, cutting me off.

"What is the right question, pray tell?"

"Questions. Many of them. When should we partner? Do you wish to reside in my quarters or would you prefer a new palace be built? What will your role with Galfrid be, as I assume you will still have one? How many times a day can I take you and still fulfill my duties?"

I was still focused on the first one.

"You wish to partner?" I asked, the answer in front of me. The way he touched me, looked at me, held me... I had no doubt. Yet I asked because the turn of events seemed even more unlikely than Kael partnering with Mev.

"I do. I love you, Lyra. Surely you know that."

I didn't mean to laugh. "Only you could make an admission of love sound as if it may be a declaration of battle, if the words were different."

"Oh, there will be one, for certain. If I tell you to get on your hands and knees for me, and you fail to do it quick enough."

Oh dear.

I'd stirred the other side of him, and wasn't sorry for it.

"The sweetest battle I could have ever anticipated," he said, his eyes dipping down to the front of my gown.

"Outside the bedchamber," I warned him, "if you order me—"

He grasped my chin, forcing my eyes to him.

"I would not dare. You are equal to me in every way, Lyra. Those are games we play, but not who we are as partners. I will be your king as much as you will be my queen. If you can accept living in a land very different"—he swept his hands out to the growing darkness, but I knew what lay beyond—"than this."

I lay my hand over his fingers.

"I can accept anything except being separated again from the stubborn Gyorian prince turned king with whom I've fallen in love."

His eyes softened, hinting of the Terran I'd come to know. That he showed so few another side of him made it all the more to relish. As he kissed me, Terran's lips covering mine in a caress that was equal parts sweet and promising, I scooted closer to him. Soon, I'd be sitting on his lap, but did not care. So much would change after this day. Everything, really.

But not this.

Not our love for each other.

But then I remembered.

Pulling back, I looked into the eyes of one who had lost his father and now, potentially, his brother.

"How long will you wait?"

Sighing, Terran looked out into the night, only the stars, and not the mountains below them, now visible.

"Decades. Centuries, I suspect."

He was being deliberately coy.

"Shall we join Galfrid? Ensure it remains open?"

"If it had not, he'd be here already, with us."

Terran made no move to get up, so I took my cue from him.

"Galfrid mentioned being a bridge between our clans," I said. "In answer to another of your questions."

"Dell has been received much better than I anticipated," he said. "Though as my queen, if any thought to disrespect you—"

"I would not win your clan over in such a way." This would be like whispering to the dead, attempting to convince them of as much.

"You will do so, I've no doubt. But that does not preclude—"

The Gate.

Terran and I jumped up and ran toward it, the sound of voices unmistakable. Mev and Kael had returned, the former already in her father's arms. Kael embraced his brother as well while I stood back, watching the scene unfold.

They were dressed differently than when they'd left, their clothing more similar to when Mev had first come through the

Gate. Though it was jarring to see Kael in such attire, Mev appeared less conspicuous.

"How long has it been?" Terran asked.

Mev looked at her partner. "A week perhaps."

"Where is she?"

That, from Galfrid.

"We tried to get her to come," Mev said. "Jon Harrow helped us get back to the States. Clara had just returned and told my mother what had happened, but thankfully, it had only been a few days earlier. Not that Mom wasn't freaking out. I won't say she didn't believe Clara, or me, especially after meeting Kael. But she was definitely freaked out." Mev looked up at the king, sadness etched in every line of her face. "She just doesn't remember."

Terran winced.

Of all the tragedies Balthor caused, this was one of the worst. Stealing someone's memories was an atrocity.

"Mom begged us not to come back. She traveled as far as York with us, even met Jon. But in the end, she was just too scared. Not that I blame her. Being back made me realize how insane the whole thing is, almost like it was a dream."

My heart broke for the king. To come so close to being reunited with the woman he loved...

"We told Jon not to allow anyone else through if the Gate stayed open," Mev said. "Which it seems to be doing. So that's good news, right? Maybe we can convince her..."

Galfrid wasn't listening any longer. He walked toward the antechamber, leaving the four of us alone.

"I'm glad you got to see her," I said to Mev. "And your friends."

"Thank God Clara didn't tell anyone besides my mom. The worst was trying to explain why I went MIA to my boss. I told him I got sick in England and lost my phone. I'm pretty sure he thought I'd lost it. But at least I was able to tie up loose ends and not leave him totally hanging."

Tie up loose ends.

Mev had never talked about what she would do, permanently, if the Gate reopened. Getting back to make sure her mother didn't worry had been her only concern.

"Does that mean—"

"We're staying here," she said, looking up at Kael, who was clearly pleased. "This is my home. When I went back, I felt like a visitor. Like this is where I was meant to be."

"If she wanted to stay, we would have," Kael said. "Maybe if the Gate stabilizes, remains open like it was, we could go between our worlds."

But in the meantime, she was staying. I was so pleased, I hugged her and Mev squeezed me back, whispering, "Thank you," into my ear. She'd already thanked me more times than was necessary.

"We're glad to have you," I said, pulling back and glancing toward the antechamber.

Mev's shoulders sank. "We tried. She came so close, but in the end... just couldn't do it."

"What will he do?" Terran asked.

It was well known kings, or queens, did not go through the Gate. Even when it had been open for centuries, there had been a fear something could happen to make the portal impassable. Especially now, when it was still considered unstable...

"I don't know," Mev said. "But Mom is going to stay in York for a bit, just in case."

The rest of her words were unspoken but we understood the implication.

Would he do it? Galfrid loved Mev's mother dearly, but he

loved his clan and kingdom too. It was much to risk, leaving Aetheria without a leader.

Without warning, the king re-entered the chamber.

"Terran," Galfrid said, his tone grim. "One of my men just brought a message from Dell. Word of the Gate's opening has begun to spread already. Loyalists to your father are gathering in the lower quarter. They claim the Gate is proof of Aetherian meddling... that your rule is illegitimate."

Lyra felt Terran stiffen beside her. His hand brushed hers, only briefly, but she read the vow in his eyes: he would have kept his promise to her tonight if he could.

But his duties, for now, lay elsewhere.

41

TERRAN

"That was quite a... spectacle." Dren surveyed the dead bodies.

It was a bloodbath, but my right hand was too diplomatic to say as much.

They had pulled me from Lyra, incited violence along the border, and took their rage out on an innocent human village. Every one of them had deserved the punishment they received, though I took no joy in such a sight.

Dren had just arrived, having been summoned as I was. Detained by another of my father's loyalists, one he'd been able to sway but by less violent means, he had just missed the reckoning.

"They took two innocent lives, guards from Ashwick, not bothering to deny it."

"To sow the seeds of rebellion, as if the cause of an ensuing battle would not be discovered."

My men had begun to bury the dead. I would help them, but needed a moment of rest. Dren had found me sitting on a log on the edge of the lower quarter's forest, where the loyalists were camped.

"What happened, precisely?"

"When we arrived, they were well-hidden among the trees."

"Not surprising, given how many trackers your father trained."

It was one of his best-honed Gyorian skills, and one Father enjoyed passing on to others. Neither Kael nor I took as much of an interest as he would have liked, but throughout the years, others enjoyed being trained by their king in such a skill.

"I felt nothing, at first. But remembered, thankfully." I patted the pouch at my side.

Dren's eyes widened. "The Stone."

"When I pulled it out, the Stone's glow was steady. Laying my palm to the dirt was a very different experience with it in my other hand. I could sense them but..." How to explain it? "Not in the typical way. It felt where they moved, where they ran, as if it were a memory."

"So not their vibrations?"

"No," I said. "Something else entirely." I shrugged. "When we did find them, I offered the same opportunity as the others."

Dren seemed surprised.

"Despite the killings?"

"With the caveat that those who'd committed the crimes would step forward."

"They declined?"

I nodded. "To accept my rule. To admit to the murders."

"Then they deserved to die."

I pressed my palms to my eyes, wishing the Stone's glow could burn the sight from my memory. "Perhaps. But I take no pride in it. There's been too much death already."

Dren frowned. "And there will be more before 'tis done, no doubt. If word spreads of what happened here..."

Standing, I walked forward, toward the men.

"I have no wish to be a ruler my clan fears."

"Those loyal to your father are not your clan. They are poisoned by hate."

"Perhaps some can be redeemed," I mused aloud, thinking of Kael and myself.

Without waiting for Dren to respond, I took the Stone from its pouch and turned it over in my hand. How some could wish for so much power, I didn't understand. The things that were possible with the Stone of Mor'Vallis should be feared, not revered.

Feeling my strength returning, I joined the men, using my hand to unearth dirt as each of those fallen were carried into their graves with the Stone still in my left hand.

"We will give them this land."

Dren wasn't the only one to look at me as if I were mad.

"To honor the guards of Ashwick whose blood was spilled here," I said, standing straighter. "Ashwick has little fertile ground, and this soil has been marked by their sacrifice. Let their kin plant where hate once rooted."

Dren's frown eased slightly, though doubt lingered. "Some will say you gift too freely."

I touched the Stone, its steady glow warming my palm. "Let them say it. My father ruled by fear. I would rather bind our clans by balance and by justice that even humans can see."

"Very well."

"Your majesty?"

It took me a moment to realize it was me being summoned from behind. I turned as the messenger dismounted, his horse clearly spent.

"Aye?" I asked, immediately, and irrationally, thinking something might be wrong with Lyra. "What is it?"

"The king. Of Aetheria," he clarified.

"What of him?"

"He's going through the Gate."

Although every Gyorian warrior who heard the message either froze in surprise or dropped their collective jaws—or both—I said nothing. Before Lyra, I'd have thought King Galfrid unfit to rule, to make such a decision. But now?

I understood it. But the implications of such an act...

"He would leave Aetheria without a ruler?"

Even temporarily, it was unheard of. And if something happened to the Gate after he went through it...

"No," the young messenger said. "He called for an impromptu Trial of the Tempest in two days' time."

By the Stones. He wasn't just going through the Gate. He was leaving Elydor for good.

"Go," Dren said. "I will see the necessary tasks here complete. You should be there."

"If there is another uprising—"

Dren laughed. "After this? If there is another uprising, it will be initiated by Gyorians with no will to live."

Dren was wrong. There would be another uprising. Whether of blades or of truths long buried, I could not be certain. With luck, Elydor would be ready to face either.

42

LYRA

"Speak with her, please. Mev will not listen to reason."

It wasn't the first time the king had made his request, but unfortunately, Mev had inherited more than strength and skill from her father. She was as stubborn as a Gyorian and refused to listen.

"She truly does not believe she should be eligible," I said, peering out from the king's solar windows yet again. The Skyway was clearly visible, and my guess was that Terran would arrive on horseback rather than by sea. He could, in theory, make better time if not traveling to the coast.

"There is little time before the Trial," I said. "Perhaps you could delay it?"

"I would, if there was any indication she would listen to reason."

I couldn't understand a parent's frustration at being unable to control their child, even as an adult, but imagined it would be frustrating. Knowing from experience what was best for them but watching them take another path... the truth was, however, Mevlida was an adult woman. And though she respected her father greatly, she also truly believed the possibility of her as queen of Aetheria was not her place.

She'd not been in Elydor long enough.

She was half-human.

The list of reasons she gave was long, but those were the two I found most difficult to refute. As to the second, we attempted to point out that perhaps it would be a good thing, now that the shared goal of all clans was for a united Elydor, including the humans.

But so far, she could not be swayed.

"Will you try?" he asked.

As if I would deny him.

"Of course," I said, the lump in my throat near constant now, as the day approached.

When Galfrid first announced his intentions, I had been as surprised as the remainder of his court. And now the day was upon us. Terran had still not arrived. Mev refused to discuss the matter. And the king became more and more distraught each day.

He'd assumed his daughter would participate. Assumed she would proceed him as queen. And while it was true, Mev was extraordinarily strong, there were others that could potentially best her.

"Remind her that a lifetime of training does not measure against the skill of a true king or queen."

I could not agree or disagree. I'd never considered anyone besides Galfrid as the ruler of Aetheria. Would there be some comfort in having his daughter as the next ruler? Aye. But she was, as Mev pointed out, the least experienced air-wielder in the land.

"I will do so," I said, hurrying toward the window. A sole rider, large enough to be him.

"It is Terran," Galfrid said.

I spun toward the king.

"I can sense his power." The corners of his mouth lifted. "Which is how I know Mevlida is destined to be our queen."

"I will greet him briefly and then find her. We've still time."

No sooner had the sun risen than Galfrid had summoned me to him and the Trial was to be performed, as was custom, at dusk.

"Report back to me," he said, clearly worried.

I bowed, leaving Galfrid just as his Council began to file inside the chamber. Since his announcement, meeting after meeting had commenced. It was no small matter to lose a king who had been in power for centuries. Eirion had attempted to persuade Galfrid to wait, to ensure all was ready for a smooth transition. But the king insisted on speed, clearly anxious to go through the Gate before his wife returned home.

Running toward the courtyard, I did not stop to speak to anyone, even those who called my name. It was the last time we'd be separated, I decided. Doing so was too painful, by far.

He dismounted just as I ran down the marble steps of the palace's front entrance. Without hesitating, I jumped into his arms, Terran catching me as my legs wrapped around his waist.

Kissing me for all to see, he stopped only when the whistles grew loud enough that they couldn't be ignored.

"Quite a greeting from a normally reserved lady. I don't believe I've seen you run before, if not in battle."

He smelled like the land. Like Terran. Felt so solid against me. Being wrapped up in his arms was where I belonged.

"You have an effect on me," I said, disengaging myself.

"Do I?" he taunted.

"Shall I take him, your majesty?"

"Aye, thank you," Terran said to the stablehand. Giving him the reins, he followed me back into the palace.

"It's set for tonight," I began, telling him all that had transpired since he left. Terran appeared less surprised than I'd been, but his brow drew together at mention of Mev.

"Why not let the Trial decide?" he said, echoing the king's words precisely.

"She refuses. Mev believes she will be humiliated and thought poorly of, for even attempting to participate. I even challenged her to a duel, one which she won easily, but Mev insisted I went easy on her, which I did not."

"Can she win?"

"Aye. Her progression of skills is unlike anything I've even seen. Galfrid believes it is because she is destined to be the next Aetherian ruler, but Mev disagrees. She will not be persuaded."

"And Kael?"

"Is useless."

Terran stopped short. Remembering this was his brother, I amended. "He refuses to take a stance on the matter. Says it is Mev's choice alone to make."

"Hmm." Terran clearly disagreed.

"The king asked me to speak with her again. Will you come with me?"

"I assumed that's where we were headed."

It was difficult not to grin from ear to ear. Terran was back, and I appreciated his unwavering support.

"I know you must want a bath and a meal—"

"I want a few things more than you can imagine," he said, "but a bath and a meal are not among them."

"No," I asked coyly. "Not even a little?"

"We can have this conversation, if you'd like, but do not expect me to care if we're overheard."

Even that, in Terran's deep voice, drew attention.

Grinning, I turned a corner. "She is in her bedchamber. Or was the last time I left her."

Heading to Mev's chamber with Terran following, I knew immediately she was still there due to the presence of her guards outside the door.

"Good day, Lady Lyra," one said, hand over his fist to Terran. "Your majesty."

"Good day," he replied back as the guard opened the door, escorting us to her antechamber and calling her name.

Kael rushed toward us, though there was no sign of Mev.

"Brother," he said, embracing Terran as the guard retreated.

"I came as quickly as I could."

"The lower quarter?"

"Taken care of. We can discuss later."

Embarrassed I'd forgotten to ask in my rush to see him, I said as much silently to Terran, who winked at me, seemingly understanding.

Winked.

Actually winked.

"Why don't you persuade her?" Terran asked Kael without preamble.

"It isn't my place to—"

"By the Stones, Kael. Then whose place is it?"

"She is a grown woman, her mind, her own. If Mev doesn't wish to participate—"

Without waiting for him to finish, Terran brushed past him and headed deeper inside the chamber. Mev stood on the balcony, her long white hair flying behind her like a banner. Dressed in pale blue with silver lining, she certainly looked like a queen, even if she didn't feel like one.

"Terran, she's not from here. Do not—"

He wasn't listening. Bracing for what he might say, I followed him out as Mev turned to greet us. At least, she'd been prepared when Terran spoke.

"There is no one in Elydor less deserving of ruling their clan than me," he began. "I allowed hate to guide me, despite being taught to love. I was nearly too late to change course, and did so only after killing my own father. But here, Princess Mevlida, we do not decide. This land"—he waved a hand to indicate the snow-capped mountains beyond the balcony on which we stood—"is not somewhere we simply occupy. Elydor lives alongside us, its will as important—if not more so—than any one of our own opinions."

Without warning, he reached his hand out to those very same mountains Terran had pointed out to us, and incredibly at such a distance, sent a boulder the size of Mev's chamber rolling downward. If allowed to continue unfettered, it would likely cause an avalanche.

It took Mev a moment to realize none of us were stopping it. The distance was so great, I would have had difficulty doing so anyway.

With a scowl at Terran, she lifted a hand and harnessed a gust of wind so strong it not only rushed upward toward the boulder, stopping its descent, but it also tore leafless trees from their roots, the wind's path left barren.

Terran twisted his fingers again, this time melding the boulder, somehow, into the mountain as if it had always been there. Then, with a sweep upward, he regrew everything in the wind's path, leaving it as if no such disturbance took place.

"She could not have done that," Terran said, speaking of me.

I didn't refute his words.

Mev stared at him and then turned to Kael. "Your brother is mad."

Kael grinned. "Aye, he can be."

"What if I hadn't stopped it?"

"Not the right question, princess," Terran said. I recalled the last time he used a similar phrase toward me.

I withheld my smile, unsure Mev would appreciate it at the moment.

"What's the right question?" she asked, not hiding her annoyance.

Terran smiled as if he'd won a great prize.

"Why aren't you training for the Trial?"

Mev opened her mouth, and shut it.

She looked at me.

I shrugged, with little to say.

Is he always this way?

Her whispers were seamless, as if she was born using them.

No, I whispered back. *Sometimes, he's worse.*

Unable to help myself, I laughed at her expression of horror which is when Kael and Terran realized we'd been whispering. And while the mountains still trembled with his power, it was Mev's silence that promised the greater storm.

43

TERRAN

"How is she doing that?" I asked Lyra, finally able to breathe.

We stood at the base of the Sky Pinnacle where candidates for the next ruler of Aetheria tested their skills against each other. The sheer rock face of vertical stone offered no quarter. Gusts of wind sliced through the air which smelled thin and cold, a reminder that in this place, only the most powerful could do battle. There were four candidates in total, Mev, thankfully, among them. Two had dropped out already with only Mev and an Aetherian noble, and long-rumored as a potential for his predecessor, remaining.

He was strong, but Mev was stronger.

"I don't know," Lyra said beside me. "Removing air is more difficult than manipulating it. I've seen Galfrid attempt something similar, but I doubt anyone taught her to do that, including him."

When the spectators realized what Mev had been doing from her position near the top of the mountain, it was too late for any of them to fight back, if this had been a battle. Making it as difficult to breathe as if we were up there with her, Mev had created a moment of stillness that kept me uneasy, even after she returned the air to normal.

It was a skill that would be difficult to counter.

"It's as if Elydor itself chose her," Lyra said.

"I agree. Maybe her arrival awakened something dormant and Elydor recognizes her as part of the Gate's balance, lending her extra power."

Since I was watching Mev and her opponent, I didn't realize Lyra was staring at me until Kael chuckled. When I looked at her expression, I may have scowled.

"That was incredibly insightful. And enlightened," she said.

"I will have you know—"

"Look," Kael exclaimed as those around us gasped.

Mev had lifted her hands, bending the high winds into a dome over the Pinnacle. Clouds ripped apart and then reformed into a roaring vortex above her opponent, pressing him down with invisible weight.

Both stayed that way until... he yielded.

For a time, no one moved. Then the mountain itself seemed to exhale and wind rushed over the stone as if carrying word of what had just taken place. The air was alive with power, with the certainty that something in Aetheria had shifted. Even the elders, usually unmoved by contests of might, stood silent in reverence. This was not merely victory. It was the birth of legend, the moment the chronicles of Elydor would mark as the day Mev of Aetheria bent the wind to her will and claimed the skies as her own.

Cheers erupted around us, giving no hint that Mev might face the same type of rebellions as I was, though so far, there had been no further reports of unrest. A new king. And now, a new queen.

"Congratulations," Lyra said to Kael as Galfrid approached

the pair. Soon they would descend, and Aetheria would have its first half-human ruler.

"I cannot believe it," he said, my brother's shock apparent.

"Mev has become quite powerful," Lyra said as the crowd began to file down the mountain around us. They would gather in the palace courtyard where Mev would be crowned immediately. She was already Aetheria's queen, the most powerful in their clan since Galfrid had renounced his claim to the crown earlier, but a ceremony, according to Lyra, would simply make it official.

"I knew she was but... this is unexpected."

"You are not happy for her?" Lyra was anything but pleased by my brother's reaction.

"She will be targeted," he said, staring at the spot where the contenders had stood. "Some may be unhappy with the outcome. Unhappy her father is stepping down. Or that she is partially human."

I knew my brother. The catch in his voice was fear.

"She has the ability to make others stop breathing," I reminded him. "Think on that, Kael. It's never been done before. Mev is as strong, if not stronger, than even her father. In time, she'll master every skill of his."

"And has already an arsenal of her own," Lyra added.

"Trust in her skills. Support her. Mev will be fine."

Kael looked at me as if we were strangers.

"What?" I snapped.

"You're just... different. Thank you," he tossed to Lyra, taking off as Mev appeared through a break in the trees with her father.

"I suppose he thinks you are responsible for this... *difference* in me?"

"I suppose he does."

I pulled Lyra toward me, knowing Kael was right.

"And I suppose you'll be wanting some sort of reward?"

"Only if you agree with him."

Only a handful of stragglers remained as the crowd had moved on. If anyone had told me I'd be standing at the base of the Sky Pinnacle with Lady Lyra of Aetheria in my arms, I'd have thought they were mad. And yet... nothing had ever felt more right.

"You fish for compliments," I teased.

"I do."

Smoothing back her hair as the wind picked up, I offered them freely.

"My brother often said our mother was the best of my father, and I understand now what he meant."

"We are an unlikely pair." Lyra leaned her cheek into my hand.

"Perhaps the reason it seems to work?"

"Perhaps."

I dropped my hand as Kael, Mev, and Galfrid approached. Mev was clearly exhausted, though she ran straight into Lyra's arms.

"Thank you," she said, "for training me. Believing in me."

Lyra squeezed her and murmured something I could not hear. When Mev let go, she looked at me.

"You have some interesting motivational methods, but they worked. Next time, a bit of warning before you cause a potential avalanche would be nice."

"A warning would have weakened its purpose."

Mev's lips twitched despite the exhaustion lining her face. "Maybe."

"Congratulations, your majesty," I said with a bow. "That was well done. A most impressive display of air-wielding."

Mev glanced between us with my brother and Galfrid looking at her proudly.

"I had no idea I could do half of that," she said, "but I just remembered what you told me when we first started training, Lyra. That the air was never mine to command but something to listen to. And today, it listened back."

"It did." Lyra beamed. "In a most spectacular way."

We began to walk, collectively, away from the Pinnacle.

The crowd had moved on, chasing the ceremony, the promise of a queen crowned at the palace gates. Mev walked ahead with Kael and Galfrid, the new center of their world.

"You don't have to play the brute all the time," Lyra said softly. The wind tugged strands of hair across her cheek, and she didn't bother brushing them away. "Sometimes, the warning matters more than the avalanche."

I stepped closer, close enough that the sharpness in her eyes caught the last shreds of daylight. "And sometimes," I murmured, "the avalanche is the warning."

Her laugh was low, unguarded... and tempting.

"Do you know what I saw up there?" she asked.

"Mev nearly killing us all with air?"

Her head tilted upward, the corners of her mouth daring me. "I saw you watching her. I saw you see yourself in her."

I should have denied it, but the words stuck. Elydor had chosen Mev, just as surely as it had cursed, and chosen, me. Power that came unasked, unwanted, reshaping everything it touched.

But Lyra... steadied it.

"I am nothing like her," I said, though my voice lacked conviction.

"No," Lyra agreed, brushing her fingers over mine, featherlight, as we wrapped them together. "You're worse. And better. And far more infuriating."

Suddenly the mountain, the trial, the crown... they were distant things.

"Lyra." My voice was rough.

She didn't wait for me to finish. She stopped and rose onto her toes as her mouth found mine. I caught her against me, one hand fisted in her hair, the other dragging her flush to my chest. The kiss was a clash, sharp edges and long-denied hunger, but beneath it thrummed something steadier.

When we finally tore apart, breathless, the world was no less dangerous, no less uncertain. But for the first time, I didn't care.

Elydor had chosen its queen. And I had chosen mine.

"After the crowning," I murmured, thumb at her throat where her pulse raced, "I collect what I'm owed."

Her slow smile made my own pulse race.

"I'm yours to command... Your majesty."

44

LYRA

The celebrations could wait.

With the door barely closed on my bedchamber, I was summarily lifted from my feet and tossed onto the bed.

"If you aren't undressed before the last of my own garments fall away," Terran said, beginning to unlace his boot, "I will make you plead for release."

In the process of already unlacing my own, my fingers froze at his tone. It was more than simply commanding. Terran's words were a definitive promise and part of me wanted to push back.

"I'd likely do so anyway," said the part of me unused to taking commands.

With an ominous look, he tossed his boot aside and began to unlace the second. "You'd best hurry."

It was the thud of his second boot hitting the floor that made my fingers fly. Heart thudding, the look Terran gave me was one that would likely petrify the most hardened Gyorian warrior.

Racing to undress before him, my mind wandered back to when he'd left. Somehow, Terran had found his way into connecting to the very essence of me. His absence had left a hole I hadn't known was there.

The way he looked at me now?

It was an almost predatory one, but I was his willing prey.

"Terranor take me," he said, his torso now blessedly bare. "Your breasts are astonishing. I am going to ravage you, Lyra."

And he did.

Thankfully, I'd beaten him by a thread, but it didn't seem to matter. Squealing as a completely nude Terran in all his glory climbed onto the bed and grabbed my ankle, I clutched the coverlet which was dragged down with me. With his other fingers gripping my second ankle, he pulled my legs apart and descended.

Without warning, his mouth was between my legs. Clean shaven, no barrier between his lips and mine, he kissed. Licked me from bottom to top. And releasing my ankles, spread me open even wider with his thumbs and plunged his tongue into me.

The authority of his every movement had me resisting the waves of clenching in pleasure that were sure to come sooner rather than later. I pushed my hips into his expert mouth, but without warning, he stopped.

Lifted his head.

"Beg for me, Lyra."

My core clenched at his words, his expression.

"I undressed before you."

"You did," he admitted, "but I'm changing the rules. Beg me, and you will find release like you never have before this day."

I would anyway if he continued to look at me like that.

"Terran..."

And then he licked his lip. A taunting, delicious gesture.

"Do it."

I didn't hesitate.

"Please," I said, my voice foreign to my own ears. "Please," I repeated when he hesitated.

He was upon me once again, this time even more relentless than before. His tongue plunged, swirled... his thumb circled me as the suckling sounds were nearly my undoing. I could feel the building of sensations but didn't want to let go.

Not yet.

But he proved too much to resist and when it came, as Terran predicted, my release didn't whisper but roared like a raging storm. Hips high, my fingers still gripping the coverlet, I screamed his name over and over.

It was only when I felt the pressure of his chest that I realized he'd driven into me. I held onto his shoulders, or tried to, as he plunged himself harder and faster.

The entire time, he looked at me. Looked into my eyes.

And it was only after we both came down, the shudders that wracked our bodies both simultaneous and all-encompassing, that Terran flipped us over, me on top of him but still joined, and kissed me.

We were one, in every sense of the word. I'd crawl further into him if it were possible.

"*Voren vel'kora.*"

"Aye," I said simply. "I am."

45

TERRAN

"How do we find ourselves here?" my brother asked.

We stood on and watched Mev and Lyra as they spoke to Eirion. Two suns had risen since Mevlida had become Queen of Aetheria, and tonight, her father would go through the Gate. It had been a brief training, but Mev had reassured Galfrid there were many around her she could trust to continue aiding in her transition. Just as importantly, she wanted him to get through before her mother left England.

"What would Mother say?" I asked in answer to his question, one that eluded me.

Kael sighed. "She would be little pleased by our actions, but maybe she would understand too."

It was more of a question than an answer.

"I suppose it matters more what we do with his legacy. If we serve Elydor well, what more can we accomplish?"

"Father thought he served it well." Kael smiled as Mev and Lyra laughed at something Eirion said. Such a short time ago, I'd not have been able to understand a love like his and Mev's, but now, I understood better than I did how to govern a bloodthirsty clan who were proving stubborn. Though no incidents required my immediate presence yet, that was not to say they all had been quiet south of us.

"The difference between him and us is that we will lead with tolerance and an attempt at understanding what we'd previously put aside. In the end, Father led with intolerance and division which served no one. Not even him."

Kael didn't seem completely convinced. Assuaging him of his guilt would be no easy task. It would take many years, I suspected, for us both.

"Lyra," Kael said, clearly pleased. "I'd not have named her as your partner of all the women in Elydor, but she clearly makes you happy. I've not seen you smile so much since we were young ones."

"She does," I said, his statement true, though oversimplified. More than happy, Lyra made me want to be better.

"I hope she will be happy in Gyoria. Lyra was made for the sky."

"And has lived here for many years. How often have we said what an adventure it might be living among another clan for a spell?"

"Something that will be possible now," I said. "Or soon, at least."

"Though more difficult for us. A king. My brother"—he slapped me on the shoulder—"a king."

"And mine." I didn't miss a beat, "The partner of a queen."

Kael smirked. "A good enough title for me. I care little for such things."

We remained there, in compatible silence, until Mev and Lyra walked back into the palace.

"An Elydor without Balthor," Kael mused as we began to follow. "I could not have conceived of such a thing."

"And soon, without Galfrid. Many times, I've wished for such a thing, but now that the day is upon us..."

The words for what I was feeling eluded me.

"He has been an enemy to Gyoria for many years. At least," Kael said as more than one head turned as we strolled toward the palace together, "we thought as much. I do not believe he ever was, and our blindness to the fact weakened our clan." My brother smiled. "I leave it to you to rectify."

"Your presence here." I waved a hand. "Will do much to aid me in that."

We stopped before entering the Aetherian palace, likely thinking the same thing. Though it was not a place either of us expected to find ourselves—on the precipice of bidding adieu to the most powerful ruler Elydor had seen during our lifetimes—it was also an exciting, if not daunting, place to be.

The palace loomed quiet around us, as if it too held its breath. Soon the silence would break at the Gate where a farewell, centuries in the making, awaited.

* * *

This time felt different.

Somehow, when Mev and Kael had gone through, even though they'd said their goodbyes, prepared for them to be final, I'd known, deep inside my soul, they would return.

Galfrid, for all I knew of him, would not. At least, not as long as Mev's mother was too frightened to come through. He'd spent years attempting to reunite with his partner and unborn daughter and would not risk being separated again.

As he'd promised, even though the Gate remained open, Jon Harrow had not allowed any to pass through. Until a new Gate Council could be formed and rules, on both sides, set in place, it was better kept a secret and nothing more than a locked Crooked Key basement.

"We will be unable to pass through," I said to Lyra, who stood by my side, looking at the swirling patterns that marked it open, "in our role, or mine at least—"

"I have all I need here," she said, reaching for my hand. "Though I will miss him dearly."

Galfrid had said his goodbyes. He'd addressed all of Aetheria at the palace, giving those gathered his daughter's support to take up his long reign. It was too soon to tell if her transition would go more smoothly, or, like mine, it would be marred with rebellion and unrest.

"As will she," I said of Mev, who held onto her father as if she might never see him again—a distinct possibility. He'd promised to relay a message once travel commenced once again between realms, or even to return himself with her mother if possible, but neither were guaranteed.

With only the five of us, soon to be four, standing before the Gate, it wasn't long before Galfrid had bid adieu to those gathered.

"Take care of her," he said to Kael, as if such a thing needed to be uttered. My brother would devote his life to such an act, as was evident by the way he looked at her now. Instead of saying as much, he bowed to the former King of Aetheria.

"It will be my honor, your majesty," he said, the courtesy title one of respect.

Galfrid turned to me.

"We built walls where bridges should have stood. We mistook fear for strength and pride for honor, and it cost us dearly. Yet here you stand beside one of my trusted and beloved charges, having chosen love over hate, unity over division.

"Elydor will not be healed in a single season, Terran. Perhaps not in a single reign. But you have already proven it can change. You have proven that the Gate does not close on us forever... It opens when we are willing to listen.

"Serve not as a ruler above your clan, but as a steward beside them. Remember that power bends to those who honor the land, not those who seek to master it. And remember this: the choices you make now will echo longer than the battles we fought to get here."

I bowed to him, as my brother had.

He spoke to me, but to Mev as well. At his words, she reached for Lyra's hand. Kael tightened his hold on hers, and I found myself grasping Lyra's other. By the time Galfrid's voice fell silent, the four of us stood bound together, a single chain before the Gate.

"I will cherish Lyra and my clan, honoring both in the name of your legacy," I said, "Your majesty."

Galfrid's quick nod of approval accompanied his step toward the Gate. He turned to face it, and then looked back at us once more.

"I go to finish what I began with the woman I love. But it is you four who will finish what was broken in Elydor. And I have no doubt you will succeed."

He was gone, but his words lingered like a vow etched into stone. Four hands still linked, we faced the Gate not as heirs of ruin, but as the beginning of a new realm forged from stone and starlight.

EPILOGUE

LYRA

It was my favorite spot in all of Gyoria, especially when sharing it with Terran.

Just beyond the palace walls, carved into the cliffs, he had a narrow terrace called the Starlight Overlook carved out for me. At night-time, as it was now, the skies shimmered brighter than anywhere else, the moon casting a silver light that turned the ice-crusted stone into a mirror.

The overlook was a quiet refuge from duty where the rest of Gyoria remained unaware of our presence in this spot.

Terran's hand brushed mine as he sat up beside me.

"What are you thinking?"

As my fingers wove through his, I pointed out one star in particular.

"From my window at the Aetherian palace, I could see Velastra clearly most nights. Do you know of it?"

Terran chuckled. "Gyorians aren't known to stargaze."

Taking that as a "no," I enlightened him.

"It's known as the Crown of the Gate and is said to shine

brightest on the nights a human comes through. Aetherian lore whispers that it's not just a star, but the lingering ember of Elydor's own magic, watching over those who dare to walk between realms. Couples often make promises beneath it, believing Velastra binds hearts as firmly as it guards the veil."

"Interesting. So it shone brighter last eve, then?"

I thought back to the whispers I'd received from Mev with a smile. "I assume so." Turning to Terran, I searched the lines of his face, wondering what he was thinking as well.

"I am happy for her. For them."

"As am I. Though I do wonder why it took nearly forty moons to relay the message. They've been coming through for half that time."

A new Council had been set up, Kael among its members. Thus far, the transition to the Gate's reopening had been going extraordinarily well. Tales of the reunions, both in Elydor and the human realm, warmed the hearts of all who heard them.

Or perhaps, not all. In Gyoria, resistance to the Gate still ranged from simmering anger to open hostility, but Terran's combination of strength and compassion had thus far tempered any additional rebellions in his father's name.

"Remember," I reminded him, "Galfrid did not simply have to reunite with his partner. She had to fall in love with him again. Not an easy feat to accomplish twice."

"I could do it," he boasted. "You would fall in love with me in every lifetime."

"So humble," I teased. "Though I do not doubt that I would."

He was my perfect complement. A rock when one was needed. A companion and friend. But also, the lover I never knew I needed.

"As I would fall in love with you again, and again."

Terran leaned forward and kissed me softly. The dichotomy of his kisses, and touches, soft at times and others coming from the king of a people forged from stone, was something to which I'd never become accustomed.

"Do you think she will ever be convinced to come through?" he asked.

I thought about it for a moment. "I do. Galfrid can be quite persuasive. And of course she will want to see Mev. It might simply ease her into the idea of our world. There is likely a block there from having been traumatized the first time, after she was kidnapped. But hopefully, there is some residual memory, too, Galfrid can explore."

The change in his expression when I mentioned the kidnapping was immediate.

"Terran—"

"Nay," he said, "do not apologize for mentioning it. Pretending it did not happen, or that I allowed myself to be so taken with the idea of hating humans for something they did not do on purpose... remembering will remind me, remind us all, to do better."

He truly had come full circle, as Kael had before him. A part of me had, as well. My own prejudices against Gyorians were stronger than I'd realized before living here.

I looked back up into the sky.

"Let this overlook be our promise," I whispered, "that no matter what unrest rises, no matter what trials await, we will always return here."

"Aye," Terran whispered back. "And that no matter how many realms divided us, love would find a way to bind us again."

* * *

MORE FROM C. L. MECCA

Another book from C. L. Mecca, *Whisper of War and Storms*, is available to order now here:

www.mybook.to/WhisperofBackAD

ACKNOWLEDGMENTS

Thank you Andrea, Katie, and Megan for encouraging me and helping bring this series to life. Without you, I might have been content to keep reading the fantasy stories I love instead of building realms of my own.

Thank you to Nate Van Coops for listening to barely formed ideas about immortal elemental wielders and lending your story-plotting expertise to *Heirs of Elydor*. A fellow member of the Tiki Bar Pals, a group of friends and writers I consider one of the greatest gifts of my career, NVC isn't just a master storyteller but also the coolest pilot on the planet.

Speaking of cool, Boo Walker not only claims that accolade but also embodies what it means to live with passion and authenticity. Boo is one of the authors, and people, I admire most, not just for his writing, but for the way he shows up in life.

To my fellow Tiki Pal, Lucy Score, who aims high and hits higher... thank you for being the perfect example of how to achieve success with skill, grace, and generosity (I even used an Oxford comma there for you). Your stories, like you, are filled with love and humor.

Rounding out this motley crew is my dear friend James, otherwise known as The Honourable James Blatch (with a 'u' because he's British). You do exactly what I hope to accomplish with stories like this one for my readers: put a smile on my face and fill my soul with pure joy.

Thank you, Tiki Bar Pals, for your support, your encouragement, and most of all, your friendship.

ABOUT THE AUTHOR

C.L. Mecca is the author of historical romance and also writes contemporary small town romance as Cissy Mecca.

Download your exclusive bonus content from C.L. Mecca here:

Follow C.L. Mecca on social media here:

    📘 facebook.com/MeccaRomance

    📷 instagram.com/meccaromance

    ♪ tiktok.com/@clmeccaauthor

ALSO BY C. L. MECCA

Heirs of Elydor Series

Whisper of War and Storms

Tide of Waves and Secrets

Fate of Echoes and Embers

Realm of Stone and Starlight

C. L. Mecca writing as Cissy Mecca

Cedar Falls Series

Fallen Hearts

Desired Hearts

Protected Hearts

Boldwood
EVER AFTER

X♡X♡

JOIN BOLDWOOD'S **ROMANCE COMMUNITY** FOR SWEET AND SPICY BOOK RECS WITH ALL YOUR FAVOURITE TROPES!

SIGN UP TO OUR
NEWSLETTER

HTTPS://BIT.LY/BOLDWOODEVERAFTER

Boldwood

Boldwood Books is an award-winning fiction publishing company seeking out the best stories from around the world.

Find out more at www.boldwoodbooks.com

Join our reader community for brilliant books, competitions and offers!

Follow us
@BoldwoodBooks
@TheBoldBookClub

Sign up to our weekly deals newsletter

https://bit.ly/BoldwoodBNewsletter